T0209237

Bridge of Shadows

IRIS MUNCHINSKY

WESTBOW
PRESS®
A DIVISION OF THOMAS NELSON
& ZONDERVAN

WestBow Press books may be ordered through booksellers or by contacting:

WestBow Press
A Division of Thomas Nelson & Zondervan
1663 Liberty Drive
Bloomington, IN 47403
www.westbowpress.com
1 (866) 928-1240

Because of the dynamic nature of the Internet, any web addresses or
links contained in this book may have changed since publication and
may no longer be valid. The views expressed in this work are solely those
of the author and do not necessarily reflect the views of the publisher,
and the publisher hereby disclaims any responsibility for them.

Any people depicted in stock imagery provided by Thinkstock are models,
and such images are being used for illustrative purposes only.
Certain stock imagery © Thinkstock.

ISBN: 978-1-5127-9162-4 (sc)
ISBN: 978-1-5127-9161-7 (hc)
ISBN: 978-1-5127-9163-1 (e)

Library of Congress Control Number: 2017909769

Print information available on the last page.

WestBow Press rev. date: 08/10/2017

Acknowledgments

Several years ago my father passed away while vacationing in Acapulco, taking with him an old secret from Scotland. Though we as a family dug for facts, we were unable to discover what it was all about.

When the shock of his death wore off, I realized this could be the beginning of a good story—the bulk of which would be pure fiction.

Thanks, Dad, for being able to keep a secret and inspiring me to write this story. Someday we'll know the truth.

For my husband, Karel, for his generosity and support,
For Elsie, who listened to each chapter as it was being written
And for my sister, Avril,
For her faith and courage during devastating loss.

Special thanks to Rick Wark for his incredible eagle eye.

Chapter One

Sela jolted wide-eyed out of the soothing swirl of ultramarine and indigo and into the jagged reality of her new norm. Her hand shot out and brought the phone to her ear.

"Hello." Her voice was low and gritty, partly from sleep, but mostly from standing in the pouring rain till her dress clung to her knees and her hands shook worse than old Mrs. Hardy's with Parkinson's.

"Joseph," the voice on the other end blared. "Sorry to call ye at home. There's not much time but we're onto somethin' big that might require yer expertise. Shades of Tanika, without a doubt."

Sela stared at the phone as if it had sprouted a set of eyes, her mind still in a cloud. Was this some kind of sick joke? The accent was broad Scottish—an older man, like Granddad. But what was he talking about? What on earth were "shades of Tanika?" Some stock market scam? And what expertise did Granddad have? The railroad? She brought the phone back to her ear. "Who is this?"

"Is this not Joseph?"

She moved to the edge of the bed and stood, her legs quaking like toothpicks holding up a wedding cake as she cleared her throat. "I just buried my granddad. Who is this?"

A lengthy silence ticked by before he finally spoke again, this time with less volume. "Pardon me, miss. I must have the wrong number." Then the phone went dead.

With jerky fingers she punched in the call-back code but no number appeared. What was going on? A racket? The wrong number? Nothing to do with Granddad. That was for sure.

She was still eying the receiver when a knock rattled the back door and the phone threatened to jump out of her hand. She let out a breathy "Whoosh." Probably the Mary-Martha ladies with their coffee and muffins. Forgetting the call, she grabbed her house coat off the floor and stuffed her arms into it. While attempting to smooth down her chaotic hair, she headed for the door.

<hr />

Her mind, though, just wouldn't let it go. Among the florists, the tears, and the welcome camaraderie of friends with casseroles, she kept trying to sort it out. Not just the phone call, but also Granddad's strange admission at the airport.

She chugged down a mouthful of coffee and tried to think. What if the phone call and Granddad's sudden revelation were somehow tied in together?

He'd been listing off the bills to pay and other mundane things to keep track of while he was away when he'd slipped something in about the hidden chapter of his life. When she'd plied him with questions, he'd taken a sudden interest in his boarding pass and mumbled something about telling all when he got home.

"Is it about the accident?" she asked in a last-ditch effort.

"Don't go jumpin' to conclusions, lass," he said. "It's long before that. Something back in Scotland."

Her eyes widened. "At least give me a hint then, Granddad. Don't just leave me in suspense."

As if on cue, an echoing voice cut in. "Boarding for Flight 503 to Acapulco will begin shortly. Those requiring assistance proceed immediately to Gate 12.

"There's still lots of time," she coaxed. "Unless, of course, you need boarding assistance."

He stood and stretched to his full five feet eight and a half inches. "Ach. How is it that I've raised such a cheeky lass? As ye can see, I'm fit as a fiddle at the ripe age of eighty-four."

"And that's how I want you to stay." She grasped the gnarled hands in her own. "Why do you need to go traipsing off by yourself? They'd probably give most of the money back if you canceled."

Her grandfather hesitated, his expression taking on a sheepish grin. "I hate to admit it lass, but the old bones need warmin' and Minneapolis is still cool and damp this time o' year. I may look the part but I'm not the young rogue I once was."

Sela sniffed. "Just don't forget about me, that's all. A month is a long time and you're all I've got, remember."

He gently stroked the side of her face. "How could I possibly forget the offspring of my only son?" He swallowed and then seemed to brighten. "Besides, every time I look in the mirror I'll think of you. That high-placed dimple of yours that charms all the young gents is a Lamont trait. It's stamped on us all."

Sela touched the frail fingers once more. "Why didn't you stay in touch with the family in Scotland? I wish I knew more than their names."

"I've been thinkin' of that," he said. "We'll see about changin' things when I get back.

And I'll tell you the rest of it then as well. Just see to it that you get on with your art project so you can support me in grand style when I arrive home. After all, you're now a full-fledged college graduate."

She stood and they walked arm in arm to the gate, their shoulders almost level. "I want you to have a wonderful time," she said. "You deserve it more than anyone."

He encircled her in a surprisingly strong hug. "And lassie," he said, pulling away and training his eyes on her, "I know how ye love gettin' to the bottom of things. Just leave everything as is till I come back." With a final peck on the cheek he turned and was gone.

Five days later the call came. "Miz Lamont, so sorry to inform you … Joseph Lamont … fatal heart attack … body shipped back …"

The room spun around her. "Granddad," she sobbed. "You can't leave me. What will I do without you?" A strong north wind whistled along the side of the house, banging the shutters relentlessly against their frames. She was utterly alone.

A week later, she'd stood side by side with the pastor, her eyes focused on his shoes which seemed to be taking in water like two old rowboats while the rat-a-tat of rain accompanied the lowering of the casket. A ragged sob escaped her. The pastor dropped his umbrella and cradled her in both arms.

"He's not here, dear," he said. "He's with the Father."

Sela leaned heavily against him, reluctant to move though a button from his trench coat was stamping its round image onto her cheek. After a while, though, her trembling subsided and she sighed audibly. Maybe he was right. Maybe Granddad was up in heaven like he said. But she'd been on the outs with God since her parents had been killed. She pressed her eyes shut, giving in to the memory of that day. "I hate Him, I hate Him," she had screamed, striking Granddad repeatedly as he tried to calm her down. "He doesn't love me. He killed my mom and dad and now I have nobody." Granddad hadn't replied in kind. Just rubbed her shoulders, soothing her without words and consoling her with kindness. From then on he'd been her only standby. He was always on her side, making things fun for her and encouraging her on. And now he was gone too. God hadn't changed much. He still took everything she had and left her with nothing.

"Are you ready, Sela?" The minister's voice was low and comforting, but there was a jagged edge to it as if his teeth were chattering together.

She nodded, pulling away. "Yes, let's go." They turned and with his arm still supporting her, they trudged, dripping wet, to the waiting car.

Now that she thought about it, Granddad having a secret past was as ludicrous as the anonymous phone call being anything more than the wrong number. She'd made a career of building mountains out of molehills and now it was time to face reality—boring as it was.

She couldn't lie on a couch for the rest of her life, though. Against her will she forced herself to the local art shop for a few sheets of two-hundred-pound cold-pressed paper but getting started was another matter. Sixteen water color paintings were supposed to be finished and exhibited in the next three months. Sure, she'd be receiving a hefty grant any day now, but just hauling out her paints was enough to send her back to bed. The theme, "The Play of Light in Nature," didn't exactly fit with her mood either. Whatever she globbed down would no doubt end up stuffed in a garbage bag, waiting by the curb for the weekly pickup. She took another noisy slurp of coffee and settled the mug on the table with a sigh.

When the attorney's office called a while later, she jumped at the chance to get out from under the gloom. Half-way through the meeting, though, her brain threatened to go on auto-pilot. She had inherited Granddad's estate, but the way it was set up was hard to understand. The lawyer wasn't exactly forthcoming and in the end, she just signed the forms granting her a modest monthly allowance until her twenty-fifth birthday. At that time she'd receive a surprisingly large lump sum—three years from now. She wasn't about to ask questions. It was more than enough and she was grateful for all of Granddad's hard work.

Six weeks from the date of the funeral she gathered the courage to open the door to his bedroom and begin going through his personal things. He had said to leave everything alone till he got back but that was never going to happen.

She sat on the edge of the bed and ran a hand across the faded chenille spread, breathing in the faint fragrance of the Eternity cologne she had bought him for Christmas. How fitting. A tear hovered at the corner of her eye but she brushed it away.

She stood and looked over the familiar room. It was Spartan, to say the least with an old- fashioned mirrored dresser and an unmatched chest of drawers. Everything, of course, was as neat as a pin, unlike her own room which sported piles of books and papers, as well as a few unwashed garments still lying where she'd stepped out of them. Some things just weren't in the genes.

Walking over to the high boy, she opened the top drawer. Sweaters, all neatly arranged. The second held T-shirts, the third boxers, the fourth socks, and the fifth pajamas. No surprises. Just like a set of railroad tracks, Granddad's life had been one of order and routine.

Maybe the dresser would offer up something more personal. Two family photographs graced the top of it but she forced her eyes aside. Opening the top drawer, she sifted through it but saw nothing hugely interesting except for a boar-bristled brush with a few silver hairs caught up in it. She snapped the drawer shut. What was she looking for anyway? Evidence of a secret past? Something inside her just wouldn't let it lie. What if Granddad actually had something to hide? And what if the key to it lay in one of these drawers? She had to find out.

She reached down and opened the bottom one. A stack of papers had been placed at the top and she picked them up and began sorting through them—a couple of paid hydro bills, an old Sunday School paper, the rules of some long-forgotten game as well as other random sheets. Surprisingly, they hadn't been thrown out or squirreled away in the basement filing cabinet with all the other bills and things Granddad kept on file in case he ever needed them. When she got to the bottom, however, a little gasp escaped her lips. In her hands lay an address book—discolored and worn thin over time—not the one used for Christmas cards, but one she'd never seen before.

She dropped the papers onto the dresser, took the book to the bed and sat down. Why would Granddad have two address books?

She opened to the "L" section and immediately spotted the name Alec Lamont—his brother. The phone number and address from Glasgow, Scotland were written neatly below. Granddad had talked of him occasionally and other than his sister Jean, she knew this was his only sibling. Why hadn't she thought to contact the family before now? Surely they'd want to know about his death. She'd have to get on it right away.

As she leafed through the remainder of the book, her mind drifted again to the anonymous caller from a few weeks back. Was his name listed here as well? Was he another relative, a friend from long ago, a co-worker? Her heart skipped a beat. Or did he have something to do with Granddad's hidden past?

Her stomach rumbled. It was almost suppertime. She'd pull out another lasagna from the freezer and while it was heating up, read through the rest of the address book. First, though, the other papers had to go back in the dresser. It was the least she could do for Granddad. Opening the drawer, she was about to chuck them inside when her eyes were drawn to a large brown envelope lying face down on the bottom. For some reason, she had overlooked it.

She picked it up and turned it over. Printed in block letters with a felt tipped pen was the word "PRIVATE." What in the world? She stared at it for a long moment, then walked back and sank down on the bed. *The hidden chapter of my life.* Was this something secretive or just another bill? She had a habit of blowing things out of proportion. She'd better not get too keyed up.

Biting her bottom lip, she drew the envelope away from herself and observed the printing once more. Definitely Granddad's. She lifted the flap and peered inside. A paper, looking suspiciously like a phone bill, sat benignly within. What was so mysterious about that? She sighed aloud as she pulled it out and opened it up. The mystery of the phone bill. Big hairy deal. Was it two days late or …

As she stared at the open page before her, though, her heart began to race. On three separate lines the name and number had been blacked out with a felt pen, no doubt the same one used on the envelope. The date on top was from the previous month—just before Granddad left. Who had he been calling?

She searched through the list of other calls but there was nothing mysterious about them. What could his reason be for hiding these particular names and numbers? Had they been made to the anonymous caller? With a sudden thought, she snatched up the envelope and looked inside. A small, thickish square of paper rested near the bottom, tucked closely into the fold. She reached in and pulled it out.

It was an old black and white photograph of a young woman, obviously from the 1940s judging by the square shouldered knee-length dress she was wearing. Sela squinted, trying to make out the blurry details. The woman was thin and pretty with black wavy hair and a small smile. She was standing in front of some kind of shop. A sign on the wall began with the letters "ULL" but disappeared behind her. Who was she? For sure not Grandma who'd been light-haired and even in old photographs, slightly stout.

She turned it over and as she took in the block letters printed neatly across the back, her heart lurched in her chest. It read simply, "Tanika." Her mouth went dry. *"Shades of Tanika without a doubt."* She flipped it back over and peered at the woman's image. Was this what the man had been referring to—some girlfriend from Granddad's past? But what was so terrible about that? And how could it possibly mean anything after all these years? Surely the two of them hadn't been involved in some kind of scheme.

She grabbed the phone bill again and looked carefully down the list. On the last blacked-out line, lighter patches could be seen where it had been dragged across the page—as if the ink was beginning to run out. She held it up to the light. The person's name was completely covered but the destination held possibilities. The first two letters looked like "SC"—Scotland, no doubt.

But what was the name of the town? Glasgow? No, the last letter was tall—"b" or "d" possibly. Jumping up, she hopped over to the window, flipped up the shade and held the paper up. It was a simple straight line. An "l".

She turned and ran to her own bedroom, plunked down on three or four pairs of dirty jeans and opened her laptop. Clicking on Google, she punched in "names of Scottish towns." She waited until the screen brought up a list of available sites, then clicked on "Scottish Cities, Towns, and Villages." Seconds later a list of towns appeared in alphabetical order. Scrolling down, she looked for towns ending with the letter "l". There was only one— "Ullapool." That had to be it. She clicked on it and immediately a map of Scotland appeared. The town of Ullapool was marked by a dot on the northern side of Loch Broom in the western highlands. Granddad had been making calls to the highlands?

With another lightning thought, she bolted back to his bedroom and grabbed up the address book. Was there anyone in it from Ullapool? Starting with the "A's," she sped through the pages like a mad woman, nearly ripping several out in her rush. Many had just names and numbers but when she got to the "M's," she let out a shriek of triumph. It read "T. McLeod, Ullapool, Scotland."

Swallowing hard, she picked up the photograph and placed it between the address book and the phone bill— "Ull-Tanika"— "Ullapool-T Mcleod." Was this girl the T. McLeod from the address book? And what did she have to do with the anonymous caller? Before she could process it further, the phone began to ring. She grabbed it up, annoyed by the interruption.

"Hello." Her tone could have doused a blazing fire.

"Sela?" The pastor's wife was sweetness itself—the perfect grandma.

Sela gave a slight cough. "Sorry Mrs. Blakely, I … uh …"

"It's okay, dear. I shouldn't be calling so close to suppertime but I took the chance you hadn't eaten. We have so many leftovers from the church dinner, I wondered if you'd like to come and share them with us."

Sela bit her bottom lip. She'd missed church again and didn't want to have to give explanations. On the other hand, the Blakely's had been the height of kindness to her since Granddad's passing. "Sure," she said. "What time do you want me to come?"

◦•◗▬▬▬▬◗▬▬▬▬◖•◦

Mrs. Blakely reached for Sela's dessert plate. "How about another piece of blueberry pie, dear. You're looking awfully thin."

Sela shook her head. "I couldn't eat another bite, but I'd go for a second cup of coffee if that's okay."

"Of course, dear." She lifted the carafe, her wrinkled hand shaking slightly as she refilled Sela's green Corelle cup. "I hope you don't mind that it's the unleaded variety," she said with a little chuckle. "Mr. Blakely and I find it difficult to sleep after drinking the regular blend."

"Oh no, this is good." Sela poured in a dollop of thick cream and took a sip, pausing to get her thoughts together. "I'd like to thank you both for your kindness. Granddad would be very relieved to know how well I've been taken care of."

"Not at all, dear." Mrs. Blakely reached over and squeezed her hand. "You're like a granddaughter to us—not that we can replace your granddad, of course."

Sela looked at the sweet old couple before her and pressed her lips into a firm line. She wouldn't let them see her cry again. They'd been extremely kind and helpful but that didn't make her part of them. She was still alone in the world with no one to call family.

"Not trying to pressure you," Mr. Blakely began, shuffling in his chair, "but we've missed you the last couple of Sundays. I know it must be hard to carry on without your granddad."

Sela looked down at her plate. She didn't want to disappoint them but she was no closer to God than on the day of the funeral. He'd taken her family for the second time and left her with no one. She couldn't very well vent her anger the way she had when she was a child, but attending church seemed like a complete farce. "I've been kind of busy," she answered, wincing at the lame sound of her excuse.

"Life's like that, dear, but I caution you to draw near to the Lord. He's our only Rock when things seem out of control."

Sela nodded, scrambling to divert the conversation. "I found a couple of things in Granddad's drawer and wonder if he ever mentioned them to you."

The minister seemed to hesitate for a fraction of a second before setting down his cup. "Oh?"

"I came across the name T. McLeod from Ullapool, Scotland. It looks like Granddad called there a few times lately."

"I know he originally comes from Scotland." His wrinkled eyes gazed off to the side. "Could it not just be an old friend from the past?"

"It could be, but I've never known him to call there before. There was a picture of a lady, too, probably taken in the 1940s."

"Maybe he's just trying to catch up with people he once knew," Mrs. Blakely said. "You know, when people get a little older, these things become more important. We tend to wonder what happened to the people we once knew."

"Could be." Sela poured more cream into her coffee. "Anyway, I just thought I'd mention it in case you'd heard anything."

"I don't think we're able to help you there," Mr. Blakely said. "but we're here for you in any other way we can."

Mrs. Blakely smiled suddenly, her hazel eyes twinkling beneath rimless glasses. "Maybe Sela should go for a little trip to Scotland to see her family over there."

Mr. Blakely's stared straight ahead, his own eyes slightly wider than normal. "I'm sure Sela can make up her own mind on that account, Edith." He gave a small cough. "I don't think she needs us to tell her what to do."

Sela had never seen so much as a hint of argument between them before. "It's fine, really," she said. "I might even go for it if I didn't have this art project to finish. But as it is, I can't even think about trips."

Mr. Blakely reached over and took his wife's small hand. "Edith and I just want the best for you, dear."

Sela threw them a warm smile. "I know you do and I appreciate it more than I can tell you." A few minutes later she gathered her things together, and giving them both a quick hug, left for home.

The house was dark as she came through the door and she switched on the hallway light. What was wrong with her? She always turned it on when she went out. She'd have to get a cat or dog or something. Everything was way too quiet and still around here. Even a goldfish would make a few cheerful bubbles. The grandfather clock in the living room informed her it was ten o'clock on the nose but she still needed to write that letter to Uncle Alec. She didn't want it hanging over her head.

Walking into the kitchen, she glanced about for the address book she'd found in Granddad's drawer, then remembered it was still on the bed in his room. She ambled down the hallway, stifling a yawn. Where in the world was the breeze coming from? And what was the clicking sound in the bathroom? She went in, turned on the light and stopped dead.

The bathroom window stood wide open, the blind waving slowly in front of it. What on earth? She hadn't opened it. Standing still, she listened to the hum of the traffic a few blocks away. Who had opened the window?

As she reached across the bathtub to close it, her eyes fell on a small patch of black dirt lying at the bottom of the tub. She shrieked and jumped back, colliding with the open door and letting out another scream. Someone had been in her house. Were they still here or had they left when she came in?

Her heart lurched into overdrive. What should she do? First, she had to call the police but the closest phone was in her bedroom. Backing out "Law and Order" style, she crept to her room, turned on the light and dashed to the cordless phone. She punched in 911 while frantically checking under the bed and in the closet.

When the operator came on the line, she burst into a breathless account of her discovery and was assured the police would arrive shortly. She waited, not daring to move until a siren chirped in the driveway, then she raced to the door and threw it open.

The officer's expression was conciliatory as she quickly recounted her story, his double chin bobbing up and down with each nod. Would he actually be able to chase down a thief? He trundled to the basement, checked that all was clear, then heaved himself upstairs once again and inspected the coat closet and kitchen cupboards before moving to the hallway. His eyes seemed to linger a fraction of a second too long on a plate of brownies the neighbors had sent over earlier but Sela couldn't be sure.

When he reached the door to her cluttered bedroom, however, she felt herself blush scarlet. She assured him it was all clear but he insisted on seeing for himself. After a cursory glance around, he allowed her to lead him to the bathroom and finally Granddad's bedroom.

"Looks like you must've scared him off, miss," he said finally. "Everything seems to be in order ... unless of course ... ah ... your own room ..."

Sela managed a slight cough, feeling her deep color return. "No ... I'm uh ... doing a little rearranging." Quickly changing the subject, she added, "Do you think he'll be back? I'm a bit nervous here by myself." She wrapped her arms tightly around her waist as she spoke.

"I'll tell you what." He scribbled something in his notebook with a pudgy left hand. "We'll first make sure all the windows and doors are locked, then I'll check the yard for anyone skulking around. If no one's there, it probably means he ran off and won't be back. Just to be on the safe side, though, I'll drive by a few times throughout the night to see that you're okay."

Sela nodded, feeling anything but okay.

"Unless you have relatives or someone to stay with."

"No," she answered. There was no way she'd bother the Blakely's tonight though she was feeling more alone than ever.

"Alright then, I'm sure you'll be fine. Just don't open the door for anyone unless you see a uniform and badge. You can come down to the station tomorrow and fill out a report." Giving her a final chin bob, he turned and went out the door.

••◦•▬▬▬▬▬▬•◦•▬▬▬▬▬▬•◦••

The pair of them stood like stick men plastered to the side of the garage, hardly daring to breathe till the footsteps receded back toward the house. "That's what ye'd call a close call," the lanky one observed, grinning.

"Shut yer yap," his partner snapped. "We're not out of the woods yet. We should've left when we first heard the scream. But no, you had to wait to see who'd show up."

"I just wanted to find out if he had any cronies this side o' the pond." He rubbed his palms down the side of his pants.

"We nearly got ourselves the American version of the "Glaswegian Siesta" for yer tomfoolery. And hand me that book. I better be the one holdin' onto it."

"Ye don't trust me? Don't forget, I'm the one who chanced a run-in while you were here, out of the line of fire."

His partner snorted. "It's a wonder ye came across anything at all, what with being terrified o' yer own shadow. Are ye sure you didn't leave a trace?"

"Of course I'm sure. Everything's just as it was—except for the address book, that is." He gave it a final tap before handing it over. "I just hope the boss knows the trouble we went to."

"We're supposed to be soldiers, man," the other spat. "Try to act the part."

They stood silently for several minutes, listening, then turned and made their way down the alley. They'd be back on familiar ground within twelve hours.

••◦•▬▬▬▬▬▬•◦•▬▬▬▬▬▬•◦••

Sela immediately bolted the door, then ran and double checked every window and door and turned on all the lights. How could she possibly sleep? Maybe she'd get into her pajamas and housecoat and at least feel comfortable. A few minutes later she climbed into her unmade bed and poofed a couple of pillows behind her back. She took her romance novel from the night stand and opened it up. After a couple of minutes, though, she snapped it shut, not remembering a single word. Worse still, she wasn't the slightest bit sleepy. She thought back to the events of the past few weeks and suddenly recalled the letter she still had to write to Uncle Alec. At least that would take her mind off her present state of affairs.

She got up and slipped down the hallway to Granddad's bedroom for the address book. It was dimmer than most of the other rooms, Granddad having insisted on sixty watt bulbs. Still though, everything was plain as day—everything except the address book.

She stared at the empty bed as if willing it to materialize. Had she put it back in the drawer with the papers? Dashing across the room, she threw the drawer open and emptied the contents out onto the floor. Nothing. She rummaged through all the other drawers on the off chance she'd stuffed it in somewhere by accident. Nothing there either. Maybe it was in the kitchen after all. She tore down the hall and searched the table, the counter, and each drawer. Not a thing. Pulling out a chair, she sat down, drumming her fingers on the table. Where could it be?

Almost imperceptibly, a tingling sensation began in her spine and worked its way up through her fingers as a new thought dawned on her. Whoever had been in the house had stolen the address book. And it wasn't some random robbery, since nothing else seemed to have been taken. She shuddered. Why would someone want it? It didn't contain anything of importance—just names, addresses and phone numbers. Or was that what they were after?

She grabbed a note pad and pen off the counter. Maybe if she put it down on paper it would make some kind of sense. First, she wrote the words, "phone bill" and "address book." Why were they hidden in the first place? Under that she put, "1940s lady—Tanika—shades of Tanika." Thinking for a moment, she added, "Granddad's calls to Ullapool—anonymous caller—Granddad's expertise." Lastly she wrote, "Granddad's secret past." Were they all related? And who would possibly know about all of them? A fresh shiver ran down her spine at the thought of someone waiting for her to leave, then searching the house. She jerked her head to the window for any peering eyes but the cheerful white shade covered the darkness.

She turned back to the paper and scribbled, "How are they all related?" She'd have to give it some serious thought, but not tonight. A sudden weariness had crept over her like a shroud. She'd better get back to bed or she'd be spending the night on the kitchen floor. She made her way into her room and dropped like a stone onto the bed.

It was after eleven when she awoke the next morning. Granddad would be having a fit. She meandered into the kitchen, put on the coffee and saw the note. So it wasn't a dream after all. Someone had actually been in her house. Refusing to let it get her down, she walked to the front door and checked the mail box, turning off lights along the way.

An official looking letter had arrived. It had to be her check from the grant office. Nothing like good news to chase away the blues. She tore the envelope open and pulling out the paper, began reading. "Dear Ms. Lamont, So sorry to inform you that your art grant will be delayed by at least three months. While your project is significant, more urgent requests have been submitted causing a substantial backlog. We encourage you to continue your work." Blah, blah, blah.

She crumpled the paper into a ball and hurled it across the floor, then sank down on the chair and sobbed. Of all the rotten luck. Where would she get the money now? The framing alone would cost a fortune, not to mention the studio rental. And who felt like painting with everything up in the air like this. Couldn't anything go right?

She shoved the chair aside, grabbed a mug out of the cupboard and poured it full of coffee. "So sorry to inform you," she mimicked in a childish voice and slammed it down on the counter. It sloshed over the sides and spread across the flat surface but she was in no mood for clean ups. First a thief, now a three-month delay. What next? Once again, God wasn't doing her any favors

Chapter Two

For the next twenty minutes, she sat in frozen silence, allowing her coffee to cool to lukewarm. Finally, she gulped it down, took a deep breath, and stood. The letter to Uncle Alec still had to be written before she forgot it altogether. How was she supposed to send it, though, without the address? Thinking for a minute, she snapped her fingers. Was it by some chance in the other address book? She'd never seen it there, but still … Turning, she raced down the basement stairs and over to the makeshift office.

She took a tentative seat at the cold metal desk chair and opened the middle drawer. The book was right where it had always been, thanks to Granddad's orderly habits. She picked it up and leafed through till she came to the "L" section. No Lamont. A bead of sweat broke out on her forehead but she ignored it. The address had to be there. Maybe Granddad had filed it under a different heading. She turned to the "S's"—"S" for Scotland. Nope, not there either. What about the back of the book? She flipped to the last page and there it was— the name, address and phone number. She could have wept with relief. Something had finally gone right.

Grabbing an envelope out of the bottom drawer, she carefully copied the name and address onto it before going back upstairs. She'd write the letter, drop it off at the mail box, then go on to the police station. Things were at last falling into place.

Half an hour later she still sat at the kitchen table, the words,

"Dear Uncle Alec" written at the top of an otherwise blank sheet. She couldn't just say, "Hi, how are you? Your brother died and I forgot to tell you." She didn't even know the man. Maybe she'd leave it till later. Getting up, she quickly dressed, grabbed her purse, threw on her flats, locked the door, and got into her black '98 Cavalier. She'd go to the police station first, then write the letter.

She was about to turn the corner leading past the church when she saw Mr. Blakely returning from lunch. He spotted her before she could zoom by and waved her over. One thing she wasn't going to do was tell him about the theft. He'd insist she stay at their house and she wasn't about to tie herself down. Besides, she didn't want them to worry.

"Lovely day, isn't it Sela," he said when she'd lowered the window.

"It sure is. I'm just on my way to … town." She breathed an inward sigh of relief.

"I've been thinking about last night." He dropped his eyes and transferred his weight to the other foot as he leaned in the window. "I guess the Lord brought you by here so I could explain something to you." He let out a noisy breath before beginning. "I wasn't entirely honest with you."

Sela looked up sharply. "What do you mean? You're always honest."

"I try to be. But last night when we were talking about your Granddad, I wasn't sure how to answer you. He had confided a few things to me a while back and I told him I'd keep them to myself."

"What kind of things?"

"Nothing really specific." He waited as the maintenance man lumbered by, thumped him on the back, and commented on the weather. "Just that he'd been forced to move from Scotland due to some kind of uproar, and he didn't want you bothered about it."

"Uproar?"

"Again, he wasn't specific. But when you mentioned finding a picture of a woman, I couldn't help but wonder …"

Sela drew in her breath, her voice catching. "That's not it. My granddad was very respectable."

"Of course he was," Mr. Blakely soothed. "He was one of the finest men I've known, but we all make mistakes."

She sat silently, staring out the window. It wasn't fair to take out her anger on him, but still, he should have told her right away. After a few seconds, she turned to him again. "So that's why you didn't want your wife suggesting I go to Scotland."

"Yes," he admitted. "But now that I've given it some thought, I wonder if it might be the best medicine for you. You could meet your extended family, and possibly clear up a few details as well."

She rubbed her fingers across the grey velour seat covers. What a disastrous few days—the theft, the postponed grant, and now Granddad's involvement in an uproar—no doubt the hidden chapter of his life.

Maybe Mr. Blakely was right about going. With her allowance from the estate and the small amount she'd saved, she'd probably have enough to cover the costs and still have a little left over. It would get her away from the house, give her the chance to meet the rest of her family, and let her do some digging into Granddad's past. And it wasn't as if she had to rush back to finish her art project. She'd attend to that when the grant came through. Maybe she'd even catch a little Scottish inspiration on the side.

"I'll give it some thought," she said, offering him a begrudging smile. After a hurried good bye, she sped off in the direction of the police station.

That evening after checking the state of her finances, she went on-line and booked a direct flight to Glasgow, then sat down at the kitchen table once again. "Please forgive me for not writing sooner," she wrote, "but Granddad passed away last month. I knew you'd want to know. I'm planning a trip to Scotland for two or three weeks and would like to stay with you if that's okay. Would you be able to pick me up at the airport?" She wrote the date and time of the flight. "Watch for a tall, skinny girl with long, curly reddish hair. I'll look for a sign with my name on it. Hope this isn't too much trouble for you. I'll pay for your expenses. Thanks again, Sela Lamont."

It was as if a huge weight had rolled off her shoulders. Two weeks from today she'd be stepping out into the unknown—away from her fears and disappointments—into something new, maybe even something exciting. "Thank you, Mr. Blakely," she said aloud. For the first time since Granddad died, she felt like laughing.

Jimmy clinked glasses with the men across from him, his dark eyes intense with anticipation. "Here's to the hunt. May we be the first to get our hands on it."

"Aye," the others murmured in assent, clinking back.

"We haven't got much to go on but we'll use every angle we come up with—and more. There's too much ridin' on this for any negligence on our part."

"We're with ye on that," a sandy-haired man replied.

Jimmy sat back, allowing the others to take the conversation. Understated leadership had always been his way and it had served him well. Few, even at school, had been prepared for his crackerjack answers and quick retorts.

His attitude had, of course, landed him in hot water far more than once but he'd laughed it off—even when it cost him dearly, like the time he'd been kicked out of school for mouthing off the teacher one time too many. Or the time Moira had pulled the ring off her finger and thrown it at him, refusing to see him again. Or the time … well, never mind that now. That was altogether different. He hadn't admitted to a soul how deeply he'd been crushed. But that was all in the past. This time the stakes were higher—much bigger than himself. He'd have to keep his tongue in check, conveying to others the image of a dullard while arming himself with the element of surprise.

The plane shuddered and lost altitude as the "Fasten Seat Belts" light flashed. Sela looked up the aisle for any sign of alarm but settled back in when she saw everyone else dozing, oblivious. Just her own jitters. Why hadn't she phoned instead of writing? The address book had both the address and phone number but she'd felt shy about speaking to her relatives directly. Maybe the letter hadn't arrived. Maybe her uncle wouldn't come. Too late now. She'd just have to keep her eyes peeled for an elderly man carrying a sign with her name on it.

The bell pinged again and she looked down to see toy cars racing to and fro across the streets of Glasgow. "You wanted me to know, Granddad, so here goes."

***

Nudging the battered case with her foot, she edged toward the bank of phones, her knock-off Gucci slung across one shoulder and her oversized carry-on clutched in both arms. Hopefully this would make a good vantage point.

She surveyed the interior of the Glasgow airport before her. A lively stream of cyan, magenta, and violet-clad women swished by, leaving the echo of some exotic tongue while clusters of weary looking travelers emerged from the baggage department and ambled down the corridor on her right. People from every location on earth, it seemed, flooded the concourse—all with smart looking spinner cases. Why hadn't she had the foresight to buy one before the trip instead of using Granddad's ancient relic? Her uncle would think she'd come for a hand-out. With any luck, he'd be half blind.

"I get you taxi, lady." A dark little man sporting a red boutonniere in his lapel hustled toward her and reached for the case.

"No thank you. I don't need one."

"You no walk. I get you taxi."

"No, I" ...

He grabbed the handle and pulled it toward himself, appraising it knowingly. "Taxi cheap."

"I don't care. I don't want a taxi." She hooked one foot around the bottom of the case and held on.

"The lady said she doesn't need a taxi. Now buzz off."

Sela let go of the case and looked up. Towering over her was a striking, fair-haired man of about thirty, dressed in a green Argyle sweater and neatly pressed khakis.

"No problems." The little man whipped the flower from his jacket and presented it to her. "A prize from city of Glasgow."

"Thanks." She took it in her hand, glancing up at the younger man as the other strolled off. "Sorry to bother you," she mumbled.

"No bother at all. A pleasure to help a lady in distress."

His accent was definitely Scottish though more cultured than Granddad's. He exuded such a disarming air of confidence, she felt instantly drawn to him. Abruptly though, the sorry state of her suitcase flashed to her mind and she stepped back to conceal its shabby condition.

"Pardon me," he said. "I didn't mean to offend you."

"Oh no … you didn't … I'm uh … just a little nervous. I'm waiting for a man." She winced, giving herself a mental kick. What a ludicrous thing to say to a stranger.

"Are you alright?"

"I'm fine, really. I just need to find someone carrying a sign." She stuck out her bottom lip and blew the hair out of her eyes.

"Well then, that shouldn't be too much of a problem," He turned and pointed down the corridor. "Take your pick." Off to the right, concealed by the telephones, stood a small crowd of eager welcomers, all holding up cardboard signs.

Sela felt her cheeks grow warm.

He looked at her unwieldy bags. "I'll tell you what. You let me know what the sign is supposed to say and I'll see if I can find it."

She could have hugged him. "Sela. It says Sela."

He stood stock still for a moment, then reaching into his pocket, pulled out a piece of paper. "Like this?" he asked softly as he unfolded it.

She gazed from the paper back to him again. "You can't possibly be my great-uncle."

"No, but I can be his son. You didn't do yourself justice in the letter."

"Sorry. Granddad never said much about the family."

"And I'm sorry to hear about your granddad."

She paused. "I hope you won't think I'm rude, but would you mind if I ask for a favor?"

"Name it."

"I know it sounds a bit crazy but would you mind smiling again?"

He stretched his lips into a wide grin but though Sela searched his face, she was unable to detect even the faintest indent. She gave a little laugh, taking a step back. "How did you manage to pass up the Lamont dimple? I thought it was stamped on us all."

He paused for a minute, rubbing a hand across his clean-shaven face. "Sorry. Yes, I guess that is a bit revealing." Looking down for a moment, he continued in a quiet voice. "I'm actually related only through Mum. My father adopted me … later …"

A familiar heat wave rose up the back of Sela's neck and onto her cheeks. "Oh … no … I didn't mean …" Would she ever learn to keep her mouth shut? With an apologetic grin, she stuck out an encumbered hand, aware of her own family trait breaking the surface of her skin. "Sela Lamont from Minneapolis."

"Dougal Lamont from Glasgow, at your service." He ignored the hand and embraced her in a hug. "Let's go meet the family."

<hr />

The blood drained from her face the instant they turned onto the M80. Taking in a ragged breath, she stared straight ahead.

"We actually live in Steppes, just north of the city," Dougal informed her.

Sela didn't care where they lived as long as they were nearly there. Vehicles by the thousands shot down the highway at breakneck speed and motor bikes darted in and out as if the drivers had a common death wish. She pressed down on an imaginary brake. If only they were on the right side of the road.

Dougal looked over and laughed. "You're not frightened are you?"

"That wouldn't be my word of choice." She cringed as another bike cut in front. "Terrified."

"Relax. I drive for a living."

"You're a truck driver?"

"I'm actually in sales—a company called "Anything Tartan." I make a round trip from Glasgow and Edinburgh right up to the highlands each month, so I should be quite adept at handling the roads."

She felt her heart skip a beat. The highlands? "You wouldn't happen to know of a town called Ullapool, would you?"

"Actually, I do. Our company does a lot of business with the tourist shops up there, especially during the summer." He paused. "It's rather a small place. How did you ever hear of it?"

"I've just been reading up on Scotland is all." She glanced out the side window, averting her eyes.

"If you stay long enough I'll take you up there."

She let out her breath. "That would be great—as long as we walk."

"That can be arranged." A few minutes later he braked and veered right onto a slower-paced thoroughfare. Turning down a narrow street, he pulled into the driveway of a large Tudor-style house. A profusion of rose buds lined both sides of a cobblestone walkway leading to cement stairs and a massive apple tree sat like a fat sentinel in the middle of the yard, its branches thick with blossoms. Dougal turned to her with a smile. "Out you get. Can't keep the clan waiting."

She opened the door but despite the hair- raising ride, couldn't bring herself to leave the security of the car. Dougal walked around and pulled her up by the hand. "They're not going to eat you, you know."

She angled her face toward him. "Do you think we could bring the cases later?"

"Whatever you want," he said, giving her a wink.

The door of the house burst open and a gray-haired jolly looking woman bustled down the steps to meet them. "It's so good to finally see you, luv." She wrapped Sela in a firm hug, then leaned back for a better view. "Just look at you—the very picture of your granddad."

Sela grinned. "You must be Great Aunt Jean, Granddad's sister."

Before the woman could answer, a tall elderly gentleman sporting a bushy beard and sparse silver hair called out from the doorway. "I see our son has excellent taste when picking up ladies from the airport." He picked his way down the stairs toward them followed by a heavy-set woman about fifteen years his junior.

Dougal shook his head. "Let's at least get her into the house, Dad. Sela, these are my parents—my mother, Agnes, and my father, Alec, your granddad's brother."

Sela gave them both a quick hug. "Pleased to meet you. I hope I didn't shock you too much with the letter."

"No, no. We're glad to have you. Just terribly sorry about Joseph. I haven't seen him in many a year but that didn't change things. Come inside and I'll introduce you to the others." They made their way through the door to a sea of vaguely familiar, smiling faces—aunts, uncles, and cousins she'd barely heard of until this moment. In a jumble of welcoming hugs and kisses, she tried in vain to match each name to a face.

After a few minutes Alec stopped the commotion. "Give the girl some space, people, before you scare her clear out of Scotland."

Sela laughed. "It's okay. I'm just glad to be part of the family. Granddad really wanted me to meet all of you."

"I'm sure he did, luv. Aunt Jean squeezed her hand as she led her across the room to a deep mocha-colored chair in front of a bay window. "Have a seat and I'll go see if Agnes has the tea ready. You must be exhausted from the trip."

"I guess I've been too excited to notice," Sela admitted. She dropped onto the over-stuffed cushion with a "Whoomp" and glanced across to a costly looking green settee flanked by matching floral chairs and backed by a bronze-framed landscape. Not bad at all. Compared to Granddad's minimalistic approach to decorating, it was the Taj Mahal.

A couple of the women pulled up chairs beside her and sat down for a chat but after a few minutes, Sela knew her chance to quiz the whole group was slipping away. Taking advantage of a pause in the conversation, she gave a slight cough and began. "Since everyone's here, I wonder if any of you would be able to clear something up for me."

Aunt Jean's eyelids fluttered as she walked in and set a blue Wedgwood cup and saucer on the end table beside her. "We can try."

"It might not be anything at all. It's just that when I was going through Granddad's stuff I kept coming across the name Tanika. Does that ring a bell with anyone? It doesn't really sound Scottish at all."

The room went dead still as if an invisible vacuum cleaner had whirled in and sucked up all the energy. The older woman's smile slipped and she appeared to be fumbling for some kind of answer. Sela glanced at Uncle Alec but he was busy coughing into a Kleenex. "Did anyone know her?" She looked from one to the other but everyone seemed to be looking somewhere else.

Dougal suddenly stood at her side. "Probably just a friend from the past, but we can talk about that later. There's someone you still haven't met."

Sela steeled herself. So her worst fears were true. There really was a can of worms, but this didn't seem to be the time to open it. She smiled up at him. "Oh? Who might that be?"

He pulled her to her feet and hooked an arm around her shoulder as he led her toward a closed door at the end of the hall. "It's your great-grandmother."

Sela stopped, he knees suddenly weak. "My great-grandmother? Granddad's mother?" She hadn't even realized she was alive.

"At a hundred and three, she's not too steady on her feet. Her mind's good, though." He knocked quietly and opened the door.

Propped up by pillows on a hospital-style bed and covered with a thick tartan blanket, lay a tiny, wooly-haired woman. Deep lines crisscrossed the skin on her face but Sela could make out a delicate bone structure under the surface. Aunt Jean, who had followed them into the room, went to her mother's side.

"Mother, your great-granddaughter's here to see you."

Sela gazed at the shrunken figure, tears inexplicably forming in her eyes. Granddad's mother—her own great-grandmother.

The woman lifted her eyes and smiled, highlighting the deep creases.

"Joseph's granddaughter." Her voice was high and shallow, the Scottish brogue accentuated with age. "Come let me see ye, lass." She held out her hand.

Sela moved forward, blinking furiously. "Great-Grandma." She took the proffered hand and found the fingers surprisingly strong.

Tears began coursing down her cheeks. "I miss him so much."

Her great-grandmother nodded. "As do I. But you can see him again you know."

"I hope so."

"Ye can be sure." She lay back, her breathing labored.

Sela looked up, alarmed.

"She's just tired. She doesn't have much stamina." Aunt Jean patted the bony hand.

The old woman stirred again and opened her eyes. "I want to see Sela alone."

"Are ye sure, Mother? There's always tomorrow."

"Aye, I want to see her alone."

Aunt Jean exchanged looks with Dougal, but conceded with a smile. "Alright then, but no overdoing it."

Grea-Grandma waited till the door snapped shut, then turned to Sela with a look of urgency. "I don't have much time, lass." Her eyes held a glassy brightness and Sela wondered if the shock had been too much for her.

"You don't have to tire yourself. I'll be staying for a while." She smoothed the pillow with her fingers.

"I've got something for you, dear. I've been keepin' it all these years in the hope that ..." She pulled a decrepit envelope from under the blanket and with shaky hands, placed it into Sela's steady palm. "Read it without judgment. Try to find the truth."

"Is it about Granddad? Does it have something to do with him moving to the United States?"

"It's for you alone to read. Keep it to yourself." Her eyes closed and Sela knew the conversation was over.

That night, encased in the fluffy white pillows and goose down quilt of the guest room, she held the faded envelope in her own shaking hands. The words stood out before her—"Joseph Lamont, Ullapool, Scotland." So Granddad had been in Ullapool. Had he been involved with that dark-haired woman? Was there some illegitimate outcome that had sent him fleeing across the ocean in disgrace? She lifted the flap. Why had he never told her about his family—his mother? They all seemed so friendly. She pulled out the paper, yellow and brittle with age, and began to unfold it.

Written in fountain pen in the English style of the day, it began. "25th January, 1945." Her heart pounded as she read on. "Joseph, new orders from the Fuhrer himself. Meet tonight at art shop 11.00 o'clock. Payment to arrive shortly. As always, Tanika."

Sela stared at the letter in bewilderment. Tanika? The Fuhrer? Her granddad had orders from Hitler? Payment? No. She would never believe it. He was no traitor. Was this the reason the family had reacted so strangely to the name Tanika? Was she a Nazi spy? Was Granddad? Is that what his expertise was all about? No! She stuffed the letter back into the envelope and jammed it inside her suitcase, her heart thumping like a jack-hammer. "Read it without judgment ... try to find the truth." She lay back on the bed and stared up at the ceiling, her original plan to discover the secret taking on a whole new significance. To Ullapool then. She'd ferret out the truth and prove her grandfather innocent if she had to raise the dead to do it.

Chapter Three

"Are you awake, Sela? It's nearly quarter of eleven." The aroma of hot buttered toast and strong coffee found its way to Sela's nose, and she opened an eye to see Aunt Agnes hovering in the doorway holding a heavy silver tray, her expression cloudy.

"I've brought you some breakfast to get you going." She strode into the bedroom and set the tray on the night stand. Then marching across to the window, she drew apart the limp brocade drapes, exposing the dim interior to an even dimmer outdoors. A loud clap of thunder completed the greeting.

"Good morning." Sela's voice sounded raspy from sleep as she smiled at the flushed face before her. "Sorry, it must be the jet lag. Breakfast smells fantastic, though."

"Dougal's chompin' at the bit. He thought you'd enjoy a day of sightseeing." She cast her eyes about the room, allowing her gaze to land on the lavender Queen Ann chair laden with a heap of yesterday's crumpled clothes.

Sela sat up and gave a slight cough. She quickly poured a dollop of cream into the cup and picked up a thick slice of raisin toast. "Sounds like fun but I'd really like to spend time with Great- Grandma."

"Your uncle had her taken back to the nursing home this morning. We can pop by there tomorrow. And don't worry about the rain. I'll lend you a brolly—umbrella, that is."

Twenty minutes later, clad in faded jeans and navy hoodie over a blue plaid shirt, Sela hurried into the living room.

Dougal stepped out from the kitchen, coffee in hand. "And aren't you looking the part of the Scottish lassie in your tartan shirt. It appears, though, we'll have to find something to cover that frantic head of hair."

"It's the weather," she said with a laugh. "I can hardly get a brush through it."

"Are you up for some sightseeing?"

"What did you have in mind?"

"I thought we'd take a little excursion downtown to Buchanan Street and see some of the shops, hit a couple of high spots at George's Square, and perhaps get a bite to eat." He peered at her over the rim of his mug.

She looked up at him and smiled. With a little cajoling, he might make that trip to Ullapool sooner than later. "What are we waiting for then? Your wish is my command." They called a quick goodbye and were off.

Dougal looked across the seat at her with a grin. "I notice you're now able to keep your eyes open when the car's in motion. Has my driving improved that much?"

"Not exactly," she quipped. "Just my state of mind. It's amazing what a person can endure after a good night's sleep." She sat back, watching the streets of Glasgow unfold between swishing windshield wipers and wondered how best to broach the subject of Ullapool.

In a few minutes she let out a breathy sigh. "Every big city is basically the same, you know. People, buildings and vehicles all jammed together."

"So I'd be quite at home in Minneapolis?"

"Sure, except for the wider streets, newer buildings, and driving on the right side of the road."

He laughed, braking abruptly for an elderly woman tottering across the street with a bag of groceries. "Sounds like the other side of the moon."

"Oh no, it's really pretty cultured. We even have things like churches and universities."

"Let me guess—you're a math major."

"Definitely not. Fine arts."

"Ah, so I should expect you to produce a sketchbook full of scenes from the Scottish countryside before long?"

She grinned. "I'd love to … but I'd have to be in the countryside first."

"Patience, my dear. I need to make that trip to Ullapool and then I've got a couple of days free. If you'd like, you could come with me. I'm sure we can find you a few sheets of sketch paper somewhere in this jungle."

She did her best to contain her excitement as they slipped past rows of century-old tenement buildings before rounding the corner to Sauchiehall Street and then on to the junction at Buchanan.

"Here we are—the Buchanan Galleries—one of Glasgow's newest shopping centers. Now, if we can just locate a parking spot." A quarter of an hour and six blocks later, they headed back toward the shops, sheltered under matching red and white umbrellas. Jostling past shoppers, strollers, and groups of shouting children, they made their way up a wide set of cement stairs, through one of sixteen doors, and into a sky-lit rotunda where escalators and stairways fanned out in all directions leading to second and third stories.

Dougal grinned. "Just like Minneapolis?"

"Worse." She rolled her eyes and laughed.

They spent the next couple of hours investigating shops of every size and description, interrupted only by the constant ringing of Dougal's cell phone. "Sorry," he apologized, finally shutting it off. "I'm afraid everyone's geared up for the tourist season."

"No problem. I'm about finished shopping anyway."

"You're not exactly the last of the big-time spenders," he observed.

"I'd rather look first, buy later. Besides, my suitcase is jam-packed as it is."

He threw her a sideways grin. "Perhaps we should find you a new case."

"I think the prices here are a little steep." She tucked a frizzy strand behind one ear.

"No problem, then. I know just the place." He grabbed her hand and headed for the doorway.

"Where are we going?"

"You'll see—and I'm sure there isn't anything like it in all fifty states."

Keira glanced through the window of the Ullapool Youth Hostel as she made her way to the door. "Are you sure you won't come with us, Professor? You shouldn't be spending your time inside on such a beautiful day."

"I promise I'll go the next time," Julia said, an apologetic grin crinkling her eyes. "I've got a few things to check on first. You'd better hurry or you won't catch up with Amanda."

"Okay then, we won't stay out late." The door closed behind her and Julia squeezed her eyes tight, a headache beginning to throb at her temples. Oh, to be eighteen again where every jaunt held the promise of adventure. She gave a little laugh. Not that she was all that far removed —just a little more worldly-wise—unfortunately.

Opening her lap top, she positioned herself on the creaky rattan chair and clicked through until she came to the file on lichens. Just the sight of them usually filled her with a sense of comfort but not today. She let out her breath with a noisy "Whoosh." What was she doing anyway, sitting alone in a room? Hiding? She'd been down this road before. She had to get over herself. By the way she acted, anyone would believe she was the guilty party.

She got up and looked through the latticed window onto Shore Street. Business as usual, it seemed, with pedestrians, cyclists, and motorists all on their way to somewhere. Still, the town appeared to be more than simply quaint. It was as if there were hidden possibilities here. "Lord," she prayed aloud, "I know you've got good plans for me. Help me to keep that in mind when I feel like falling apart."

She moved into the bathroom, and finding an elastic, scrunched her ebony hair into a frizzy ponytail. She stood on tiptoes to peer at her image in the vintage mirror. Not bad. Creamy brown skin, black eyes, straight white teeth set in a wide mouth and a small, dainty chin.

Retrieving her purse from the back of a bedroom chair, she turned and grabbed the door handle, giving it a forceful twist. "Take that," she said. "Here's to open doors."

⁘⁘

"It's called 'The Barras'?" Sela peered through the rain-smeared windows as Dougal negotiated the narrow streets.

"Yes. Glasgow's version of the Paris flea market. It's just off the Gallowgate Road. You can buy anything you like there—although I must warn you—some items have been known to have a slightly questionable origin."

"Sounds intriguing. Will we get ourselves arrested?"

"Not likely, but Maggie McIver would be turning in her grave if she saw the place as it is today."

"Maggie who?" She held her breath as they roared past a silver Jaguar.

"The woman who started the whole thing. She began renting out barrows in the 1920s for hawkers to sell their wares. From there it turned into a market with a life of its own." He swung into an oversized parking lot where crowds of people streamed toward an arched gateway ahead. Thankfully the rain was letting up so they'd no longer need umbrellas.

"It looks like a circus."

"You might say that. In any case, stay close. I don't want anyone trying to make off with you."

A minute later they were swept into the carnival-like atmosphere of raucous laughter, bartering, bantering, and general camaraderie. Sela caught a whiff of unwashed bodies and greasy fish as her eyes brushed past row after row of cluttered stalls. Hawkers, claiming to be Scotland's biggest suppliers of everything from CD's to antique lamps, blared out a cacophony of enticements and last-chance offers while children, oblivious to the noise, darted about playing hide-and-seek.

"What do you think?" Dougal asked, bending to be heard above the din.

"I think it's fabulous! It's so alive." As she glanced about, her eyes were drawn to two men in sleeveless shirts and army fatigues standing off to the side eyeing her. Identical tattoos reached from their wrists, clear up to the top of their arms. Why were they looking at her like that? Were they planning to mug her? Abruptly they stepped forward and began shouldering their way through the crowd toward her. The closest one moved in as he approached and sneered into her face, his arm grazing hers just before he veered away. Sela shuddered and grabbed Dougal's arm. "On second thought ..."

"They're harmless," Dougal said. "It's just a big show."
"Do you think so? I read a newspaper article on the plane about neo-Nazi activity up in the highlands."

"The only activity you have to concern yourself with is right here." He stopped in front of a bulky stall overflowing with an array of handbags and cases in every imaginable hue—tangerine, fuchsia, sage, apricot, aqua, and more. The rich aroma of fine leather wafted toward them, mingled with others of a more uncertain nature.

Sela gawked at the display and immediately forgot the incident. "This is really amazing."

Dougal nudged her forward. "Go ahead. See how well you do at bartering."

She did her best to straighten her hair with one hand and stepped inside. Before long a man of about forty sauntered from the back, smiling broadly through a picket fence of yellow teeth. "Can I help ye, luv?" He gave her a slow up and down. "A woman of your breedin' must be wantin' something high class. How about Italian leather—dark, like the color of your eyes."

Sela stepped back as the stench of stale tobacco threatened to take her breath.

"The lady's looking for a spinner-case if you don't mind." Thankfully Dougal had decided to join her after all. "Just show us where they're at."

"Why didn't ye say so in the first place?" the man whined. "Us business folk aren't mind readers, ye know." Straightening, he swaggered to the back, the successful entrepreneur. "We keep our finest stock back here—so as to shield them from the young louts, ye understand." He indicated a set of cases against the wall. "As I said, they're high quality items."

Sela reached over and pulled out the nearest one—black, with a broken zipper.

"Ach, that must be my partner's doin'." He led her to a navy-blue case a few feet away. "How about this one? It's pure dead brilliant."

She took in the fine lines and sturdy material, imagining herself pulling it along with ease.

"Of course, it'll cost a bit more. This type was originally sold by Harrods of London."

"How much more?" cut in Dougal.

"I'll have to charge ye a pony at the least." His voice was low, conspiratorial.

"Twenty pound and that's it."

"Twenty pound! How do ye expect a man to make a livin?"

"Twenty-three," cut in Sela.

"Sold, to the lady wi' the beautiful eyes."

•◦◈◈◦————◦———————◦◈◈◦•

"What in the world is a pony, anyway?" she whispered under her breath as they made their way out of the stall, the spinner-case jostling behind Dougal.

"I thought you must know, the way you charged right in."

"I know what a pound is. Do you think I should've let you decide on the price?" She looked up at him, her eyebrows slightly arched.

"Dinna be daft, girl. It's yer own money."

Sela laughed. How come you don't speak with a Glaswegian accent like everyone else around here?"

"Oxford."

"Oxford?"

"No matter how you go in, you come out speaking the Queen's English."

"So you went to Oxford?" She gathered her hair in a knot behind her and let it go, sidestepping two women who were pushing matching strollers.

"Yes. I studied Scottish history."

"Ah," she said. "So it all comes together."

"All what?"

"The accent, the poise …"

"Like I said, dinna be daft."

She spent the next hour rummaging through old books, paintings and other paraphernalia while Dougal went off in search of his own treasures.

"Is your stomach beginning to speak to you?" he asked later when he found her.

"Yes," she said. "It's telling me to find some other place to eat."

"Well then, I've got the perfect spot—but you can't leave here without some token of Glaswegian culture." He took his hand from behind his back and held out a blue and green tartan beret. On one side, in small letters, was the word "Barrowland." "It's the Lamont tartan. Do you like it?"

"It's gorgeous," she gushed, smiling from ear to ear.

He reached over and placed it firmly on her head. "That should keep your hair in line."

Sela took a small mirror from her handbag and admired her image. "Well, I've got to admit —it's pure dead brilliant."

⁘═══════◆═══════⁘

The maitre d' guided them to a secluded softly lit corner. "Enjoy," she breathed once they were seated.

Sela gazed around. "Quite the culture shock."

"We're not all from the Barras, you know." He looked at her over his menu. "This part of Glasgow can compete with any world city."

"Do you come here often?"

"Occasionally. The art gallery and university are nearby."

"It's a beautiful place." She silently took in the dove-grey plaster walls, metal artwork, and contemporary chandeliers. "I'd be here every day if I lived in Glasgow." She opened the menu. "Or maybe not. I think I'll just have coffee."

Dougal grinned. "Not to worry. It's on me tonight."

"I hope I didn't sound destitute. Grandad left me his estate but I want to be careful with his money."

"You must've cared a lot for him."

"I do—did. He was everything to me." Her voice faltered and she tried to blink back a tear but it coursed down the curve of her cheek. "I feel so lost without him. Sorry … I must still be overtired."

"Are you alright? We don't have to stay." He reached across the table and touched her hand.

"I'm fine … really. Anyway," she said, recovering, "you're not getting out of buying my supper that easily."

"Okay, then. Let's see what damage we can do."

An hour later they were poking at the last remnants of smoked salmon in dill sauce with wild rice and artichokes. Dougal pushed back from the table. "How about dessert? They've got a wonderful sticky toffee pudding."

"Ordinarily I'd go for it," she said, "but today I think I'd explode. Coffee would be nice, though."

He ordered two coffees and they sat for a while in comfortable silence, enjoying an old Ella Fitzgerald jazz tune.

Sela held the steaming cup in both hands. She'd love to find out if he knew anything about Granddad's past but pushing it might cause him to clam up. Perhaps she could employ a little finesse. Batting her lashes, she looked up at him with a smile. "So how closely are we related, anyway? Would you call us cousins?"

Dougal grinned. "As I intimated before, we're not actually related at all—at least by blood. Your granddad was my adoptive father's brother. My father's first wife died and he married my mother when I was three.

"So what are we then—second cousins?"

"I believe I'd actually be something of an uncle—though we're of the same generation."

Sela smirked. "That's a little too weird for me. I think I'll just call you my cousin."

Dougal sipped at his coffee, changing the subject. "What was your main reason for coming, Sela? Was it just to meet your long-lost family?"

"That was a big part of it." She crossed her legs.

"And the rest?"

"What makes you think there's more?"

"I don't know. I guess it's just that we've never had any contact in the past."

"You must've heard about the accident."

He nodded, lowering his voice as another couple took a seat directly opposite them. "Sorry. I didn't mean to bring up past tragedies."

"It's okay. It was a long time ago. When my parents and grandma were killed, it took Granddad and me all our energy to go on. I moved into his house in Minneapolis and we made a life for ourselves. But I was always curious about the rest of the family."

"So you decided to come over and get acquainted with the clan."

"That's pretty much it." She paused, weighing her words. "There's one other thing, though."

He looked up.

"Remember yesterday I mentioned the name Tanika? I think Granddad was in contact with her—in Ullapool."

She waited while a server stopped to refill their cups. As the woman turned to leave, the coffee pot bumped against Dougal's shoulder, sloshing a few drops onto his pant leg. He jumped back and grabbed a napkin, painstakingly wiping off the offending splotches. "Do you have any idea how much …" He stopped mid-sentence. "Sorry. Please forgive me. It's just that I've newly had these pants dry-cleaned."

"It's completely my fault, sir" she said. "I'll be happy to pay for them to be cleaned again." Though her smile was in place, Sela noticed her lips had gone chalk white.

"Really, it's no problem at all." He glanced at the other couple, nodding as they looked away. "Let's just forget about it."

When the waitress had gone, he looked sheepishly at Sela. "Sorry. I tend to like things neat and clean."

Sela smirked, recalling the clump of clothes she'd stuffed into her suitcase that morning. Thankfully he hadn't witnessed the mess. "I guess it's not the biggest problem in the world."

"Anyway, what makes you think your granddad contacted someone in Ullapool?"

"The old picture I found of her had a building in the background with the letters "Ull" on it. There was also a phone bill with three blacked-out calls made to someone in Ullapool. He must not have wanted me to find it."

"But why would he be phoning her now?"

"I don't know, but before he left on his trip, he told me there was something in his past."

"Here in Scotland?"

"Yes. I'm thinking maybe it was something he wasn't proud

of … although I can't really imagine what. He stuck to his faith through thick and thin."

Dougal shifted in his seat.

"Do you know something?" She leaned forward.

"No—it's nothing. I'm sure your granddad was a very reputable man."

"Of course he was. He was the best person I've ever known—along with my parents of course. But if you know something …"

"Don't worry. It's nothing. I just want you to have a good time."

She sat quietly for a bit. There were lots of things she'd like to talk to him about—the phone call, the break-in, and now the letter from Great-Grandma—but was that wise? He'd probably think she was some kind of drama queen. Besides, Great-Grandma had told her to keep the letter to herself.

Changing the subject again, she asked, "Don't you think it's a coincidence that you've been going to Ullapool?"

"Possibly, but like I said, I deal with some of the tartan shops on the main stretch."

She put her coffee cup down. "When did you say you're going?"

"I was planning to leave in a few days but I could go sooner if you're really anxious."

"I don't want you to change your plans. What about the day after tomorrow? That way I could spend a little more time with your parents and Great-Grandma."

Dougal smiled. "I'll make a few calls."

They spent the rest of the day strolling through the Kelvin Grove Art Gallery viewing paintings by Monet, Degas, and Renoir. Her heart raced at the sight of so many originals.

"Degas is my favorite," she said. I love his Dancers in Blue. What about you? Are you a fan of his?"

He hesitated. "Actually, I prefer a more contemporary artist—a Scotsman named Jim Dewar. I like his untamed seascapes where the wind is tossing huge waves all about."

"So you're really saying that you're wild at heart."

"You might say that—but it's yet to be decided whether I'm the wind or the waves." He laughed and guided her toward the door. "Mum will be wondering where we've got to. We'd better head back."

The following day her aunt and uncle took her to see Great-Grandma at the nursing home. They found the tiny woman seated in a lounge chair, cocooned in a soft-looking white blanket.

"I've brought your great-granddaughter to see you today, Mother," Uncle Alex said. "Remember she came to visit us?"

"Of course, dear. I'm not a dunderhead, ye know." She looked over at Sela. "Have they been treating you well, luv?"

"Like the queen herself. And Dougal's been showing me around the city." Sela took her hand. "It's so good to see you again."

"And you as well, luv. It's like seeing Joseph all over again."

"Do I really look like him?"

"Aye. It's that reddish colored hair with the dark eyes—not to mention the Lamont dimple. I'd have known you anywhere—even with my poor vision."

Uncle Alec pulled over some chairs and they sat down next to her. After a few minutes, Aunt Agnes brought out her knitting, apparently settling in for the long haul. Sela blew out her breath. It would be nice if they'd take a walk or go buy a crumpet or something so she'd have time alone with Great-Grandma. It might be her only chance to ask about the letter. Her aunt and uncle, however, seemed rooted to the spot.

Half an hour later Aunt Agnes brought the visit to a close. "We can carry on with this another time. Mother's starting to nod off. We don't want to tire her out completely."

As Sela leaned forward to kiss the old woman goodbye, she heard a hushed whisper in her ear. "Don't forget about the letter, luv." Sela squeezed her hand and stood. Leaving her in the care of a young nurse, they caught the next train back to Steppes.

Dougal arrived a few minutes later. "I've made all the arrangements," he said. "How are you at backpacking?"

"Backpacking? I thought it was about two hundred miles from Glasgow to Ullapool?"

"One hundred forty-five, to be exact." He slouched onto the sofa, his long legs stretching out in front. "Of course, we don't have to walk the whole way. I thought we'd take the train to Inverness and then catch a bus to the Corrieshalloch Gorge—a mere twelve miles from Ullapool. That way you can see some of the sights first hand."

"But I can't backpack with a suitcase—even my new one."

"That's why I'm going to lend you my other backpack." He smiled smugly.

"Maybe Sela doesn't like walking," Uncle Alec said. "Did you ever think of that? It's just like you to consider yourself before everyone else."

Dougal's mouth formed a thin line. "That did cross my mind, Dad. It's not set in stone."

"I think it would be fun," Sela cut in, "Backpacking up in the Highlands. It sounds so romantic."

"It won't be quite so romantic with a foot full of blisters." Aunt Agnes huffed into the kitchen to put on the tea.

Sela smiled. "I've got my sneakers with me. I ran a half marathon in them so they should be okay."

"It's a done deal, then." Dougal stood up, his own smile returning. "I hope you brought a few warm things. It can get chilly up there. Get your duds together and I'll get the backpack to you first thing in the morning."

"How long will we be gone?"

"Let's say four or five days at the outset."

"I'll have to go to the bank machine before we leave," she said, grinning. "All I've got on me is a pony."

Dougal laughed. "How in the world did you come across the meaning of that expression?"

"It was easy. Great-Grandma told me."

He shook his head in amusement. "I can see I'll have to keep my eye on you. Bad companions, you know."

She sat back, thankful when the family began another topic of conversation. Tomorrow they'd backpack to Ullapool. What would she find? Whatever it was, she couldn't get there fast enough.

Chapter Four

The steadily changing landscape brought to her mind one of those old flip-book animations where the character moves as you release the pages with your thumb—Olive Oil sashaying down the street to meet Popeye or Felix the Cat pouncing on an unsuspecting mouse. As they traveled north, the lowlands had spontaneously turned into a wilderness of heathery mountains, gorges and gushing waterfalls. An artist's dream, she thought. And me without my paints.

She looked over at Dougal who was leaning back in the seat with his mouth slightly ajar, snoring. Surely that sprint at Inverness hadn't done him in. They'd taken off at a dead run from the train station, barely making it to the bus before it pulled out in a wide diesel-belching arc, the driver apparently intent on announcing their departure to the world.

Soon they'd be at Corrieshalloch Gorge, whatever that was. She bent down and retied her laces. Tonight she'd sleep in Ullapool.

The driver's animated voice cut in on her thoughts. "Ladies and gents, we are now approaching one of Scotland's most amazing wonders—the Falls of Measach, plunging one hundred fifty feet down the Corrieshalloch Gorge. Straight ahead there's a Victorian suspension bridge for any brave souls who …"

Sela was straining to see the falls when she noticed a man about four rows ahead remove his cap and turn to stare directly at her, his mouth forming an ugly sneer. She averted her eyes. Was she imagining it? Who in the world could he be and why was he looking at her like that? Her heart began to thump. Something about him was familiar. "Dougal," she whispered, "Could you wake up? There's a man up there looking at me."

Without opening his eyes, Dougal began to quietly chuckle. "Surely this isn't the first time you've come up against that."

"I'm not kidding." She glanced toward him again. He had turned back around but his arm was draped over the seat, revealing numerous tattoos including a thistle reaching from wrist to shoulder. As she took in the shaved head, skeletal-like facial structure, and muscular arm, it suddenly dawned on her. "Dougal," she whispered again, "He's one of those creeps that nearly charged into us at the Barras. What do you think he's doing here?"

Dougal unfolded his long legs and sat up. "Where is he?"

She pointed ahead but the man had once again donned his hat and sat slumped, half hidden among the other passengers.

"We're getting off here anyway," Dougal said, "but I'll see if I recognize him on the way by."

The driver wheeled into the parkade. "We'll be stoppin' here for a few minutes, ladies and gentlemen. Feel free to get out and explore."

As the bus pulled into the assigned space, the couple ahead stood and moved into the middle of the aisle where they painstakingly rearranged their paraphernalia in the overhead carrier.

Dougal looked at Sela helplessly as the man vanished into the crowd. "So much for that. I'll keep my eye out for him, but chances are it was just coincidental." They made their way out of the bus to recover their backpacks from the undercarriage.

"Ye must stop for a few moments to view the falls," the driver told them, his pudgy face glowing. "Why don't ye leave your bags here for the time being. It's just a twenty-minute walk through the Kissing Gate and then over to the bridge." He paused, giving Dougal an exaggerated wink. "Ye may earn yourself a wee peck from the lady for your trouble."

Dougal threw Sela a mischievous smile. "Sounds scrumptious, doesn't it darling."

She shot him a look. "Positively dizzying."

They left their bags and made their way across the lot. "I wonder if the Kissing Gate is for kissing cousins?" he said, laughing. Sela noticed that his eyes lingered a moment on her lips and her heart began to flutter. What was the matter with her?

He grabbed her hand and led her through the gate. "This way, mademoiselle. Believe me—you'll be wanting to hold onto something when we get there." They followed the dank path before them. A spongy forest floor carpeted the ground on either side and colonies of toadstools sprang from rotting logs and fallen branches. Tattered rags of Spanish moss dangled overhead from birch, oak, and hazel trees.

"Do you see those mushrooms over there?" he whispered, pointing to a darkly-shadowed area between the trees. "Don't go near them. They're said to be hallucinogenic."

"That's all I need," she said, rolling her eyes. She was becoming aware of a steadily growing roar. "We must be close to the falls." They stepped into a clearing and saw the bridge directly ahead—long and narrow and swaying slightly as two people alighted on the other side. "Do you think it's safe?"

"I haven't heard of anyone plunging into the depths recently."

Sela took a tentative step forward and stopped. Her heart seemed to be pounding louder than the falls. "I can't do it. For some reason, I'm terrified."

"I've got an idea." Dougal spoke softly. "Just trust me. Hold onto the rails, close your eyes and take ten steps forward. When you open them you'll be in the middle of the bridge and I'll be right behind you."

She took in a deep breath. "Okay, I'll do it." She closed her eyes, resisting the heady sensation. Holding tightly to the rails, she stepped forward. The bridge swayed as she took another step and counted out loud—two, three, four. A gust of wind lifted her hair and pulled it back away from her face. She clutched the sides but kept going.

After the tenth step she opened her eyes and looked behind. Dougal was still back on the ledge. She peered dizzily down at the vertical rock walls and rushing water far below. She was alone in the middle of space. "Dougal!" she screamed. "You said you'd be right behind me." White dots danced in front of her eyes and her knees began to buckle. She was going to faint. "Granddad!"

Within seconds Dougal's arms were around her as he pulled her to her feet. "I'm so sorry. I wanted you to get the full impact of the falls. I didn't imagine it would scare you like that."

She took in a ragged breath, clutching him with white-knuckled fingers. "Get me off here." They backed up, a step at a time, until they were once again on the bank. Sela sank down on the cushiony moss and lay still. Slowly her breathing returned to normal and she sat up. "I'm sorry." Her face still felt bleached white. "That only happened once before—when I was alone at the top of a Ferris wheel the year after my parents died. Granddad had to get a man to stop the whole thing and bring me down. I've never been on a ride since."

Dougal squeezed her hand, and gave her a sheepish grin. "Can ye forgive such a lout?"

After a moment, she grinned back. "Och aye—just as long as he brings me my backpack and serves me my lunch."

"It's as good a time as any," he said, and was gone. Sela closed her eyes again, allowing the cool breeze to quiet her mind. Poor Dougal. She'd probably scared him half to death. What was the matter with her anyhow?

It wasn't long before he was back, spreading a cloth between them and setting out Drunileish cheese, oatcakes, dried apricots, and a thermos of tea. "And now, m'lady," he said, when their appetites had been assuaged, "the piece de resistance." From under one of the packs he produced a small white paper bag. "Do you trust me?"

She paused. "Of course."

"Then close your eyes and open your mouth."

Sela slowly closed her eyes, her mouth opening slightly.

"You can do better than that."

She opened her mouth wider and was rewarded with the luscious taste of milk chocolate. "Where in the world did you find that?" she asked, savoring the silky texture.

"Let's just say I have my sources."

She leaned back against a smooth stone and regarded him lazily. "I could lie here forever. You've almost made me lose my focus."

His eyes fixed on hers. "We can stay as long as you like."

Abruptly she sat up. "But what about Granddad? That was the whole purpose."

"You're right," he said with a sigh. He checked his watch. "And if we're to reach Ullapool tonight we'd better be off." They quickly donned their backpacks, deposited the remnants of lunch into the waste bin and set off on the A835.

Directly overhead the sun broke free of a roguish band of clouds, warming her skin and clearing her mind of every recalcitrant thought.

<hr />

It took until suppertime to reach Ullapool. The changeless backdrop of purple hills along the winding road, coupled with the fragrance of honeysuckle, hawthorn, and wild rose had left her exhilarated but weary. "I think your mother was right about the blisters," she said, arranging her socks more comfortably into her shoes.

"That's Loch Broom on your left. Try to hold on. We're nearly there." As they started downhill, a long strip of land came into view, jutting out from the harbor. "I give you Ullapool," Dougal said with a flourish of his hand.

From their vantage point, Sela looked down on a gleaming row of whitewashed buildings following the shoreline. Blue, red, and white fishing boats bobbed about close to the docks, struggling for freedom, while out at sea a massive ship lurked in the deep water.

"It's one of the last factory ships," Dougal said, seeing her look. "It's called a Klondiker. The fish are caught, processed and packaged all in one fell swoop."

Sela shuddered. She preferred to look out at the surrounding mountains and distant Summer Isles. "It's breathtaking," she said, feeling a sudden thrill.

The hike down to the town took only a brief time, their first order of business that of finding accommodations. Dougal looked over at her expectantly. "I've heard the Ullapool Youth Hostel has a good name. And the location is perfect—it's right on Shore Street, close to all the amenities."

"Spoken like a true business man," she laughed. "Let's go check it out."

They found their way through the narrow streets to the hostel and entered the whitewashed door. The woman at the desk appeared friendly but Sela didn't like the way her eyes darted back and forth. "Canadian or American?" she asked, taking in everything from dusty shoes to unruly hair.

"I'm from Glasgow and my cousin is from the United States." Dougal's voice was all business.

"I see. You'll be wantin' to room together then?" Her brows arched almost to her hairline.

"No," Sela cut in. "Separately."

"Well then, there's three girls from New York in Room Two. I can put you in with them."

"That's fine. Are they here right now?"

"No, they won't be back till late. Gone treasure hunting on the strip—no doubt for the two-legged variety, if ye know what I mean." She laughed at her own joke. "And you, sir? Haven't I seen you around these parts before?"

Dougal smiled. "Possibly, but I'm usually here on business.

Today it's pure pleasure. Do you have a single room? I'm afraid I can't hack the snoring of some of the chaps."

Sela stifled a grin, thinking back to the bus trip.

"There's a small room next to the laundry," the woman said after checking her register. "Not much but it's private."

"Perfect. I'll take it."

They decided to meet back in the lobby at six-thirty.

She stood, head back, in the tiny shower allowing the hot spray to saturate her skin and draw the weariness from her muscles. In a few minutes she'd crawl into the unclaimed bed and sleep for an hour. After supper she'd start the search for Tanika.

Her eyes closed as she breathed in the humid air. Suddenly, with a loud splutter the shower head began swinging wildly, spewing icy blasts out into the mist. She jumped back with a gasp, fumbling with the unfamiliar handle. By the time she was able to shut it off the drowsiness was long gone. "Perfect."

"Ah, I see you've been christened," a female voice laughed.

Sela quickly reached for the towel and gathering it around her, stepped out into the room. Cross legged on a bed, laptop open in front of her, sat a petite young African-American woman, her hair pulled back in a frizzy pony tail and a wide smile alighting her features. "I heard we had company. I'm Julia Kalahadi."

"Sela Lamont. Sorry. I didn't hear you come in. You're from New York?"

"Staten Island. And you?"

"Minneapolis. I see we have a similar problem." She pulled at the ends of her hair.

Julia laughed. "Maybe it's a North American phenomenon. Are you here on vacation?"

"Sort of. What about you?"

"Half business, half fun. I'm teaching a botany class at the

University of Aberdeen. Since this is reading week, I came with two of my students to take in the sights while we finish up our project."

"Sounds like fun. What are you working on?"

"We're studying a rare species of lichen that grows on hazel trees—a type of 'Graphidion Scriptae,' if that means anything to you."

"Not really, but it sounds interesting." Sela pulled a clean outfit from the middle section of the case and quickly dressed.

"I don't suppose you know any of the local people?"

"Not really. Anyone in particular?"

"Just a friend of my granddad's. I think her name is Tanika McLeod. It's kind of a long shot, actually.

"Sorry, I haven't heard that name." She tapped her slender fingers on the skimpy quilt. "Have you checked the phone book? They usually list nearly everyone."

"I took a quick look when I first got here. There were about twenty-five T. McLeods, so …"

Just then two girls, about eighteen years of age, burst into the room. "Hey Julia, we found some terrific botany and we're 'lichen' them," the tall one said with a giggle.

"Quite rare, too," the blond countered.

Julia crossed her arms in mock sternness. "Doesn't sound like A-plus material to me." She introduced them as Keira and Amanda, both natives of Aberdeen.

"I thought the woman at the desk said all of you were from New York."

"I'm afraid the woman at the desk doesn't always get her facts straight. Be careful what you say to her." She gathered her things together and turned toward the door, the girls in tow. "If you get any free time, we'd love to have you join us."

Sela pulled the backpack up onto the bed. She'd just dab on a bit of makeup, stick some anti-frizz gel in her hair and go meet up with Dougal. It was already 6:20. She was about to unzip the front section when the door swung back open. "Just me again," Julia said.

"Forgot my keys." She grabbed them off the bed and with a quick wave, was gone.

Sela opened the zipper and reached in to pull out her makeup bag. Suddenly her finger poked into something sharp and she jerked her hand back, startled. What in the world? Her finger was bleeding.

She peered in and let out a strangled gasp. The makeup bag lay open. Inside, the containers lay strewn about in a jumbled heap. All the lids had been removed and the contents scooped out and smeared together as if by a naughty child. Lying lengthwise at the top was a long, wilted thistle.

Her hands began shaking and she wrapped her arms and legs tightly about her, staring at the chaos. She wished she were back home in Minneapolis sipping tea with Granddad on the deck. Nothing like this had ever happened when he'd been around.

She sat curled up for a long time, afraid where her thoughts might lead. At last she forced herself to think. Who would have done this? She hardly knew anyone here.

Think backwards. That's what her Math teacher had suggested when she couldn't figure out an algebra question. Think backwards. Slowly, she began to retrace her steps. When had she been away from the backpack? During her shower. Julia Kalahadi could have done it when she was showering. Why had she come back to the room anyway?

No. That was crazy. What possible reason would she have for destroying her makeup? If anything, she might have borrowed it— not ruined it. Where were they before that? Backpacking to town. And just before that they'd had lunch at Corrieshalloch Gorge.

That was it. The man on the bus. He probably saw them leave their backpacks with the driver when they went to look at the falls. He'd had the opportunity, but what in the world was his motive?

A sudden chill ran through her. His arm had been tattooed with a long thistle. She looked over at the case, the dead thistle lying like a wordless threat. What could he possibly have against her? Sure, he'd nearly bumped into her at the Barras but that wasn't such a big deal.

Maybe she'd given him a dirty look. Maybe he didn't like Americans. Maybe—stop. This was ridiculous. How could he have known where she was from? And why would he care?

And what was the significance of the thistle? Was it some sort of gang symbol? Had he mistaken her for someone else?

She felt violated. His hands had been rifling through her things. How could she ever wear them again?

"Sela. Are you in there?" Dougal's voice, coming from behind the door, sounded anxious and she realized he must have called her more than once.

She leaped up and ran to the door, flinging it open.

"What's wrong? It's almost 7 o'clock." He stepped back and took in the scene before him. "What happened here?"

"Oh, Dougal," she said, tears beginning to stream down her face. "Somebody hates me." For the second time that day, he took her in his arms and patted her hair as she choked out the story.

"We'll exchange backpacks," he said when she'd finished. "You take mine and we'll buy you some new things. Don't worry. Someone was just playing a nasty prank."

She pulled herself away and blew her nose. "I don't know what's going on. If it wasn't so important to me, I'd leave right now."

"Sela, you don't have to prove a point to anyone. Your granddad was a good man."

"That's why I want to make sure … I mean … I'm not letting that creep scare me away from here."

"Alright then," he said, "let's go have a bite to eat and then pick up some incidentals at the chemist. They're open quite late."

She offered him a cautious smile. "Are you sure you want to be seen around a red-eyed girl with frizzy hair and no makeup?"

"You could be wearing a burlap bag and you'd still be the most beautiful woman in town." Dougal lifted the backpack and took her arm as they went out the door.

Chapter Five

Marching to the beat of the drummers, twelve young pipers in Mackenzie kilts and green Barathea jackets puffed out their cheeks and blew into the blowpipes, their fingers deftly sliding along the chanters as they produced a rousing version of "Scotland the Brave."

Sela and Dougal stepped out from the drug store entrance and clapped along with the spectators lining Quay Street. "It's the Junior Pipe Band," he said. "If we had more time we could watch the whole performance."

"I'd like that, but it's getting late." She looked up at him. "I'm starting to feel anxious about finding Tanika."

"Don't worry," he said. "Perhaps we can see it another time. Let's go." They turned and made their way toward Shore Street.

"Have you ever tried your hand at the bagpipes?"

"'Try' would be the operative word. It's more complicated than it looks. Something to do with keeping the air pressure constant between the blowpipe and the bag."

"Well, at least no one can accuse you of being a windbag."

"Very funny."

They passed by the Ullapool Bookshop, its narrow windows revealing wooden tables stacked high with reading materials. A handwritten sign was taped to the glass—Internet Facilities Within. "I'll have to keep that in mind in case we don't come up with anything.""

Dougal checked his watch. "So what's the plan? Should we just visit the shops and see if anyone knows of Tanika?"

"I've got a better idea," she said. "I think we should look for older businesses and try to find someone close to Granddad's age. Maybe we'll come across the shop I saw in the photograph."

As they approached the intersection of Argyle Street, Dougal slowed his step. "We'd probably cover a lot more ground if we split up, you know. Why don't you take this street and I'll take Shore Street? We'll meet at the Ceilidh Place at 9:30 to compare notes. It's right here on Argyle."

Sela looked down at her feet. "Sure … I just thought we could go together."

"And we will. But I think we'd get more accomplished tonight if we did it this way." He cupped her chin in his hand and spoke softly as he looked into her eyes. "Don't worry. If she's here, we'll find her."

She swallowed. "I know it probably sounds dumb but I'd feel safer if I was with you. What if that guy shows up?"

"Don't worry, he's long gone. And I'll only be a street over." He squeezed her shoulder and left.

She could still feel the gentle pressure of his fingers a block away as she squinted into the setting sun. "Concentrate," she told herself. "You're not here to find a boyfriend—especially one related to you". What was she thinking?

Getting down to business, she entered the next shop she came to but no one seemed to know who she was talking about. Heaving a sigh of frustration, she was about to continue on when she noticed a weathered stucco building on the other side of the street. The peeling sign above the door indicated it was a butcher shop. Maybe someone there would know about Tanika.

She crossed over and looked into the darkening window. Suspended from a meat hook, hung the carcass of a skinned sheep, its lifeless eyes staring vacantly onto the street. She looked away disgusted, but in spite of herself, was compelled to look back. She was about to leave when something caught her eye. What was it?

She stood still. There it was again. The nuance between dark and darker. Her heart began to pound. Was it something in the window or a reflection from the street? She whirled around.

Facing her stood an overweight middle-aged man, his yellowed butcher's apron spattered with blood and his eyes lit with amusement. A long cigarette dangled from his sausage-like fingers. Where had he come from? She stepped back.

"May I help you?" He blew a thick stream of smoke through rubbery lips.

"No … I was just looking …"

"Are ye interested in buying some lamb, then?" He nodded sideways toward the window.

"No thanks. I'm just trying to find someone."

"In the butcher shop?" He smirked.

"Of course not. I can see it's closed." She glanced at the nicotine stains on his hands. "Excuse me." She turned to leave.

"If you want to find someone, ye might try the pub at the Ceilidh Place just down the street. The old man there knows everybody."

"Thanks." She hurried away, the heels of her shoes clicking loudly on the sidewalk with each fleeting step. What was wrong with her? He was just a butcher.

She could hear the music and laughter a block away. A series of connected, white-washed houses came into view as she rounded the curve of the street, their pointy roof lines emerging like a miniature castle. Above each doorway was a decorative sign—Art Gallery, Restaurant, Pub. Judging from the number of people milling about, the pub was definitely the place to be.

Why had she let Dougal talk her into splitting up? Everyone would think she was a loser walking in alone. As she hesitated, a group of men in dirty work overalls looked toward her. "Are ye not coming in, lassie?" one of them called out. "There's a seat with your name on it."

"Aye, right next to mine," countered another, his eyes mocking her beneath an oily cap. He opened the heavy wooden door, bowing at the waist in an exaggerated welcome while the others hooted in laughter.

Sela cringed. There was no turning back now. She'd look like a fool. "I'm just waiting for someone," she said, her cheeks burning as if they'd been scorched.

"Why don't ye wait with me?"

"Why don't you get lost?" a deep voice behind her countered.

Sela swiveled around and saw Dougal. He placed a bouquet of miniature carnations into her hands and taking her arm, led her through the door while the others stepped aside, their eyebrows raised in surprise.

"Sorry. I meant to arrive ahead of you."

"How'd you get here so fast," she whispered in relief. "I thought you'd be at least half an hour."

"I didn't realize Ullapool rolled up the carpets quite so early. I'm usually here in the daytime." He guided her through the haze of boisterous customers to an empty booth where they took a seat on the broad wooden benches. "It seems I'm always rescuing you from admirers."

"I'm just glad you showed up when you did. Where'd you get the flowers?" She fingered the delicate petals.

"The flower shop was one place that was still open. Other than that, I didn't have any luck. What about you?"

"None, except for some creepy guy at a butcher shop. He said the old man who runs this place knows everyone."

"Let's find out if he's right." They looked up and saw a woman maneuvering through the crowd toward them with menus in hand. She had a youngish appearance but as she approached, Sela noticed the brassy sheen to her hair and deep vertical lines around her mouth.

"What'll it be, luv?" she asked huskily. She appraised Dougal through thick layers of mascara.

"Could you tell us if the proprietor's in?" he asked.

"I'm afraid not, luv. Taken the night off, he has. Are you a friend of his?"

"We'd like to talk to him if we could. Would you be able to tell us when he'll be here?"

"Not till morning, I'm afraid." She leaned forward. "If you're needing help, I'm sure I could be of assistance."

Sela gave her best impression of a smile as she placed her hand on Dougal's arm. "Do you happen to know someone called Tanika?"

"Doesn't ring a bell." The waitress kept her gaze fixed on Dougal.

"Have you worked here long?" Sela persisted.

The woman paused, her eyes closed in studied patience. "Let me know if you're meanin' to eat." She dropped the menus onto the table and huffed toward another booth.

"Ouch," Dougal said. "I don't think she's too happy with you."

Sela smiled sweetly. "I guess it was my turn to rescue you for a change."

An hour later they trudged back to the hostel, none the wiser for the evening's efforts. When they reached Sela's room, she turned toward him with a sigh. "I hope we'll have better luck tomorrow."

Dougal nodded. "We'll get an early start in the morning. There's a place I'd like to show you before we begin, if that's alright. Afterward we can investigate to our hearts' content."

"You're full of surprises, aren't you. She looked down at the carnations. "Thanks again for the flowers. They're beautiful. And for lending me your other backpack. I can't tell you how glad I am you're with me."

He bent his head and brushed her cheek with his lips. "Not as glad as I am." With that he turned and ambled down the white-washed corridor. Sela leaned against the door, her knees weak and her heart thumping. Was that a cousinly kiss?

A short time later she was settling into the lumpy cot at the far end of the room, her mind working overtime with the events of the day. She drifted into a troubled sleep, dreaming of Granddad on a swinging bridge and men with tattoos chasing her. She was only vaguely aware of the door opening and three giggling girls fumbling about in the dark before they, too, settled in for the night.

<hr />

She awoke with a start and rolled over to check the time. Just after seven. The room was quiet except for the chirping of a few sparrows outside the latticed window. She stood and picking up her towel, tiptoed across the squeaky floorboards to the bathroom.

Gingerly, she turned on the tap. The shower-head seemed to hesitate, then suddenly sprang to life, swiveling once again from side to side as it belched out freezing cold water. "Deja vu," she groaned as she washed up in record time and turned off the offending blast.

Wrapping herself in the towel, she opened the bathroom door and peeked out.

Two of the beds showed no sign of life but on the closest one, Julia stirred and sat up, her hair sticking out in a mass of errant curls. "We meet again," she whispered with a grin.

"Sorry," Sela grimaced, creeping back across the room. "There must be a knack to that thing."

"I think the knack would be in the form of a new shower head. Did you sleep well? I hope we didn't wake you up when we got back."

"I barely heard you," she said. "My cousin and I had an early night. What about you? Did you have a good time last night?"

"It was okay—if fending off unwelcome attention counts." She threw her legs over the side of the bed and stood, stretching. "Just some slightly inebriated jerk trying to impress us with his knowledge."

"Did you tell him what you do for a living?"

"The girls mentioned it. At that point he became highly interested in the rare species of lichens. Finally I told him to take a hike."

Sela laughed. "Good for you." She pulled out a pair of khakis, a light blue T-shirt and navy sweater. Dressing quickly, she did her hair and makeup. "Sorry I have to run off."

"Hey, where'd you get the flowers?"

"A little gift from my cousin. He's been a real sport about showing me around. It should be me getting him something."

"Don't forget my invitation to join us sometime."

"I won't." She stuck on her beret, grabbed her purse and went out the door.

Dougal was already waiting in the cramped lobby, his knees brushing the desk in front of him as he sat stiffly on the bare wooden chair. He looked up as she approached. "Ready to go?" His smile was bright but Sela noticed a hollowness to his eyes. Hadn't he slept well?

"Aye aye captain. Lead the way."

"What will it be first—breakfast or point of interest?"

"You decide."

"How about point of interest- breakfast-investigation?"

She stroked her chin. "Hmm … sounds like you've got it all figured out, Sherlock. Let's go." She grabbed his arm and they left.

"Right this way," he said, leading her west on Shore Street.

"Now can you tell me where we're going?"

"You'll see." The fragrance of freshly baked bread wafted toward them as they passed by a bakery and turned left on Mill Street. Sela's stomach growled loudly. "May I ask the point to this point of interest?"

"Just a little sight-seeing before a busy day." There was something forced about his banter but it didn't seem like the right time to mention it. They were now out of the town limits and past the sign to Blughasary. "There we go." He pointed to another sign. "Postie's Path."

"What's that supposed to be?"

"It's the path the postmen used to take when they were delivering the mail. It's not in decent shape anymore but it affords such a beautiful view of the coast I wanted you to see it. Shall we?"

They left the main road and began following a narrow trail uphill through a wooded area. Before long the trees disappeared and a panoramic view of Loch Broom came into sight with a steep hill standing guard behind. In the distance, bands of low-lying fog shrouded the heathery hills.

"It looks like we jumped into a fairy tale," Sela said, taking a step forward.

"Just be careful of your footing," Dougal warned her. "You may look like a nymph but I doubt you'll be able to fly if you go over the edge."

"I wish I had my sketch pad with me. It's so beautiful."

"We can come back any time you like." He reached into the small knapsack he was carrying and handed her a thermos. "Have some tea. I don't want you fainting before breakfast." She took a sip and they walked on in silence. Taking off her beret, she let her hair stream out behind her in the soft breeze as the pungent fragrance of salt water prickled at her nose. She looked over at Dougal. "You seem a little stiff this morning. Is everything okay?"

He smiled but his eyes didn't seem to be in it. "Everything's fine." He paused before going on. "There is one thing though …"

"Yes?" She looked up at him, trying to gauge his mood.

"I haven't been entirely honest with you. I need to tell you something."

She swallowed, her throat suddenly dry. Mr. Blakely had said the same thing a few weeks ago. "What is it?" she asked.

"Let's sit a moment." He pulled her down beside him on a grassy knoll by the edge of the path.

Sela felt her heart begin to flutter. She was afraid to look at him. "Just tell me. Are you sorry you brought me here with you?"

"No, no, it's not that at all." He put his arm around her shoulder and gave it a little squeeze. "I really like being with you. And I don't want to hurt you. I've been trying to devise a way out of telling you this, but I think that not knowing would hurt you more in the long run."

She pulled away. "Telling me what?"

He hesitated, seeming to weigh his words. "It's about your granddad leaving Scotland."

Sela stared at him. "What about it?"

"I'm sure it's just a rumor, but there still seems to be a lot of old gossip about it."

She couldn't breathe. "Just tell me."

Dougal sighed and went on. "Apparently, he was mixed up in some kind of espionage with that Tanika woman during the Second World War." He lowered his voice. "He would've been arrested if he'd stayed on in Scotland."

Sela jumped up and glared at him. "Who told you that?"

"Please, Sela. I'm just the messenger. This is hard for me, too."

She turned her back, the words of Great-Grandma's letter searing into her brain— "New orders from the Fuhrer himself … Payment to arrive shortly." How did he know about that? She thought it was a secret.

She looked out over the peaceful water, the reflection of the hills now boldly painted on its placid surface. In a minute, she felt him place a hand on her shoulder and turn her around. "I know you loved him." His voice was soft as velvet.

She looked into his eyes and saw the hollowness again. So this was the reason he'd been so strained. He hadn't wanted to break it to her. "How long ago did you hear this?" she asked in a whisper.

"I've known for a while." They stood that way for a long time, the tension between them tangible. For some reason she was strangely drawn to him, as if the news about her grandfather was somehow losing significance. What was wrong with her?

"There is one other thing."

"What is it?"

"I just got word from the company that I have to get back to Glasgow. I need to leave within the hour."

She heaved a sigh. "I thought you had a few days off. You said we could investigate to our hearts' content."

"That was before. The company is a wicked taskmaster. Believe me, I'd rather be here." He tried to take her arm but she pulled away.

"Sela, I want you to come back with me. There's really nothing for you here."

Her head shot up in disbelief. "Nothing for me? Do you think I'd leave now that I'm here and let my grandfather's name be dragged through the mud for another half century? Besides, it's just a rumor."

"It's not just a rumor." He paused. "There's proof."

"Proof?"

He looked down. "Your grandfather was apparently instrumental in leading the Nazis to some sort of treasure."

She sprang back from him. "That's not true. How dare you."

"Sela, do you think I like this?"

"I don't know what you like. I just know you're wrong."

"Think for a minute." He paused as though embarrassed to go on. "Did he leave you a fairly substantial inheritance?"

"None of your business. He was a hard worker. Anyway, what's that got to do with it?"

"Where do you think he got the money?"

"I told you, he was a hard worker."

"You think the railroad pays that well?"

Sela opened her mouth to speak but nothing came out. She'd been a bit surprised herself. He'd always been so Spartan in his spending.

"Look," Dougal said, taking both her hands. "There may be a

logical explanation but I don't think you'll find it here. Come back to Glasgow with me. I promise we'll have a wonderful time together."

She shook her head. "I can't. I'm committed to seeing this through to the end and I won't leave until I do."

"Alright then," he said with a sigh. "I've done what I could." They turned and as they made their way back down the trail, Sela felt her spirit as broken as the path itself.

Chapter Six

So much for all his support. Sela kicked the spindly desk leg on her way by and threw her purse over the back of the chair. Was he nothing but a puppet on a string?

Sinking down on the limp bedspread she let out a sob, "I really needed you with me, Dougal."

"Are you alright?"

She whirled around and saw Julia coming from the bathroom, a toothbrush stuck in her mouth and her brow creased with concern.

"Yes," she stammered, "of course. What are you doing here?"

"I'm staying here too—remember?" She took out the toothbrush and wiped her mouth with the back of her hand. "Look, I really don't want to interfere, but is everything okay?"

"It's fine." She swiped the back of her damp cheek. "It's just that my cousin had to leave." Great. Now she sounded like a two-year-old.

"I know the feeling," Julia said. "It's no fun being on your own." She paused for a minute, thinking. "Listen, the girls and I are hitting the trail this afternoon to search for more lichens. Why don't you join us?"

Sela turned and made a show of poofing up the pillow. "I don't know. There's still some things I need to take care of in town. Besides, I don't want to get in the way of your work."

"You won't be. Really, we'd love you to come. Anyway, we're not leaving until two."

Sela gave the pillow a final thump. "I suppose I could go just this once and get in a little sketching practice—if you're sure I won't be in the way."

"Not at all. We'll count on it, then." She grabbed her purse and went out the door.

Sela let out a long sigh. She had to get a grip. Going to the sink, she splashed cold water on her face and tried to focus. She had to let Dougal off the hook. After all, he hadn't even known Granddad. She made a face at herself in the ancient mirror. Grouch! She'd better get to work if she was going to find Tanika.

<hr />

Two hours later, after a futile search along Argylle Street, she came across the same pub she'd been to the night before with Dougal. There'd probably be a different crew on during the day—maybe even the old man who supposedly knew everyone. She stood near the ancient doorway and pretended to look over the posted menu. The thought of walking in alone didn't thrill her but the need to find out information spurred her on. Besides, her stomach was rumbling. Swinging the door open, she stepped inside.

"A table for ye, lass?" boomed a voice just off to her left.

"Yes, please." She squinted, adjusting her eyes to the dimly lit room.

"Are ye alone?" This time she made out the tiny shape of a man who, though standing straight as a stick, appeared to be about the same vintage as the door.

So he was here. She wondered if he could possibly lower his volume. "Uh, yes. Alone."

"Then I've got the perfect spot for ye. Just follow me." He turned on a dime and strode through the cramped quarters, nodding to everyone along the way, until he reached a small table smack in the middle of the room. Waving his little hand with the finesse of a Persian rug dealer, he pulled out the chair. Sela felt her cheeks flush scarlet. The place had grown uncomfortably quiet. "I'll give ye a minute to look over the menu and get acquainted."

She sat down and stared at the menu, seeing nothing. Was she required to strike up a conversation with perfect strangers now? This was ludicrous.

After a moment she heard a slight cough and looked up. Seated close by was a crudely dressed young man with a grin on his face. "There's a fish tea that'll stick to your ribs," he offered.

"Thank you." She quickly looked down again. Someone nearby chuckled. She wiped her sweaty palms on the legs of her jeans and clenched her jaw. "I might just try that." Her voice sounded annoyingly high-pitched.

"You're not from these parts?" Again the grin.

"No, just visiting."

"Alone?"

What was it with these people? Was everyone in Ullapool joined at the hip or something? "I'm traveling," she said, her shrill tone once again betraying her embarrassment.

Mercifully, the resident elf appeared out of nowhere, bill in hand, and held it out. "You'll be wanting this, Jimmy."

"What makes ye think so? I've as much right to be here as anybody."

"Come now, being the gentleman that ye are, I'm sure you'll want to pay up and make room for others."

Jimmy shuffled in his seat then stood, his eyes staring straight into Sela's. "A pleasure."

With that he swaggered off, apparently unaware of the oily aroma left in his wake. If she hadn't been so mortified by the attention she would have admired him just a little. Where did that kind of confidence come from?

"What will it be for ye, lass?" asked the little man.

"Fish—fish will be fine." She'd wolf down a giant squid if everyone would stop looking at her. She reached into her purse and pulling out a trusty number six pencil, began doodling on the rough paper place mat.

Slowly her heart resumed its regular beat as the image emerged. She hadn't consciously noted the details of the young man's face, but here it was, staring up at her. Deep-set, inquisitive eyes, straight nose, cocky grin, and a shock of unruly black hair. Something about him was familiar but she couldn't put her finger on it. Maybe the little waiter could help. He knew everybody, didn't he? No, she thought. He'll think I'm a floozy for asking. Still, there was something about that guy that didn't add up. Was all that bravado a cover-up for something else? He'd sure left in a hurry when the waiter gave him the bum's rush.

"Oh, I see you're quite taken with our Jimmy." The little man had reappeared like a genie, bringing with him a plate of deep fried cod, chips, and peas. Sela's stomach rumbled again. With all the hullabaloo, she'd forgotten how hungry she was.

"I like to draw people." Taking courage, she added, "He's quite a character. Does he live around here?"

The old man's craggy face took on a wary look. "He comes in now and then. A regular toerag he is." Sela cast about in her mind for the meaning of the expression. She'd heard Granddad use it occasionally. Something to do with a con artist. That was it, then. He was nothing but a crook. She reached for the oversize plate and deliberately set it down in the middle of the face.

It wasn't until she was outside the pub, having gobbled down her food and paid the bill, that she remembered Tanika. Was she entirely incompetent? She'd have to go back but now wasn't the time. He'd know something was up. In frustration, she sent a small stone flying onto the street with her toe.

"Ye'll have to watch that, miss," said a male voice coming alongside her. "A stubbed toe can cause a great deal of pain."

Sela recognized the tone before she looked up and saw Jimmy's grin. She groaned inwardly. "I'd pay more attention to my own toe if I were you. A little polish would go a long way."

He chortled with laughter and pushed his cap back on his head, revealing once again his dark tousled hair. "I wasn't meanin' to be cheeky—just looking out for the tourist industry is all."

"You're the official guide to Ullapool, then?" She quickened her step but he matched her pace with his own.

"I try to keep an eye out for the young ladies—in case they run into any difficulty of course."

"If you don't mind, I have things to do." She started to turn onto the street but he stepped in front of her.

"I'm sorry, miss. I seem to have gotten off on the wrong foot, so to speak. I'm really not what I appear to be."

She was about to snap out a retort when she stopped mid-step. Last night outside the pub. The same oily cap and mocking eyes she'd seen when the door had been opened with such a flourish. Her cheeks burned again in mortification.

"What's wrong—cat got your tongue?"

"No and I'd appreciate if you'd leave me alone. I don't take to being followed."

"Followed? I can assure you I'm not followin' you, being that I was the first to arrive on both occasions."

"So you remember me from last night. Well, I'm certainly not the one following you, if that's what you're implying."

His mouth twitched in amusement. "Of course not, of course not. You were with your boyfriend after all."

"He's not my boyfriend—he's my … ah … cousin." She blushed again as his eyebrows shot up in apparent surprise. Why was she explaining herself?

"Look," he said, sticking out his hand in her direction, "would it be alright if we started this over again? I'm Jimmy." His eyes crinkled once again though not mockingly this time.

She noticed he wasn't nearly as tall as Dougal, though by the way his shirt sleeves bulged, more muscular. He must be a manual laborer. She looked at his fingers and stopped dead. "I really have to get going."

"Can't you at least tell me your name?"

"Sela," she snapped. She turned and without looking back, strode off in the direction of the hostel, leaving him standing alone. Good. She hoped he felt like a fool. That's how he'd made her feel last night. What was he up to anyway? He hadn't actually stated what he did for a living though he'd given the impression he worked with his hands. But if that was the case, then why were his fingernails clean as a surgeon's?

The woman lifted the phone and punched in a familiar number.

"Highland News," said a voice at the other end.

"Dell?"

"Just a minute and I'll get her."

The woman glanced down the hallway. "Hurry it up," she hissed, tapping her toe on the wooden floor.

"Dell speaking."

"It's me— Maggie. Are you still in the market for some tourist-type info?"

"Could be. But none o' that boring business about who's visiting who. Just some juicy facts—well, as factual as possible." She gave a snort.

"I've got a few ideas up my sleeve what with all the networking I've been doin'. What's it worth to ye?"

"I can probably persuade them to dish out a bit more than the last time—but don't stretch it too far. I'm not about to get myself fired."

"I'll keep it to a minimum." She hesitated. "And Dell, you know the state I'm in, what with Ian running off and all."

"I know, I know. Get me something succulent and you'll be well paid." The line went dead.

Thankfully, she was the first one back to the room. It gave her a chance to mull things over in her mind for a few more minutes before the others got back. What was going on anyway? First the guy on the bus with her makeup bag, then the rumor and now a scruffy admirer. What next?

She thought of the newspaper article about the neo-Nazis in the Highlands. Could this Jimmy be in cahoots with them? She sucked in her breath. Was he by some chance the anonymous caller? No, his voice was too young. It had to be someone else—possibly an accomplice. But he could have broken into her house to get the address book. He certainly had the physique to jump through windows. Then again, maybe she was jumping to all the wrong conclusions. How could he possibly even know about Granddad's book? And what on earth would those names mean to him? Just the same, if she ever saw him again she'd mention an address book and watch for his reaction.

"Anybody home?" Julia burst in, lugging a bag of groceries which she deposited with a thud on the desktop. "Some goodies for the afternoon coffee break. I'm not sure where the girls went, though. I thought they were right behind me."

Sela grinned. "Maybe they found more 'botany' to study."

A minute later the snickering duo appeared in the doorway. "You'll never guess what I just caught on camera," Keira sighed. "A real fun-guy."

Julia rolled her eyes. "Never heard that one before. Will you two be ready to go soon?"

"Got everything right there, commander." Amanda pointed to a sturdy cardboard box in the corner.

"Check to see if we have enough brown paper bags. We can't use plastic, as you know, or the lichens will mold. Rummaging through her purse, she added, "Just about ready Sela?"

Sela grabbed three sketching pencils, a moldable eraser, and a small pad of drawing paper and stuffed them into the canvas bag she'd brought along. "All set."

A few minutes later she climbed into the passenger seat of a ruby-red Land Rover as Amanda and Keira piled into the back. She fingered the cool leather of the seats. "You really travel in style."

"Compliments of the University of Aberedeen. Julia turned on the ignition and pulled into the street. "In return I'm supposed to come up with a nice sized collection of rare lichens."

"Is that all?" she laughed. "Do you know where to find them or is it just hit and miss?"

"Nothing's hit and miss with Professor Kalahadi," Amanda chimed in from the rear.

"She's got it all covered—except the driving, that is."

"And the hair," Keira added. "She keeps talking about getting a new 'do' but we haven't seen any evidence of it yet."

"Whatever," Julia chuckled. "Actually though, I did spot a salon on the main drag that looked decent. You never know when I might stop by and see what they can do."

"I'll believe it when I see it," Amanda huffed.

"Anyway," Julia continued, "I have a good idea where to find the lichens. There's a nature reserve ten miles north of town called Inverpoly. We should see some nice pockets of hazel woodlands there. That's where the lichens will be."

Sela sat straight up as Julia turned onto the A835, relieved the traffic was thinner here than in the south. Julia was a New York driver on the wrong side of the road. They whizzed by heathery moorlands and foggy hillsides and finally spotted the sign for Drumrunie.

"Slow down. You have to turn here." Keira's voice was an octave higher than normal.

Julia braked and steered left onto the single-track road, bouncing over pot holes and narrowly missing a sizable elm before roaring to a stop. "Piece of cake." She gave the horn a blast, apparently for good measure.

Sela let out her breath. At this rate, Dougal could have made driver of the year.

"Oh, oh," Keira pointed ahead. "It looks like you've stirred up a hornet's nest." Over the rise of the hill, a shaggy brown beast had appeared, its elongated horns batting the air furiously. The remainder of the unkempt herd suddenly emerged from behind, jockeying for position as they nudged one another into a race to the bottom of the hill.

"Long-horned cattle. I sure hope they don't damage the car," Julia said, her eyes wide.

"You might be more concerned with what's bringing up the rear," observed Sela. A stocky herdsman advanced from behind, his notched stick pounding the ground and his mouth set in a straight slash. She wondered fleetingly if assault had been included in the car insurance.

"Are ye daft?" called out the man as he shoved his way to the vehicle, now surrounded by cattle. "Did ye not ken they could break their legs stampedin' down the hill with all that racket?"

"Sorry, sir." Julia's voice was all apologies. "We had no idea there was cattle on this road."

"What did ye expect—the Queen's Guard?"

"No, of course not. We're doing research for the university. I sure hope they'll be alright."

"Is the university settin' up shop here?" he demanded. "You're the second ones through from there today." He leaned against the vehicle, his breath coming in gasps. Sela couldn't help but notice his weathered features and tartan cap set against the leafy green background. He'd make a great subject to sketch but she doubted he was in the posing mood.

"We're looking for the hazel woods," Keira intoned, her soft Scottish accent more pronounced as she leaned forward from the back seat and smiled up at him. Her straight black locks cascaded over her shoulder and caught the light. "Would you be able to tell us where they're at?"

After a moment, he let out a resigned sigh and pointed up the road. "I'll tell ye what I told the others. Take the first left and follow the path for three or four miles. Then take a right. You'll have to walk at that point."

"Thanks so much," Julia smiled. "We really appreciate it."

He harrumphed in disgust, then suddenly thrust his knobby finger inches from her face. "And see that ye dinna drive like a lunatic from now on." Turning on the spot, he continued on down the road.

The minute he was gone the girls burst into giggles. "Amanda wiped her eyes with the back of her hand. "Consider yourself told."

"Please don't tell anyone from the university." Julia reached for a Kleenex. "That's all I need—to be dubbed a lunatic."

They drove on, turning at the first left and threading their way through jutting sandstone cliffs and rock towers that rose up around them.

Sela turned to Julia. "By the way, who do you think is here from the university?"

"Who knows? I guess we'll find out when we get there."

Before long the heather gave way to long stretches of birch woodlands, their white skins shiny against the green. "Look, there's a hazel," Julia said. "We're nearly there."

They spotted the path to the right and pulled onto it, parking close to the side.

"My, what a cautious driver you've become," remarked Keira.

"Very funny. Now how about getting the stuff out of the back."

Sela grabbed her own things as they exited the vehicle and began making their way down the path.

After a few minutes of hiking, Julia trotted ahead and looked around. "I think we should get off the road. There'll be thicker hazel patches in the middle of the woods."

As they turned deeper into the forest a hush surrounded them. Beside the twitter of a few birds, a thick silence filled the air. Before long, multi-trunked hazel trees began popping up, spreading their foliage like girls at a prom.

"It's beautiful here," Sela sighed, taking a deep breath and inhaling the pungent fragrance of the plant life. "It makes you want to lie down and fall into a deep sleep."

"Not so fast, Snow White." Julia stopped and pointed to the tree ahead. "See those leafy-like protrusions on the branches?"

"I think so."

"They're called 'Lobarion lichen'. If we keep going we'll hopefully come across some 'Graphidion scriptae.' That's what we're after."

Sela tilted her head. "This might be a dumb question, but what are lichens actually?"

"It's not dumb at all. Amanda, why don't you give this girl a lesson in Botany."

"You mean the non-human variety?" she grinned. "Okay, okay. Lichens are plants that have no leaves, stems or roots. They act like sponges, retaining everything dissolved in rainwater. Now can I put this box down? My arms are killing me."

"All in due time. Right this way, team." Julia urged them on past the last remnants of birch, oak, and ash trees.

Suddenly Amanda let out a shriek, fracturing the tranquility about them. "There they are!"

Sela whirled around to see if the cattle had put in a second appearance, but Amanda was pointing toward the trees. "See the script against the white? It's got to be 'Graphidion scriptae'."

"Spoken like a true scholar," Julia said, smiling with professor-like approval. "Can you see them, Sela?"

Sela squinted at the trees ahead. "All I can see is black dots on a white bark."

"Exactly. The bark is actually brownish-grey, not white at all. That's the lichens. And now that we've found them, you can do your thing and we'll get busy collecting."

Sela found a smooth spot next to the base of one of the larger hazels, and sat down with her sketch pad and pencils. A long branch was fanning out directly in front of her, giving her a good close-up view of the leaves. She began drawing, every now and then stopping to watch the others and listen to Julia's instructions.

They were busy scraping sections from the trees with small knives and wrapping them in tissue paper. "They're exceptionally fragile," Julia was saying. "When you consider how long it takes for this population to recover, you ..." She suddenly stopped talking.

Sela looked up. Coming toward them were two young men dressed in army fatigues. Who in the world were they? Surely they weren't from the university, dressed like that.

"Hello, ladies," clipped the one in front. "Looks like we might get some rain."

She hadn't noticed before but now that he mentioned it, she detected a definite chill in the air. Not that they were there to talk about the weather.

"I'm afraid I'm going to have to ask you to pack up if you don't mind. Official business."

"But we have permission from the university," Julia protested. "I'm teaching a botany class on lichens. This is part of the program."

He scratched his head. "Well, I suppose we can allow you to take what you've collected but that's all. I'm afraid we have orders."

Sela sniffed. "Orders, out here in the middle of the woods?"

The man looked over at her for the first time, his eyes lingering slightly longer than necessary. "I'm afraid that's not the business of the private sector, miss."

"Haven't I seen you in Ullapool?" Keira asked, peering at the lanky man on the left.

"It's possible. I'm there off and on." He shifted his weight to the other foot.

Julia arranged the samples in the box, sticking the lid on with a thunk. She turned to the two of them. "I'm going to be checking into this."

"Quite alright, miss."

As they started to leave, Sela felt the first raindrop strike her face. "We better get going before we're soaked," she said. Abruptly a crack of thunder cut the air and seconds later the rain was falling in sheets. She stuffed the canvas bag under her T-shirt and dashed through the woods behind Julia.

"This way," Julia shouted over the clamor, clutching the box with both arms.

"Give me that box," Amanda ordered. "I'm bigger than you."

Julia handed it to her on the run. "Be careful with it."

Sela noticed her hands trembling. Was she that cold?

"There's the road," gasped Keira. "We're not far now."

They shot out of the forest and tore down the road at a dead run, splashing mud up onto their pants as they sprinted toward the car. Julia fished the key out of her pocket and clicked the unlock button. The lights winked in recognition. They reached the car and scrambled in, a soaking mess of matted hair and muddy clothes.

"Let's hope this thing has a good heater." Sela's teeth were chattering like a buzz saw. "I'm chilled right through to the bone."

Chapter Seven

Julia cranked the heat up full blast as they watched the rain lash against the windows. She glanced over at Sela who was groping for the seat warmer. "I wouldn't turn that up too high if I were you. It'll give you second degree burns." She backed onto the road and took off, her tires squelching into the soft mud.

"Just so you know," Amanda commented from the back, "I'll be suing the university for whip-lash if you soar over any more pot holes."

"Promises, promises."

They drove on in silence, welcoming the hot blast of air. "You're all awfully quiet," Julia said after a few minutes.

Keira let out a breathy sigh. "I was just thinking."

"What about? Those army guys?"

"Yes, if you must know. I was wishing I'd brought my camera along. Do you think they really were from the army? And where were the people from the university?"

"I was wondering the same thing." She signaled right and turned onto the A835, surpassing the speed limit as she crept up on the van ahead. "Didn't you say one of them looked familiar?"

"Yeah. I'm just trying to figure out where we saw him before."

Suddenly Amanda thumped the back of Julia's seat. "I've got it! Remember that jerk who was hitting on you the other night? I think this guy was with him."

"Really? I guess I was too busy warding off the other one to notice." She thought for a minute. "Anyway, we better not get ahead of ourselves—they're probably just doing their job."

"What did the other one look like?" Sela asked, ignoring the comment. "Was he wearing dirty, oily-smelling clothes?"

Julia arched her brows as she looked across the seat. "I try to stay away from the oily types."

"Would you say he was just a little taller than me—about five nine or ten?"

"Hard to tell." She pulled out and passed the van with a roar. "He was sitting down the whole time. Why? Are you familiar with some of the grubby men in town?"

"Hardly. But there was a guy who was trying to talk to me when I went for lunch today. He seemed suspicious somehow."

Keira leaned forward. "Really? What was he doing?"

"Nothing. He was just annoying and nosey."

"You probably just miss your cousin." Julia zoomed around a slow-moving truck, forcing the driver to hug the shoulder of the road.

Sela peeked through the rear-view mirror and spotted a fist waving behind frantic windshield wipers.

"That also goes for any whip-lash incurred when driving like a lunatic," added Amanda.

"Yeah, yeah, whatever."

"Just keep your eyes open. I think there's something fishy going on." Sela slid her hand down the side of the seat and turned the warmer to the off position.

A few minutes later they pulled into Ullapool and followed Shore Street to the hostel where Julia found a space and parked.

Sela looked over at her and burst out laughing.

"What?"

"That's quite the 'do' you've got going. Are you sure you don't go for the oily types?"

"Well, if that isn't the pot calling the kettle black. Take a look in the mirror."

Sela folded down the makeup mirror and let out a gasp. Her hair was a wild array of cork-screw curls and a mud smear reached from the side of her mouth up onto her nose. "Touché. Let's get inside before somebody sees us.

"Not only that," Keira added dramatically, "I'm dying for a hot cup of tea."

They gathered their things together and splashed their way into the building.

Later, after splitting a take-out Hawaiian pizza with the other girls, Sela considered going out again to search for Tanika, but between the intermittent rain and the late hour, that was enough to call it a day. With all she'd accomplished, she might as well have gone back to Glasgow with Dougal. She'd have to get some information soon, though. He had said he'd be back in a day or two and she wanted to prove she was serious about clearing Granddad's name. She had to find something the next day.

⚬⚬❖❖⚬⚬━━━━━❖━━━━━⚬⚬❖❖⚬⚬

Jimmy sat alone in his makeshift "office" at the back of the gentlemen's club. Much as he was in this for the long haul, he needed time alone, away from the continual yakety-yak, to think his own thoughts.

His cell phone buzzed and he brought it to his ear with a sigh. "Jimmy."

"It's me. Anything yet?"

"I'm working on it." He shifted in his seat.

"I hope I don't have to remind you to stay on it. You don't get to walk away from this one. You start, you finish." The line went dead.

Jimmy clicked off the phone and shoved it in his pocket. Just what he needed—more pressure. One screw-up and that's all anyone could think about—especially that guy. Didn't he realize how good he'd become at his job?

Fine. He'd start with the girl. A crooked smile curved his lips. She was a stunner to say the least, though a bit on the obnoxious side. Her dark eyes, however, conveyed a deep curiosity. Why was she here? Was it just for a holiday or was she onto something? And where exactly would she stand if she did know the details? Her background alone had sent up a dozen red flags that told him to watch out. He'd have to keep an eye on her. Still, the image of her wild hair, beautiful eyes, and lithe form kept running around his head, rendering the memories of his ex-girlfriend almost a blur.

⚫

It was nearly ten when Sela woke up to an empty room. It must have been the mountain air or the wet weather or something. She threw on a pair of stretch jeans and a maroon hoody and biting into a two-day-old bagel, stuffed the picture of the 1940s woman into her purse and left.

"Not keeping the other girls company today?" asked the desk clerk.

"Not at the moment."

"You'll be lonely what with your cousin leaving and all." She emphasized the word "cousin."

Sela hurried to get out the door. "He'll be back soon."

"I hope he's not the jealous type."

She turned back around but the woman had her nose down and was sorting through files.

Leaving the building, she walked along Shore Street where fish vendors scurried about, setting up shaky metal stalls that advertised catches of prawns, lobsters, and scallops. From a nearby radio, a newscaster blared out the bad news of the day. Her head started to ache.

It was Friday. They must be gearing up for the weekend. Already the streets were lined with noisy tourists and the little tartan shops were swelling with customers. How would she find Tanika in this mess? She should've thought of that before.

What she needed was a map of the town. She'd been up and down the main drags but what about the small side streets? She made her way over to a newspaper stall and found one free of charge. Locating a nearby bench, she sat down and unfolded it on her lap. It was easy to read, clearly marking out all the streets and lanes as well as some of the larger businesses. With her finger, she traced Seaforth Lane, Pulteney St., and Market St. Each one looked small—possibly old. This would give her a good starting point.

She was about to fold it back up when someone took a seat next to her on the bench.

"Afraid ye'll get lost?"

Sela looked up into Jimmy's grinning face. She had to admit he cleaned up well. The oily clothes had been replaced by a soft blue shirt, dark jeans, and fashionable tan shoes. The cap was missing too, and she could tell he had tried to do something with his hair.

"Hi," she said. "What are you doing here?"

"I'm just takin' a rest—same as you by the look of it."

"Sorry, but I was just about to leave." She began refolding the map but in her rush to get away, doubled it against the crease, leaving the corners sticking out in a bulky mass.

"My, my, you've made a right midden of that." He took it out of her hands and carefully put it together, lining it up perfectly.

"Thank you very much, Mr. Hospital Corners," she quipped. "Who would've known?"

"Forgive me if I'm readin' into things, but have I done something to offend ye?" His dark brown eyes were the picture of innocence.

"No, not at all. I've just got stuff to do." She stood, taking the map from his hands while blowing the hair out of her eyes.

"Are ye looking for any place in particular?" He jumped up beside her. "I'm quite good at directions if I do say so myself."

She was about to give him the brush-off when a better idea

occurred to her. Maybe she could use him to help find Tanika. She didn't need to tell him anything.

Offering a begrudging smile, she went on. "I'm actually looking for an old shop and can't seem to find it. It's just a bit of family history I read about."

He thought for a moment. "How old is old?"

"It was here during the war, I know that." She bit her bottom lip.

"There's a number of shops like that around town."

"Well, it isn't on any of the main streets. Hopefully it wasn't demolished."

"Ye could look on Market Street. I think there's one or two up that way."

"Thanks. I'll try that." She turned to go.

"I'd be happy to accompany you. It's my day off." He swung into step beside her.

"Suit yourself." She marched ahead but a jab of conscience nudged her and she slowed down to let him catch up. Why was she acting so stuck-up anyway? He was just being a guy. He probably wasn't involved with the whole neo-Nazi business. Sometimes she let her imagination get too overblown. Then again, why would he pretend to be a manual laborer? And what about the address book? It was still possible he'd crossed the ocean to search out information on Granddad for the gang. She thought again of the envelope marked "Private". She had to find out.

Flipping a frizzy lock over her shoulder, she casually looked his way. "Ever hear of an address book?" She peered into his eyes for any sign of uneasiness.

He stared back with a look of astonishment then burst out in a cheeky grin. "Now that's what I call gettin' down to business. I don't happen to have one on me at the moment but I'll take your number down on a piece of paper if that's alright."

"That's not what I meant and you know it," she spluttered, her face heating up like a blowtorch. I was referring to something completely different."

He scratched his head in apparent confusion. "Seems to me there's only one purpose for an address book."

"Just don't worry about it." She stared straight ahead, promising herself never to consider the private eye industry.

He led her left on Argyle and down Ladysmith toward Seaforth Road. Passing that, they continued walking until the sign for Market Street came into view. "Here we are," he said. He put out his hand, guiding her by the elbow. Sela felt her face flush again but this time with something akin to pleasure. Was she coming down with a cold?

They strode the length of the street, but nothing even vaguely resembled the building from the photograph.

"There is one other place." Jimmy seemed to be weighing his words. "There's a little street farther up off Ladysmith."

"Lead the way, then," she said, favoring him with a slight curve of her lips.

A few minutes later they reached Custom House Street. Sela stopped and looked down the narrow road. It was tiny—no more than a couple of blocks in length but unlike the rest of town, the buildings were spaced several feet apart and were constructed of varying materials. Mature trees—oak, elm, and maple—lined the pavement on either side. Her eyes were drawn to the small white stucco building standing alone on the corner. Above its tiny window were the printed words, "Ullapool Art Shop." *"Meet me at art shop . . ."*

She shuddered, hardly able to breath. The dark-haired woman had been standing in front, the letters "ULL" clearly visible. This was the place. She knew it in her heart. The photograph was beginning to burn a hole in her purse but she wasn't about to pull it out in front of a possible felon.

"What do ye think?" he asked.

She glanced his way. The look of curiosity in his eyes was unmistakable. She'd have to mask her mounting excitement. Steeling herself, she attempted to breathe normally. "It's worth a try."

She followed him up the wooden steps and through a heavy door to a room that looked to be straight out of "The Pickwick Papers."

Heavy wooden tables were stacked high with canvasses, palettes, drawing paper, and an assortment of paints and brushes. Near the door, a clunky cash register sat on a Victorian style desk, and across the room wooden frames leaned stiffly against a flowery back wall. A row of narrow boxes, each stuffed with a variety of unframed paintings, stretched out in front. Sela felt a twinge of nostalgia as if the heavy fragrance of the place had brought on a latent memory. The musty scent of old paper mingled with the pungency of turpentine tickled her nose and she sneezed.

"Gezundheit," Jimmy laughed.

"Thank you—and excuse me." She grinned back.

Hearing a muffled swishing sound, they turned and saw a thin, middle-aged woman step out from behind a curtained opening.

"Hello," the woman said, looking quizzically at Jimmy.

"Hello," he answered, quickly adding, "My friend here is from out of town and is interested in seeing your shop. Would ye mind if she looks around?"

"No, not at all." She smiled brightly at Sela. "If you need anything I'll be right here." Reaching for a cloth, she began dusting one of the shelves.

Sela ran her fingers along the desk, trying to still their trembling. It wasn't the same woman of course. The other must be over eighty by now. There was a chance this one might know something though and she didn't want Jimmy eavesdropping on her conversation. Maybe she'd even show the woman the photograph and watch her reaction.

She turned to Jimmy as he lounged against one of the tables. "I might be a while. I'm sure you won't feel like waiting."

"I don't mind. We could go for lunch after you're done."

She looked away. "I'm really not that hungry. Maybe I'll catch you later."

For once he took the hint. "Okay, then. I'm sure I'll be seeing ye around." He winked at her as he turned to leave.

She paused, giving a slight cough. "Thanks—for everything. I really appreciate it."

"Dinna mention it." He grinned at the woman. "Be sure to take good care of her. She's right good at drawing." With that he was gone.

Sela blinked. How did he know she was "right good at drawing"? He'd never seen any of her work. Or had he? She picked up a sable brush and pretended to look it over. The only time she'd drawn anything was yesterday at Inverpoly. Maybe the army guys had told him about it. Suddenly she had another thought. She'd sketched a picture of him on the place mat at the pub. Had the little proprietor shown it to him? Had the disdain simply been a cover for something else?

"Do you work in oils?" The woman was looking at her intently.

Sela jerked her head up. "Sorry. No, I usually use watercolors but I like oils as well."

"We have a good variety of canvases if you're interested."

"Thank you. I'll just have a look around." She moved off, noticing again the boxes of unframed paintings. "Are these for sale?"

"Most of them."

She began looking through the first one. It contained mostly amateurish oils of Loch Broom and the Ullapool area. "Are they categorized in any particular order?"

"We sort them according to the approximate year they were painted. The ones in that box were done within the last ten years. They become older as they get closer to the window."

Sela silently did the math. There were six boxes. Could there be something here that would point to Tanika—or Granddad? Her hands shook as she moved toward the window and took out the first painting in the last box. It featured a docked fishing boat and the date said 1941. She was in the right era.

Placing it back, she pulled out the second where two lovers were standing in front of an old brick building, apparently in 1943. The artist was someone named Alex Morrison, whoever that was. She flipped through three more, looking for anything that might serve as a clue. The dates were right but there was nothing apparent in the names or subject matter. Two were left. She lifted out the last one. It was an interesting composition of the harbor, done in 1949. Too recent.

With quaking breath, she began to reach for the one in front when a shadow crossed in front of her.

"I'm afraid we'll have to close for lunch now."

Sela jerked her head back up. "I won't be a minute. I just wanted to see this …"

"Sorry," the woman insisted, "but we keep rather rigid hours. We'll be open again at two."

Sela stood up, not wanting to make a scene.

The woman smiled sweetly. "Please feel free to come back at that time." She held her expression but there was a faint flush to her cheeks.

Sela nodded. "Alright. I'll come back after lunch. Thank you." What was she thanking her for? She hadn't done her any favors.

She left the shop and began walking back toward Ladysmith Street. Would it have killed the woman to let her finish looking? And what would she do till two? It was just twelve o'clock now. If she'd bought a piece of drawing paper she'd at least be able to sit by the dock and do a little sketching.

Without another thought she turned and ran back to the store. Flinging open the door, she called out, "Would I be able to get some …" Her mouth fell open as she took in the scene before her. A white-haired woman was bent over the last box of paintings, her cheeks flushed as she pulled one from near the back.

When she saw Sela, she dropped the canvas as if she'd just stolen a cookie from the cookie jar. Reaching for the table, she stood upright. "Weren't you told we're closed?" Her head wobbled slightly and Sela wondered if she was about to faint.

"Sorry. I just needed to get a piece of drawing paper but I can see you're busy." Without another word, she turned and fled.

Chapter Eight

Sela's mind spun as she hurried back down Ladysmith. She turned left onto Market and came to a T-intersection. The sign said Mill Street. She cut right. With any luck there'd be a park nearby where she could sit down and try to figure out what was going on.

Before long a narrow cobblestone path came into view and she followed it to a small unkempt garden. Along one side, wild flowers reluctantly spelled out the name of the town. Next to them, propped against a low wall, was a sagging wooden bench. She sank down onto its chipped surface and let out a breathy "Whew."

Who was that woman? Could it have been Tanika herself? She was the right age though she didn't resemble the woman in the picture. Then again, it was over sixty years later. With shaky hands, she unzipped her purse and pulled out the photograph.

It was the same building without a doubt. The letters matched perfectly even though they'd probably been given a few paint jobs over the years. She peered into the woman's smiling face. The expression was slightly similar but the image wasn't clear enough to make out any real likeness. Her build wasn't the same either, but that probably had more to do with age than anything else.

She lowered the photo onto her lap and tried to replay the whole episode in her mind. She'd been just about to lift the painting out of the box when the first woman had stopped her to say they were closing for lunch. It couldn't have been more than a couple of minutes later that she'd burst back in. Where had the second woman come from and why was she removing the painting? It wasn't as though she knew who Sela was or what she was looking for. Or did she? Maybe it was a good thing she hadn't shown the other one the photograph.

She exhaled loudly and tried to clear her head. One thing she knew for sure. Something was up with that painting.

She glanced at her watch. Twelve-twenty. Hearing a sound, she looked up to see a young mother cooing to her baby as she wheeled it along in a stroller. At least some things in life were uncomplicated.

She stood and retraced her steps out of the garden. Her stomach rumbled, reminding her she hadn't eaten. Maybe she'd find a hot dog stand, or crumpet stand or whatever. It would take more than a few calories to work up the courage to go back to the art shop but she knew it had to be done.

A few minutes later she reached Shore Street where she purchased a doughnut, a green apple, and a coke from the corner market. So much for healthy eating. She perused the street for a vacant bench and finally spotted a picnic area farther down the block. Crossing over to it, she took a seat at one of the granite tables.

She took the apple out of the brown paper bag and sank her teeth into its tart juiciness, wincing as saliva dripped down the side of her mouth. Reaching into her purse for a Kleenex, she stopped dead when something on the other side of the street caught her attention. The stream of tourists had abruptly thinned out, revealing a shadowed doorway in which two men stood huddled together, deep in conversation. Something about them looked familiar.

Before she could pinpoint it, though, a group of animated teenage boys strolled directly in front of them, stopping to flirt with several girls and obscuring her line of vision. Straining to see, she stood and managed to glimpse a beefy hand as it raised a cigarette up toward smirking, rubbery lips. The butcher from the other night. She shivered. That was the last person she wanted to see. As the teenagers moved off, the door suddenly opened and a third man emerged and joined in the discussion. She gasped as she took in the soft blue shirt and tousled hair of Jimmy.

They knew each other? What was going on? She'd had a bad feeling about that butcher guy right from the start. He'd seemed cunning, not to mention disgusting, with his blood-splattered apron and nicotine stained hands.

She looked at her watch. Five after one. Enough time to see what they were up to before going back to the art shop. She glanced up at the doorway again but a Highland Adventures tour bus had rolled to a stop directly in front of her and didn't seem in a hurry to leave. Dropping her apple into the bag, she jogged up to the sidewalk, excusing her way through the crush of disembarking tourists, but by the time the door was once again visible, the men were gone.

She was still peering in frustration when she heard her name and looked up to see Julia striding toward her, her tiny figure accentuated by a slim khaki skirt and white T-shirt—her face lit with a mysterious smile.

"Are you lost?" she asked with a laugh.

"No, I thought I saw someone I knew. What are you up to?"

"You won't believe this. Hey, have you eaten lunch? Why don't we grab a bite and I'll tell you what I found out." Frizzy strands of hair fluttered across her face in the slight breeze giving her the appearance of an ingénue rather than a professor.

Sela looked at her brown bag. "I don't know if you'd call this lunch but I've hardly touched it anyway."

"Save it for supper. Come on. There's a great place to eat up here."

They turned west and passed a home-made-chocolate shop, a chemist, and a newsagent before reaching a chain of low, white-washed buildings collectively called the "Ferry Boat Inn."

"Wantin' your tea, ladies?" a greeter called out from the restaurant doorway. "We've got a fresh catch of anything you'd like today." He winked boldly at Sela who sniffed and looked the other way.

They followed him inside where he turned them over to

a sweet-looking server. Smiling shyly, she led them through the carpeted dining area to a plaid-covered table overlooking the loch.

"Isn't it a fabulous view?" Julia peered out the window as she took her seat. "I'm surprised you haven't already been out there with your sketch pad."

"I will be as soon as I can." Sela turned her gaze from the bobbing fishing boats back to Julia. "So what's your news? I'm dying to hear."

"Let's order first. Then we can talk without interruption."

They leafed through the menu and settled on shrimp appetizers and a bowl of Greek salad.

"Okay, let's have it," Sela demanded after the server had gone. "I can see you're dying to tell me."

"Are you sure you're ready for this?"

"Just tell me."

Julia paused. "There was no-one from the army out at Inverpoly yesterday."

Sela sat still, letting the news sink in. "How can you know that for sure?"

"I phoned the Inverness army office to complain. They checked and said it wasn't them. They haven't got anything going on up there at all."

Sela blew out her breath. "Who do you suppose they were, then?"

"I don't have a clue. They didn't exactly say they were from the army, did they?"

"Come to think of it, no. But they sure led us to believe it." She clicked her tongue. "Official business—right."

The server returned with the appetizers and a giant bowl of salad topped with gleaming black olives. She smiled sweetly. "I'll be back with your tea in a wee minute."

Julia looked at the bowl with wide eyes. "I hope the girls find us. There's enough here for an army—pardon the pun."

Sela grinned. "Do you think you'll go back to Inverpoly?"

"I'm considering it. We didn't collect nearly enough lichen samples."

Sela picked a shrimp up with her fork and jabbed the air with it as she spoke. "I'd be careful if I were you. Did you hear about the neo-Nazi activity in the Highlands? I read about them on the plane coming over. Maybe that's what those guys are involved in."

"I don't know. They looked pretty clean-cut." Julia lifted her fork as well, but before taking a bite, bowed her head in a moment of silent prayer. Sela waited, surprised. It was like sitting down for lunch with Granddad.

She pretended not to notice. "That's just it. The new breed of neo-Nazis tries not to look the part. That way they can carry on without anyone suspecting them—at least according to that article."

The server returned with a steaming pot of tea and a pitcher of warm milk which she deposited on the table. Julia reduced her voice to a half whisper. "But that doesn't explain what they would be doing up there in the middle of nowhere."

"Who knows? What do neo-Nazis usually do?"

"Maybe they're planning to overthrow Ullapool."

"That would be quite the heist, wouldn't it? There's nothing here except tartan shops and fishing boats."

Julia put her fork down and paused, looking directly at her. "And which one of those are you here for?"

Sela stopped, taken aback. "Neither, I guess."

"I'm really not trying to pry, Sela, but I get the idea you're here for more than the scenery. I've got big shoulders if you care to share."

Sela looked over at her tiny frame. "I trust you're not speaking literally."

"I'm serious. I know when something's eating at a person. I've been there myself ... and I've also discovered where to find the answers."

Sela wasn't about to take the bait. She'd become expert at slipping past similar situations with Granddad over the years. "It's nothing, really." She stuffed a forkful of cucumbers and tomatoes into her mouth and looked out the window.

"Are you sure?"

Sela put the fork down again and chewed, evading Julia's eyes. It would be nice to unload on someone other than Dougal for a change. And Julia did seem real. It wasn't as if she'd go running through town blabbing about Granddad. She swallowed and opened her mouth to speak but at that moment Keira and Amanda rushed in from the doorway, breathless.

"I'm so glad we found you," Amanda gushed, her face beaming. "We'd never have known you were here if it hadn't been for that hunk at the door."

"He thinks you're good looking, Sela," Keira chimed in. "Maybe he'll ask you out if you give him half a chance."

Sela hadn't seen Julia irritated before, but by the way her brows knit together and her mouth turned down, she knew the girls were on thin ice.

"Did you ever think we might be having a serious conversation?" Julia asked.

"Sorry." Keira glanced away.

Sela took a quick look at her watch which said one fifty-five. "No problem. I have to be somewhere else anyway. Why don't you two finish up the salad." She stood and retrieved her purse from the back of the chair.

Julia smiled up at her. "Maybe we can chat later,"

"Sure, I'd like that. When are you heading back to Aberdeen?"

"We don't have to leave until Sunday afternoon."

"I'll see you later then." She dropped a five-pound note onto the table, turned, and left, not knowing if she was relieved or disappointed.

<hr />

The sun shone brightly as she made her way back up Ladysmith. For the tenth time since leaving the restaurant, she tried to figure out what to say to the woman at the art shop. She couldn't very well just barge in and demand to see the painting. Perhaps a subtler approach would work, like a bomb threat for instance. She smirked at her own joke.

The younger woman was on duty when she arrived and apparently had done a little rehearsing of her own. "Glad to see you made it back." She offered Sela a studied smile. "My aunt was afraid she may have frightened you off when you came back in."

Sela countered with a gleam of her own. "Tell her not to worry. I don't frighten that easily."

"Was there something you wished to purchase, then?"

"Actually, I would love to see the painting I was just about to look at before you closed for lunch." Her jaw was beginning to ache but she maintained the beam.

"Oh, that." The woman fluttered her hand as if to dismiss the painting as less than trivial. "It's really just an amateur piece of the countryside. My aunt is protective about it for sentimental reasons only." Her teeth still showed but the smile itself had slipped south.

Sela chuckled as though highly amused. "Oh, I wasn't meaning to buy it. I'm doing an art project on paintings done during World War II. I was hoping to compare it with others I've seen." The lie just seemed to flow from her lips.

"I see." The woman hesitated, tapping her spindly index finger on the desk. "Well, I don't suppose she'd mind if I just let you see it."

"I promise. I won't even touch it. I'll just look."

She sighed with relief as the woman turned and pulled back a curtain, revealing a small, windowless office filled with accounting books and art supplies. An easy chair sat in one corner and a makeshift table at the far wall. On it was the unframed canvas, approximately sixteen by twenty-four inches. "Thank you so much," she said. "I'll just be a minute."

She stepped over to it, holding her breath. The woman was right. It was no Monet. Nondescript trees surrounded a too-blue lake and pointy hills jutted into the cloudless acrylic sky. It could have been a paint by number. She looked down at the bottom right. No signature or date.

Glancing over her shoulder, she realized the woman had gone back into the shop. She hesitated, then picked it up with both hands, inspecting it closely. What was so special about it?

She placed it back down on the table and ran her fingers over the surface. It seemed slightly gritty in places as if the paint might be peeling away. What on earth? The only way that could happen was if it had been painted over an existing coat of oil.

She checked behind her again and seeing she was still alone, picked it back up, studying it against the light for more signs of peeling. Could there be a hidden oil painting under the top layer? She'd heard about things like that during art school. She turned it over and looked carefully at the back. Something had been written in pencil on the left-hand side but it was blurry and hard to distinguish. Blinking furiously to clear her vision, she was finally able to make out the letters "KA."

"I trust you've had ample time to look it over?" The woman had re-entered the office soundlessly and was standing directly behind her.

"Sorry, yes." Sela's face was growing uncomfortably warm as she quickly placed it down on the table. "I thought there might be a date on the back."

"If you've finished then …" She held the curtain open and Sela walked through.

"Maybe I'll take a sheet of two-hundred-pound water color paper." She looked at the floor.

"You have your paints here with you here in Ullapool?"

"Uh … no." Her face was becoming hotter by the second.

"Then I wouldn't recommend it. Have a nice day."

"Yeah, you too." She scooted around the desk and out the door, feeling like she'd just received a tongue lashing from the principal.

Once outside she found herself back on Ladysmith Street which she'd begun to identify by the square inch. Slowly, her glowing skin returned to normal as the embarrassment subsided. What should she do now? Dougal probably wouldn't be back until tomorrow, she didn't trust Jimmy as far as she could throw him, and she'd blown her chance to talk to Julia. Just perfect. Maybe she should go back to the hostel and lie down. Her brain couldn't stand any more complications.

A few minutes later she lay feteled up on the lumpy cot, a worn woolen blanket cocooning her from head to toe. Hopefully the girls had gone back to Inverpoly. She didn't feel like talking to anyone at the moment. Though it was only the middle of the afternoon, drowsiness began to overtake her like a thick fog. Before long it seemed that she was observing the events of the last few days from a distance—like a stage performance with actors entering and exiting in the fast, stilted walk of the 1920s silent movies. Jimmy's eyes alternately mocked and befriended her as he opened and closed the heavy pub door. Dougal, with his arm around her waist, dragged her toward a high waterfall, and long-horned sheep rammed her from behind as she fled screaming past the hazel trees at Inverpoly while Julia and Granddad bowed their heads in silent prayer. The rain was falling heavily but not as heavy as her tears as she stood by her parents' gravesides with Granddad's arms tightly around her. She would not listen to his prayers for comfort. God didn't care or He wouldn't have taken them.

"Listen to me. You're alright."

"No. I'm not listening. I hate Him. I hate Him." She began striking at him, balling up her fists and hitting him over and over.

She felt her arms being pulled down as a heavy weight plunked on top of her, immobilizing her. She couldn't breathe. "Listen to me. You're alright."

Her eyelids flew open and she stared into the startling green eyes of Dougal.

Chapter Nine

"Dougal?"

"In the flesh. If I get off will you promise to stop beating me up?" He raised his head and she caught sight of a trickle of blood coming from his nose.

"What in the world? Don't tell me I hit you."

"I'm sure it's not as bad as it looks." He rolled off the bed and reached into his pocket for a tissue.

Sela sat up, throwing the cover aside. "Sorry. I must have been dreaming. I thought I was back at the … well, never mind." She jumped up, straightening her clothes. "I don't normally go around punching people."

He grinned, rubbing the top of his nose. "I wouldn't want to get on your bad side, that's for sure."

"Are you okay? Do you need a washcloth or something?"

He held up his hand. "No, no, I'm fine."

"I thought you'd be gone until tomorrow. How exactly did you get into my room?"

He smiled sheepishly, raking his hand through flaxen hair. "I managed to leave Glasgow a day early. When I came to register, the desk clerk asked if I would look in on you. She thought something might be amiss." He paused before continuing. "I'm afraid I had to hold you down so you wouldn't do yourself any harm."

Sela groaned. "How embarrassing. I must have fallen into a dead sleep."

"Don't worry about it. Besides, I couldn't stay away—especially when you were angry with me."

"I'm not angry with you Dougal. I know you're just trying to keep me from getting hurt." She turned and began straightening the bed. "So will you be able to stay for a while?"

"Let's see," he said, "This is Friday afternoon. Tomorrow I've got just a few small items to attend to, and Sunday I have to get back to the city. That gives us a bit of time to be together."

"That's great." What did he mean by together, she mused—friends … or something more? "You're staying here at the hostel again?"

"Same room—just like I never left."

She let out a sigh of relief and turned to face him again. "I'm so glad. For some reason I always feel safer when you're around." He opened his arms to her and she stepped into them, grateful for the security of his embrace.

After a moment, he held her at arm's length. "I'll tell you what. You get yourself straightened up, I'll go freshen up a bit, and we'll meet out in the lobby in fifteen minutes."

"It's a deal." When he'd gone she quickly dashed to the mirror to assess the damage caused by her tumultuous nap. What a mess. Her T-shirt was rumpled and her hair was wild. Would the man ever see her looking normal?

Twenty minutes later she stepped into the lobby wearing strappy white sandals, a deep brown safari jacket, and a flowy tan skirt. Dougal rose from his seat giving her an appreciative up and down. "A new woman." He pumped his eyebrows like Groucho Marx.

"I don't always look like a bum, you know." She steered her eyes away from the front desk as he held open the door for her.

"You never look like a bum."

"So what's the plan? It's only four forty-five—a little early for supper, don't you think?"

He grabbed her hand. "How about a walk. I want to know what you've discovered so far."

Sela's heart thumped like a base drum when he linked her arm tightly in his own and led her down Shore Street toward the Ullapool pier. The influx of weekend tourists had swelled the sidewalks to capacity causing an overflow onto the street. Drivers crawled along at a snail's pace, their horns blaring incessantly as they attempted to line up for the car ferry. Fish mongers, anxious for a sale, bellowed out the price of their greasy, newspaper-wrapped fare.

"Let's get out of here." He pulled her in the opposite direction, away from the commotion. "We'll come back later when the 'Isle of Lewis' is gone."

"The what?" She sidestepped an energetic cluster of tourists and tried to keep up.

"The car ferry. We'll come back when it's gone. It'll be quieter then."

They stopped at the corner and stood waiting while a stream of vehicles turned onto Shore Street. With his arm around her shoulders, he leaned down and whispered into her ear. Sela giggled, a hot glow running from the pit of her stomach through to her fingertips.

Was she falling for him? He was so handsome, so confident, so … Her eyes cut to the street where a dark grey Volvo honked at the car in front. Glancing at the other driver, she realized with a start that the mocking eyes staring back at her belonged to none other than Jimmy.

She looked away, recalling how his eyebrows had shot up when she'd told him Dougal was her cousin. So what? She didn't need to explain to him they weren't blood relatives. She looked back defiantly but he was already through the intersection, well on his way to the next block. Jerk.

Dougal squeezed her shoulder and looked down questioningly.

"It's nothing." But the tender moment had passed.

He seemed to sense her change of mood and chucked her playfully under the chin. "Let's go get something to eat."

⁘⸻•⸻⁘

They sat huddled together at a tiny table in the "Mountain Supplies Café" on West Argyle Street, straining to hear each other above the hullabaloo. Dougal looked directly at her. "I have a confession to make."

She looked at him sharply. Now what? Did he have to leave again? Had he heard more rumors about Granddad?

"We're not actually going to eat here."

"We're not? Then what are we doing here?"

"I took the liberty of reserving a seven o'clock table for us at the Seaforth Inn. I hope you don't mind. Right now we're just killing time."

A lock of thick, blond hair had fallen down on his forehead and she was tempted to reach out and touch it. If this was killing time, she was all for a slow death.

She picked up a spoon and inspected it, trying to mask her feelings. "It's really good to be with you. Like I said, I always feel safe when we're together."

"Just safe? Nothing else?"

She swallowed and looked away, a smile tugging at the corners of her mouth.

A pudgy waiter appeared at their side with pad in hand. "What'll it be for the two o' ye? There's a right good special on the Guinness tonight."

"Have anything you like." Dougal looked at her intently before glancing up at the waiter. "One for me. And my lady friend will have …"

Time to do something reckless for a change. Granddad had imposed a strict no-drinking policy and she had adhered to it even when her university friends had teased her. That was then, though.

This was now. Granddad wasn't here anymore and sweet Dougal was prompting her with an encouraging look. She wanted more than anything to enjoy his company without something standing in the way.

"I'll have … tea," she finally sighed.

"You're sure?"

"I'm sure." Granddad still held the upper hand. She crossed her leg, laughing nervously as the toe of her sandal accidentally bumped his shin. "Sorry, I wasn't trying to beat you up again."

"I'm not exactly fragile." He shifted his weight. "Why don't you tell me what you've learned about your Granddad. Have you solved the case?"

"Not yet, but I think I'm onto something."

He leaned toward her, just inches from her face. His lashes were thick and dark though his hair was fair and the cologne he wore enticed rather than overpowered. She was having trouble concentrating.

"Are you able to tell me?"

"Of course." She wondered how much to include. Should she tell him about Jimmy? "I met a guy who took me to an art shop," she blurted out. "There's a painting there that I think has something to do with Granddad."

He raised his eyebrows fractionally. "How so?"

She paused as the waiter served their drinks. "I'm not sure, but an old lady tried to keep me from seeing it. When I finally did get a look, I noticed that the top layer of paint was flaking off."

"And on that basis you believe it has something to do with your Granddad?"

"Don't you see?" She leaned even closer and felt the warmth of his breath. "The woman could have been Tanika."

He sat back. "The one your granddad was conversing with?"

"Yes. She's about the right age and I'm sure there's an oil painting hidden underneath the acrylic."

"Why would you think that?"

"It's the only reason the acrylic would flake off. It can't adhere to the oil for an extended period of time." She sat back smugly—the "Antiques Roadshow" queen.

"But how can you be certain?" He sipped the amber foam.

"There's a few different ways. It could be X-rayed—although I don't think the woman would allow that—or a palette knife could be used to chip off a little more of the outer coat, or it could be wiped away with a solvent. Of course she wouldn't allow any of that either."

He looked at her with renewed interest. "You really are an art expert. There's only one thing that bothers me."

"What's that?"

"You mentioned a guy. Are you interested in him?"

"No!" The people on either side stopped talking and stared in their direction. "I mean, of course not. He's a grubby type of guy. I just met him when I was having lunch. I don't even like him."

He let out his breath. "You had me worried for a minute." He leaned forward till their forehead nearly touched.

"Any more for ye, miss?" The waiter's smile was all business.

Dougal stopped leaning and looked at his watch. "No, I think we're finished here, thank you." He discreetly paid the bill and they left.

Thunder rumbled in the distance and the wind whipped Sela's hair back from her face as they headed down Argyle Street toward the Seaforth Inn. "We'd better hurry," he said. "These storms can come up quickly."

The street lights flickered in the premature dusk and raindrops spattered their head and shoulders. He grabbed her hand and they broke into a run, turning right on Quay Street and left onto Shore as the storm gathered strength. By the time they reached the restaurant they were drenched. Sela's flowy skirt clung to her bare legs and her soggy hair dripped like a faucet down her back. She looked up at Dougal as he attempted to shrug the water from his jacket and burst out laughing.

"What's so funny?"

"Just you—you look so cute all messed up like that."

He pointed down the hall to the restrooms. "We'd better get ourselves dried off before we catch our death."

A few minutes later they met back in the foyer, slightly less waterlogged. Sela looked down at her crumpled jacket and skirt. "Well, at least you saw me at my best for a few minutes."

He gave her a long look. "You always look your best to me."

Hearing a lively Scottish melody, she glanced into the dining area and spotted a kilt-clad ensemble near the far wall. Next to them a fire roared from a massive stone hearth. "Do you think they'd let us sit over there? I'm freezing."

"Anything for you." He hailed a passing waiter.

A moment later they were led to a white-clad table so close to the blaze Sela felt an instant warmth pass through her. She looked at him accusingly. "You had this all arranged."

"Everything but the storm."

She smiled, dropping her eyes. "It's fantastic, but I sure hope they bring the menus soon. I'm starting to feel light headed from hunger."

"No need. As I said, I took a few liberties."

She glanced up as the waiter returned, balancing a tray of appetizers on one hand. When he'd gone, she picked up a celery stick and loaded it with dill sauce before gobbling it down.

"I didn't realize you'd be so hungry," Dougal apologized. "I assure you, there's more coming." A musical note sounded close by and he grabbed at his jacket pocket. "My cell phone. Sorry."

Clicking it, he held up an index finger. "Dougal here." After a moment he covered the phone with his hand. "I'm so sorry. This will only take a minute." He stood and walked back in the direction of the foyer, speaking quietly into the receiver.

Sela attacked another celery stick. Why was she always sitting alone in restaurants? Tapping her foot to the beat of the music, she picked up the "Highland News of the Day" paper, which was wedged between the salt and pepper, and glanced at the headline.

"Rare Lichens Destroyed at Inverpoly." With a start, she grabbed the paper and read on. "It was recently discovered that clusters of rare lichens were mutilated and destroyed near the town of Inverpoly. Who could be guilty of this monstrous crime against our Scottish countryside? Though we welcome tourists to our area, some of the antics of certain visitors beg the question, 'What is going on here?' It has come to light that a number of young men and women, under the guise of student activities, have been sneaking about doing who knows what. Could they be the guilty parties? Stay tuned for more tidbits."

Sela dropped the paper, her head beginning to swim. So, she'd been right all along about the soldiers. They were nothing but a gang of thugs. But what had they been up to? Tearing up rare lichens didn't seem to be a typical neo-Nazi pastime. Suddenly another thought popped into her head and she took in a sharp breath. The article had referred to girls as well as guys. Was it trying to point a finger at Julia and the girls too? And hadn't Julia said they might be going back for more samples? What if the neo-Nazis decided to go back as well? The girls could be in grave danger.

Where was Dougal? She had to get back to the hostel and see if the girls were alright. Rummaging through her purse, she found a pen and wrote, "Be back soon" on a paper napkin. She stood and was about to make her way to the door when a beefy hand clasped her arm and she found herself swung into the middle of a lively Scottish jig.

"Take a look at this bonny lassie, folks," called out the leader of the group as he twirled her around to the tune of "A Hundred Pipers." The audience, catching his mood, began clapping along.

Sela tried to twist away from him but he grabbed her by the waist and skipped her across the stage area. "Please, I have to leave," she pleaded.

"Och, we're just getting started," he bellowed and sent her for another spin amid the whoops and hollers of the crowd.

As he reeled her in again, she tried once more to flee from his brawny embrace but she was no match for him. Frantic to escape, she waited till his foot came down beside her and planted a spiky heel directly on his toe. He yelped and jumped back, much to the delight of the spectators. Seizing her opportunity, she bolted to the foyer, threw the door open, and ran out into the street.

Sheets of rain lashed at her face and clothing but she wasn't about to turn back now. Shivering, she hurried past darkened doorways and glowing windows. What would Dougal think when he returned to an empty table? It seemed like he'd been gone an hour though it was merely a matter of minutes. She'd explain later.

She jerked her head around as a vehicle roared up beside her and squealed to a halt. The driver opened his window. "Get in," he growled.

In less time than it took to form a complete thought, she realized it wasn't a friendly suggestion and spun around in the opposite direction.

Grappling with her flailing skirt, she splashed full-tilt down the sidewalk as she heard him crank the gear shift into reverse and speed back toward her. A narrow alleyway opened up to her left and she darted through it, scraping her arm on the jagged stucco wall.

She ran the length of a block before stopping to gasp for air. Listening for the sound of an engine, she could hear nothing but the thumping of her own heart. Was he gone? She leaned back against the wall, panting. Who was he and why was he trying to get her into his car? His face had been shrouded in darkness making it impossible to see who it was.

The street lay directly ahead and she crept slowly toward it, her eyes darting about in all directions. This private investigator business wasn't really her style at all. She preferred safer pastimes like painting pictures of hills. She held her breath, trying to pick up the slightest sound. Rain pinged off something metal beside her foot and she stopped, waiting. Suddenly a paper bag, driven by a gust of wind, flew up from the street in front and she let out an ear-shattering scream. Realizing what it was, she ducked back against the wall and stood still, holding her breath.

It was the absence rather than the presence of sound that made the hair on the back of her neck stand up—as if the alley itself was on guard. And then she heard it—a controlled exhalation of breath coming from behind her. He had followed her into the alley.

Acting on survival instinct alone, she recalled the piece of metal by her foot and bent down, feeling frantically along the ground to find it. Her hand touched something cold and she pulled it toward herself, relieved to find that it was a section of pipe.

"I'm not going to hurt you," said a deep voice, breaking the silence.

She screamed again, and grasping the pipe with both hands, swung like a batter betting on a home run. She heard a thud, then a groan, and knew it had hit its mark. She dropped the pipe and ran.

She tore down Quay Street, turned west onto Shore, and raced toward the hostel, letting out a sob of relief when its white-washed exterior popped into view. Once inside, she plowed past the front desk, leaving the clerk wide-eyed, raced down the hall to her room, and threw the door open.

Sitting cross-legged on the bed, lap-top in front of her, was Julia. Sela stood in the doorway with her mouth gaping. Then, without uttering a sound, she slowly crumpled to the floor.

Chapter Ten

The two sat stiffly in the darkened vehicle, oblivious to the storm around them. "You let a terrified girl take you down?" sneered the first.

The other looked at his feet. "I wasn't expecting her to pick up a pipe." He cradled his swollen arm.

"Do you realize what you've done now? It's not just fear tactics anymore. She knows she's being watched. That's the second time you've bungled things up—first, at her house across the pond and now this."

"Ye wouldn't have been privy to all those names if I hadn't got the address book. Anyway, maybe she'll be frightened enough to leave now."

"Don't count on it. This one's likely to bring the military down on us. No … we'll have to come up with something else—and fast."

***

Sela didn't remember getting into bed but here she lay, shivering under a pile of quilts, listening to the commotion in the hallway. She could make out both Julia's and Dougal's voices but not the words. Suddenly the door burst open and Dougal charged through with a frantic expression on his face. He ran straight to the bed and sank down onto his knees.

"Sela … are you alright? Please tell me you weren't hurt."

She opened her mouth to assure him she was fine, but only managed a croak.

"This is all my fault. I kept saying to my boss that I'd call him back but I couldn't get off the phone. Please ... tell me what happened."

"I already told you." Julia stood behind him, her hands on her hips. "She's not well enough to be talking. I'm going to get her a bowl of soup and then she's going to sleep for the night."

"No, it's okay," Sela said thickly.

He stood and paced back and forth for a moment. "I'll tell you what. I'll go down to the Ferry Boat Inn. They have wonderful chicken noodle soup. I promise I'll let her sleep as soon as she's eaten."

"You've got ten minutes to be back," Julia snapped.

He returned with time to spare, bearing a steaming Styrofoam bowl of the savory liquid. Sela sat propped up with pillows, trying her best to smile as she looked up at him. "Smells fantastic."

Julia rolled her eyes. "I'll leave you two alone for a few minutes." She went out and shut the door behind her.

Dougal dragged a chair over to the bedside with his foot and carefully sat down, balancing the bowl on his knee. "Open up." He dipped a spoon in and held it out to her.

"I'm not a child. You're not feeding me."

"Don't argue. Just open your mouth."

She did as she was told, savoring the spicy flavor. "Mmm, good." After a few mouthfuls she shook her head. "That's enough. I feel better now."

He put down the spoon and took her hand. "Can you tell me what happened? I looked everywhere in the restaurant for you but you were gone."

"Sorry." She lowered her eyes. "I saw a newspaper article about the lichens being destroyed and thought Julia and the girls might be in danger."

"And did you think you could rescue them by yourself?"

"I just had to find out if they were okay. Sorry ... I should have waited for you."

He dropped his voice. "Julia said something about a man in an alleyway. Did he try to hurt you?"

"He didn't really get a chance. I was so petrified I hit him with something and took off."

"Oh Sela." He gave her hand a squeeze. "I had hoped this was just a prank but it's gone too far. I think it's time for us to call in the police."

"No!"

He sat back. "I'm not taking a chance with your life. You could have been kidnapped—or worse. We need to tell the police."

She attempted to sit up straight. "But don't you see? If I get the police involved I'll never find out the truth about Granddad. I'll never be able to clear his name." She broke into a cacophony of sneezes and lay back against the pillows.

"That's it for tonight." Julia had flung the door open and now marched across the room like a miniature sergeant major. "You can see her tomorrow if she's up to it."

"I'll be here first thing in the morning," Dougal conceded, rising. He gave Sela a long look. "Try to get some rest."

When he'd gone, Julia fluffed up the pillows and straightened the blanket. "Men," she scowled.

In spite of the situation, Sela nearly burst out laughing but soon the warm, comfortable nether land of slumber claimed her and she drifted off without another thought.

⁕⁕⧫⧫⧫⧫⧫⧫⁕⁕

Dell opened the unmarked envelope and looked over the short report, a smirk forming on her lips. People were already beginning to talk. That alone could bring sales to a new level, increasing profits and expanding her pockets all the more. She'd have to watch, though. None of it could be verified. If asked, she'd just say it was unsolicited material—the kind you're allowed to print in a free country, thank you very much.

◦•●━━━━━━●━━━━━━●•◦

It seemed only a few minutes till Sela's eyelids fluttered open. She looked up at Keira who stood by the foot of the bed holding a pot of tea.

"I think she's awake girls."

Amanda plopped down on the bed beside her. "You had us right worried. Are you feeling any better this morning?"

"I'm fine."

"Did you really belt somebody over the head with a pipe?" Keira asked, wide-eyed.

"Let's not quiz her just yet." Julia held out a blue stoneware mug for Keira to fill with tea. "Here you go. Dr. Julia at your service."

Sela managed to sit half-way up before breaking into a cough. "Sorry. I must've gotten a chill."

Julia's brow creased with concern. "Maybe we should take you to a medical doctor. We don't want you getting pneumonia."

"It's nothing like that." She took the cup and swallowed a mouthful. "Ah, that hits the spot."

"Julia said you were worried about us," Keira said softly.

"I was. It might sound silly but when I saw that article about the lichens being destroyed, I was afraid you'd run into those army guys again. Anyway, I should've waited for Dougal. I'm afraid I made him look bad."

"He'll live." Amanda scooted over to a more comfortable spot.

"So you didn't go to Inverpoly at all?"

"No." Julia took a seat on the other bed. "We decided to try another location—a place called Corrieshalloch Gorge."

Sela shuddered. "In that case, I'm glad I didn't go with you. I tried to cross that swinging bridge on the way here but couldn't make it all the way over." She lifted her cup and took a sip. "But

112

I'm still worried about the newspaper article. It seemed like they were blaming you girls for the lichen damage along with those awful men."

Julia waved her hand away. "Not to worry. There's no way the university would go along with it. Anyway, I don't think that particular paper is taken too seriously."

Just then there was a knock at the door and they all turned toward it. "Prince Charming, no doubt," whispered Amanda. "Come on in," she called out.

Dougal peeked into the room, waving a bunch of blood-red roses like a white flag. "Is it safe to enter?"

"Dougal, nobody's blaming you," Sela gushed. "And you certainly didn't have to buy me anything. But thank you. They're beautiful."

"It's the least I could do."

Amanda rolled her eyes. "I think it's time we went for breakfast." She swung her feet onto the floor and stood. "Do you want us to get you anything, Sela?"

Before she could answer, Dougal spoke up. "You girls go and enjoy your breakfast. I'll make sure she doesn't go hungry." He paused. "First, though, would you be able to find a place for these?" He held the roses out to Julia but as she reached to take them, they dropped from his grasp, landing with a swoosh on the floor. He laughed sheepishly and picked them up. "Sorry. I seem to be in a bit of a dither with all the commotion."

Julia gave him a look, then turned to search for a container. "I'm sure there's something around here." Rummaging through the cupboard, she found a stainless-steel thermos, popped them into it, and filled it with water.

He looked directly at her as she placed it onto the counter. "Thank you so much for all your help."

"Don't mention it." With the girls in tow, she went out the door, leaving the two of them alone.

"Here we are again," he said. "I hope you won't beat me up this time."

"Only if you say you're leaving." She smiled and looked down at her hands.

Dougal lifted her chin with his fingers. "I don't think I can do that."

She glanced downward. What did he mean? Did he think she was too much of a dunce to be left to her own devices or was he actually falling for her?

"Right now, however, I need to take care of some business while you get a little more rest."

"I really don't need any more sleep," she protested. "Besides ..."

He gently pushed her back onto the pillow. "Please. For me."

"Okay then," she smiled. "Just for you."

***

Half an hour later she woke up restless and hungry. She looked at her watch. Nine-thirty—too early to expect him back. The sun was streaming through the window, enticing her out-of-doors. Maybe she'd slip to the bakery for a croissant or something with a cup of tea. She was beginning to feel better already. Throwing on the navy hoody with white capris she splashed water on her face, ran a brush through her matted hair, and left.

Shore Street was just coming to life with shopkeepers bustling about opening blinds and setting out colorful pots of petunias and geraniums as she followed the aroma of freshly baked cinnamon rolls from the Tea Store Café just ahead. But as she reached the intersection at Quay Street, another idea wedged its way into her head. The Ceilidh Place was close by. Maybe she could kill two birds with one stone and have a bite to eat as well as a chat with the little proprietor.

She reached the ancient doorway and tugged on the handle. Closed. Just her luck. Possibly there was another way in. Walking around the corner she spotted an unpaved alleyway and tentatively picked her way back toward the pub.

Halfway down the block she caught sight of a rusty metal sign dangling precariously above a peeling doorway. It read, "Ceilidh Place Back Entrance." No one seemed to be around. Reaching the door, she turned the handle and pulled, holding her breath when it swung open. She paused for a moment, then stepped inside. The hallway was empty and dark and reeked of stale tobacco but the crackly voice of a radio announcer droned somewhere in the near distance.

Coughing as quietly as possible to ease a slight tickle in her throat, she took another cautious step forward but froze on the spot when a loose floorboard complained loudly. So, this was how it felt to be a thief. Should she leave or shout hello? It didn't take long to decide when a door yawned open somewhere down the hall and a man's voice roared out, "Ye can't be serious!"

Sela stopped breathing and flattened herself against the wall, "Nancy Drew" style.

"I am. She was there alright," the second voice boomed. It sounded like the little proprietor.

They'd be in the hallway any second now and the outside door was still hanging open. She could either run or stay, but if she stayed, there wouldn't be time to shut it. And how would she explain why she was sneaking down the hallway? She looked frantically about for a place to hide and spotted another door just ahead. Darting inside, she shut it silently behind her.

"She wouldn't know what to look for anyway," the little man said, his voice much closer now. "It's just a simple painting as far as she's concerned."

Painting? Were they talking about the acrylic painting from the art shop? Was it that important? And who was the "she" they were referring to? Herself? She felt like a fly on a wall but as she stood listening, another thought entered her head. Was one of these men the anonymous caller? They both fit the bill with their old-man Scottish accents but she couldn't be sure.

"The thing that amazes me," the first one went on, "is that no one's picked up on it before now."

"Don't forget," the little proprietor said, "it's just a small part of the picture, if ye'll pardon the pun. Besides, you know what they say about hiding things in clear view."

Sela peered around her hiding spot, praying that an exit sign would light up but the only illumination came from a computer screen on the opposite side of the room sitting in the middle of a cluttered desk.

"Look, ye've gone and left the door open," the first man complained. "Were ye born in a barn?"

"Ach, it must've been the cat. He pushes it open when he wants out."

"Better not get careless. We don't need any prying eyes."

Sela stilled herself. What were they afraid of? Was the painting stolen? Maybe it was a Rembrandt or Degas or some other old master. She'd heard of things like that before—people hiding things for years and then suddenly selling them for millions. Still, that wouldn't explain why they wouldn't want prying eyes in this place— unless, maybe they were in cahoots with the old woman.

A bead of sweat trickled down the side of her face as she considered what to do next. It would be impossible to sneak out with them standing this close to the door. What would Granddad do in a situation like this? Knowing him, he'd probably be down on his knees—or would he? Maybe all his religion was just a cover-up. Maybe he was in on the theft after all. Maybe that's what the commotion was all about. No, she couldn't believe that.

With thumping heart she took a cautious step toward the computer, taking care not to fall over anything on the way. Bending down, she peered at the screen. Nothing out of the ordinary. She clicked on Google and when the screen opened, pressed the history button. Nothing. Everything must have been hidden or deleted. And it wasn't as if she could hack her way into someone else's computer. She was no guru. Her eyes slipped to the documents cluttering the desk. Maybe someone had been careless enough to …

"Yer on your way then, Jock?" The little man's booming voice broke in on her thoughts. "We've got to act fast. He lowered his volume to a near-normal range. "You know what's at stake if they find the goods before we do."

"Aye."

"Before ye go I just want to show you one other thing. Ye'll find it most interesting."

Sela's heart seemed to perch on the edge of her throat. Were they coming into the office? As she stood frozen in place, the back of her throat suddenly constricted and she shielded her mouth with both hands to keep from coughing. Perfect timing!

"Can it no' wait until later?" Jock asked, oblivious to the panic just a few feet away. "I've got to get to an appointment right away. That young upstart of a doctor wants to have another look at my knee."

"Don't worry about it then. I'll show it to ye when we meet with the others. Come and I'll walk with ye to the car."

When the door banged shut, Sela nearly collapsed with relief. Covering her mouth with the sleeve of her sweater, she let out a strangled noise somewhere between a cough and a sneeze. She had to get out of there fast but those papers needed to be checked out first. It might be her only chance. She picked up the one on top and held it to the screen. Too dark. Did she dare turn on the light?

She crept to the door, flicked the switch and raced back across the room. Grabbing the paper once more, she scanned the first few lines—a bill for restaurant supplies. Quickly she sifted through the next few documents—advertisements and bills—nothing even remotely mysterious. She glanced at the other side of the desk and noticed a brown envelope sticking out from under a similar pile of papers. She pulled it out and read the label— "University of Aberdeen."

With a quick look over her shoulder, she slid the contents out onto the desk and began reading. "Inverpoly and Corrieshalloch Gorge: Locations of rare lichens in the Scottish Highlands—Particularly Graphidion Scriptae."

Her hands began to shake as she took in the implications. She had to get out of there now. Stuffing the papers back into the envelope, she tip-toed to the door, turned off the light and listened for a sound from the hallway. Cautiously she eased the door open and waited. After a minute she poked her head out. Seeing nothing, she scurried down the hallway and out the back door, careful to close it behind her. Once in the alleyway, she ran like mad till she reached Argyle Street.

When she was safely out on the street she slowed her step, trying to appear casual as she caught her breath. Could the little proprietor actually be mixed up with the neo-Nazis? It was unbelievable but there had to be a connection. And what was the common denominator between the painting and the lichens? The thing was, she couldn't tell Dougal what she'd discovered or he'd insist she go back to Glasgow.

Turning down Shore Street, she lifted her head as she made her way to the bakery. She didn't need to tell him anything. She had just gone out for a leisurely breakfast. The rest, she'd keep to herself and try to piece together on her own.

Chapter Eleven

Leaning back against the vinyl-covered chair, Sela immersed herself in the cheerful atmosphere of the Tea Store Cafe. Her pounding heart had finally recovered and for once the crowded seating arrangement felt comfortable. She tried to imagine the place as a water color painting and mentally dipped her brush into a solution of light cadmium yellow as she defined the jauntily striped curtains.

The woman beside her offered a toothy grin and raised her gritty voice a notch. "Can ye pass the sugar, luv?"

As she reached for it, she glanced toward the doorway and felt her inspiration dry up like rain in the Sahara. Standing at the counter, paying for his take-out drink, was Jimmy. She handed the sugar bowl to the woman and tried to keep out of his line of sight. Too late. His eyes crinkled in recognition.

The woman spotted him as well as he made a bee-line for the table. "Here's your boyfriend, luv," she said. "We'll scoot over and make room for him."

Sela felt her cheeks burn.

Reaching them, Jimmy waved his free hand expansively. "No need to move," he offered. "I'll just squeeze in close." He whipped off his oily cap with a mischievous grin and dropped it next to her cup, fitting himself into the tiny space beside her.

"I really have to get going," she ground out between clenched teeth, moving as far from him as possible.

"But you just got here," the woman protested. "You two haven't had a tiff, have ye?" She laughed out loud.

Sela's jaw tightened.

"No, no, nothing like that." Jimmy stretched his arm across the back of the seat. "We've never actually had a falling out, have we, luv." Sela leaned in toward the table.

"It's the same with me and my man," the woman continued, warming to the topic. "We've been together thirty-odd years and never had a fallin' out yet. Isn't that right Jack?"

"Jack" took a noisy slurp of his tea and continued with the sports page. Mercifully, a woman across the way began expounding on the merits of her own marriage.

Sela let out her breath and turned to Jimmy. "Do you mind? I've got things to do."

"Ach, and what could be more important than conversing with your boyfriend over a wee cup o' tea?" He chuckled under his breath.

"You're not my boyfriend. I wouldn't know you at all if it wasn't for your talent of popping up in other people's business."

"But I thought we were going to have lunch together." His eyes creased again and in spite of herself she burst out laughing.

"So we're friends after all?" He held out his hand.

"Acquaintances." She smiled as she took his hand and shook on it, oddly disquieted by the ease of the gesture.

"My, my, what a cozy corner this is."

Sela looked up, her hand still in Jimmy's. Standing over them was Dougal, his perfectly pressed taupe jacket skimming the table's edge.

"Dougal." She tore her hand away and accidentally bumped Jimmy's cup which shot forward, delivering a smattering of the brown liquid up onto the jacket.

"Sorry, mate," Jimmy said with a smirk. "I'm sure it won't stain. They're all washable these days."

Sela glared at him and looked across at Dougal. She had to admire him for his composure though his pupils were pinpoints and his mouth a thin slit. Grabbing her used napkin, she began mopping up the mess.

"That's it, then," Jimmy said, beginning to rise. "You know what they say—'no rest for the wicked'." He maneuvered out of the seat, brushed off his greasy shirt, and after retrieving his cap, looked directly at Sela. "If you ever need more art advice, don't hesitate to ask."

She gawked at him stupidly. What was he talking about?

"Let's go." Dougal steered her out ahead as he stepped in front of Jimmy. She wasn't about to protest. The room had grown uncomfortably quiet.

As they made their way to the door she heard the grainy voice of the woman behind her—"Oh what a tangled web we weave."

⋅⋅◦◈◦⸻◈⸻◦◈◦⋅⋅

They sat together on the grassy slope of Postie's Path, looking out at the Summer Isles. Their fingers touched and a spark of electricity ran through her.

He leaned toward her. "I've got something for you."

"Another chocolate?"

"No—a better surprise this time."

She giggled as he took a small gift bag from his jacket pocket and handed it to her.

"Dougal, you're way too kind to me. Let me guess what's in it."

He grinned playfully. "Go ahead but I doubt you'll be able to."

She gave it a rattle. "Hmmm. I believe this is going to take some concentration. It's not too heavy and it's not too jiggly. I can't wait any longer—I give up."

"Open it then."

With delicate fingers she reached in and removed a small black box. Her heart began to race and she looked up at him.

"Go ahead," he whispered. His green eyes seemed to glow in the mid-day light.

Slowly, she lifted the lid and let out a gasp. It was like nothing she had ever seen. Lying on a bed of creamy satin, encircled by a sparkling chain, was an exquisite heart-shaped gold locket.

"Dougal," she cried, tears forming in her eyes.

"Do you like it?"

"I absolutely love it. I've never had anything like this in my life." She trembled as she removed it from the box and fingered its fragile beauty. "Is there something inside?"

"Why don't you look in and find out."

Holding it between her thumb and index finger she clicked a tiny button on the side and the top sprang open. Smiling up at her, dimple intact, was a miniature photograph of Granddad as a young man.

"Oh, Dougal!" she gasped. The tears that had threatened before now spilled over and coursed down her cheeks. "How did you ever find this?"

"As I said before, I have my sources."

"Thank you so much." Her fingers tentatively touched the sleeve of his jacket as she blinked back the tears.

He smiled. "I think you should try it on. I'm sure it would look a lot better around your neck than buried in your hand."

"She giggled again and held it up to her throat, twisting to allow him to fasten it.

Turning back around, she preened like a fashion model. "Do I do it justice?"

He gave her a long look. "I think the better question would be, 'does it do you justice'?" After a moment he lay back on the grass. "More than anything I'd like you to come back to Glasgow with me today."

She sighed, running her fingers through the soft grass. Her resolve was beginning to slip but somehow it didn't seem to matter so much anymore. Did she really need to prove anything? Wasn't it enough that she herself was convinced of Granddad's innocence?

After a moment she looked over to him. "I'll do whatever you want."

"You'll never regret it," he whispered, tracing the line of her cheek with his fingertip. Slowly, his hand moved to the back of her neck and he pulled her down until her head rested on his arm, her hair splayed out around her. With one smooth motion, he rolled over, his mouth only inches from hers, his eyes searching her own. Sela's heart fluttered and leapt as his hot breath warmed her face. She reached up and grasped the locket around her neck.

Suddenly the tiny photograph of Granddad as a young man sprang to her mind. He had been about her age when he was forced to leave Scotland yet she'd never heard him utter a bitter word about it. When his wife, son, and daughter-in-law had been killed in the crash, he had been more concerned for Sela than himself. And in spite of everything he had kept his faith. Could she just let all that go without giving it another shot?

"But I'll need to stay until Sunday."

Dougal's jaw clenched slightly and he let out a resigned little laugh. "I guess I'll have to live with that," he said at length, raising himself to a sitting position. He checked his watch. "We really should be getting back."

As they made their way along the craggy path toward town, Sela felt the locket jostling against her skin with each step and smiled inwardly. Just before they reached the main road, Dougal turned to her again, his eyes probing hers once more as he cupped her hand in his own. "You know, we could actually stay a bit longer if you'd like. Nothing's set in stone, is it?"

She hesitated, but only for a second. "I'd really love to, but I can't let Granddad down."

He lifted her hand and kissed it. "A woman of honor—most appealing."

Julia walked along the water's edge and watched the sea gulls as they swooped down and snatched a few crumbs from the picnic table ahead. The girls had decided to shop rather than search for more lichens and who could blame them. She wouldn't have minded checking out a few stores herself under ordinary circumstances. Today, though, her mind was on other things.

It had been two years but the memory was still fresh, like the sting of a slap. Who could have predicted the way it had all turned out? She reached the table and sat down. Taking off her sandals, she squished her brown feet into the warm sand as she looked across at the distant hills.

Her thoughts traveled back to her first position as teaching assistant to the famed Dr. Theodore Hendricks of the University of New York. As a well-known botanist, his knowledge and power had awed her. Julia had been his willing prodigy—along with Cyril Branford, third generation faculty member.

Together they had scoured Long Island, refining the classifications of the lichen population in that region. It had been long and tedious work but she had loved every second of it. Besides, having her name acknowledged in Dr. Hendricks' upcoming book would be worth any effort she could give.

She had been caught completely off guard when an e-mail had directed her to the office of the university president, Dr. Eugene G. Pierson. Was she about to receive special commendation? The cold eyes had puzzled her but the document he'd slapped down on the desk had mystified her still more.

"Did you think you'd get a jump start on Dr. Hendricks?" he'd asked, his finger underscoring her name beneath the title, "Long Island Lichens Reclassified." "No periodical worth its salt will accept plagiarized material."

Denial had been useless. She had been allowed to resign quietly with the understanding there would be a three year disciplinary period in the United States.

When the money had run out, she'd taken a temporary

waitressing job to tide her over. One night while serving tables on the far side of the room, she'd heard the words, "Get my fellow author another bottle of your finest wine," and had looked over to see Cyril and Dr. Hendricks clinking glasses together. Dr. Hendricks had had the grace to look away when he saw her but Cyril's expression had revealed a great deal about his character—smug, self-satisfied, and oily.

It had taken months to begin to move on. With Pastor Dane's support and recommendation she'd been able to secure a few locum terms outside the USA. With God's love and grace she'd finally been able to forgive. Her naivete, though, was gone. She could spot the look of a predator a mile away. And she'd seen it today as she'd been about to walk into the Tea Store Café. Sela's head had been down but Julia hadn't missed the look on the face of one of the men behind her—secretive and smooth—just like Cyril's. She couldn't allow an innocent like Sela to walk into a trap without trying to help.

Hearing her name, she looked up and saw Amanda and Keira walking toward her, loaded down with shopping bags. "You should've come with us," Amanda called, her face lit with a huge smile. "There was a half-price sale. We pretty well bought out the town."

"I hope you got it out of your system," Julia said. Tomorrow is our last day and there's a few things we still need to finish up." She stuck on her shoes and grabbing a couple of the bags, made her way with them to the street ahead.

Chapter Twelve

Grey billows gathered overhead and a blustery wind whipped strands of hair into her face but none of these mundane matters disturbed Sela who was officially on cloud nine. She giggled to herself, reliving the sweet kiss Dougal had planted on her cheek at the edge of town and once again fingered the locket around her neck. Everything was beautiful—especially his eyes which were luminous and seemed to plumb the depths of her soul.

A car horn blared and she jumped back onto the sidewalk. She'd better get a grip or he'd be plumbing her soul in a hospital bed. Looking both ways, she crossed the street and made her way toward the Ullapool Museum on West Argyle Street.

They had agreed that until Sunday evening she would do everything in her power to clear Granddad's name. Monday morning she would return to Glasgow with him. She checked her watch—twelve fifteen. That gave her just over a day to accomplish the impossible. No problem.

Walking past an arts and crafts shop, she reviewed what she had learned thus far: 1—there was a distinct possibility the elderly woman in the art shop was Tanika; 2—the acrylic painting in the woman's possession might be covering something of much greater value; 3— the little proprietor and his cronies were also connected to the painting, and in some way to the lichen damage as well, and last but not least; 4— Jimmy was somehow linked to everything. Now all she had to do was figure out how it all fit together. There had to be a key and maybe she would find it at the museum.

Ahead of her was the Ceilidh Place. Beyond its white-washed exterior stood the rectangular stone structure of what was once known as the Thomas Telford Parliamentary Church. She had passed by it several times since coming to Ullapool and had even stopped once to read the sign out front. Built in 1829, it had apparently closed for worship in 1935 and had remained vacant until being converted into a museum in the late 1980's. Not that any of that was of much interest to her. What was of interest was the fact that it contained a full index of archives and photographs—at least according to a leaflet she had picked up on her way out of the café.

Nearing the building, she stood for a moment by the low stone fence. She reached into the pocket of her hoody and touched the letter entrusted to her by her great-grandmother. "Read it without judgment," she had said. "Try to find the truth." Sighing, she opened the heavy wooden door and went in.

A smiling grey-haired matron in a tweed skirt, lacy white blouse, and sensible shoes greeted her at the front desk and handed her a brochure. "Welcome, dearie," she said in the sing-songy accent of the highlands. "You're in luck. It's the slow time of day and ye'll have the place to yourself."

Sela took it from her, hoping this wasn't an invitation for a long drawn-out chat. She offered a polite smile. "Thank you. I'll just look around for a while."

"That'll be three pounds—unless of course you're a member."

Sela opened her purse and began fishing around for change. "Sorry, but I don't live here."

The woman smiled sweetly. "A lifetime membership is only fifty pounds and includes full voting rights plus a bi-annual newsletter."

Sela counted out the three pounds and handed it to her. "I'm afraid I won't be here long enough to take advantage of it."

"We have friends from all over the world—Canada, the United States, even Australia. Ye don't have to live here at all."

Sela thought for a moment. She didn't have time to waste and the woman might be able to lead her in the right direction. "What's the annual fee?"

"That would be five pounds—just two pounds more and ye'll be able to utilize our resources for the rest of the year."

She pulled out a two-pound coin and handed it over. "If I need help finding something will you be available?"

"Of course, of course, dearie. As ye can see we have everything from tapestries to touch-screen computers. I'm familiar with them all. Now, if ye could just fill out this wee form you'll be good to go."

With an inward sigh, she scrawled down the information in record time and handed it back. Looking around at the well laid out room, she took in the mahogany display cases and numerous exhibits. Bright quilts and tapestries hung from floor to ceiling along the left side while the right side was lined with audio-visual screens silently playing out the history of Loch Broom. "I wish I had more time," she said. "I'm sure there's a lot here to learn."

"Oh, ye must come back," the woman gushed and pointed to a large, multi-colored quilt hanging with the others. "That alone is worth the visit. It was hand-stitched by local residents in 1988 to celebrate Ullapool's bicentenary. It depicts over two hundred scenes of the Loch Broom area." She spoke in a voice high pitched with enthusiasm.

Sela looked at her watch. "It's beautiful, but I'm actually interested in seeing the reference material."

"Right this way, then." She stepped spryly to an obscure corner on the same side as the quilts. "This is our archive and photography section. As ye can see, everything is organized in the drawers according to topic and cross-referenced by date." She indicated several large filing cabinets. "And, of course, the photographs are in the albums on the desk. Feel free to browse to your heart's content."

A surge of excitement ran through her. Could she really be on the verge of a discovery? "What about old newspapers?" she asked matter-of-factly. No need to draw unwanted suspicion.

"They're all right there, dearie. What date did you have in mind?"

"I'm, uh, interested in the Second World War. Do you have much information on that?"

The woman chuckled in amusement. "Scads, dearie, scads. Ye could be here all night."

"Thank you," she said. "I'll just have a look, then."

Dropping her purse onto the chair, she scanned the labels in front until she found one near the bottom entitled "World War II." She opened the drawer. The woman was right. It bulged with documents and newspaper articles of every size and description. She sat back on her heels and thought for a minute. Where should she begin?

Taking the letter from her pocket, she read it over again. "25th March, 1945 …

… Joseph … New orders from the Fuhrer himself. Meet tonight at art shop 11.00 o'clock. Payment to arrive shortly. As always, Tanika."

At the front of the drawer a folder listed all the information by the date. Perfect. She leafed through and found the year 1945. Examining the long list of entries, she once again considered what to look for. Art, espionage? Alphabetical order then. She'd begin with art.

⋅•●━━━━━━━━━━━━━━●━━━━━━━━━━━●•⋅

Julia checked her purse for the keys and slipped on her sandals. "Remember, girls, I'm trusting you with the lichen entries. The university needs them for their records and you need them for a passing grade."

"Yes, professor," Amanda quipped. "How can we go wrong when you've repeated the instructions twenty-five times?" She ducked as Julia pretended to throw the purse in her direction.

"Not to worry," Keira soothed. "We won't let you down. Just get them to do something funky with your hair so you can finally nab a guy when you get back home."

Julia rolled her eyes and headed for the door. "Be back at about three."

Moments later she pulled onto Shore Street., doing her best to drive slowly to attract as little attention as possible in the bright red Rover. Going to the hairdresser wasn't a lie. It just wasn't her main objective.

She turned right at the intersection, then left onto Argyle and managed to find an empty parking spot. If anything turned up she'd be prepared. Leaving the vehicle, she walked towards the "Hair Today Beauty Salon" where a girl in short shorts and halter top, sporting flaming pink locks sashayed her way out the door. Oh boy, this ought to be good.

Inside, a tall waif of a girl stood at the reception desk leafing through the appointment book, her fingers drumming out the rhythm of the heavy metal rock band.

"Would you happen to have an appointment open this afternoon?" Julia took in the girl's lip, nose, and ear rings. "I realize it's late, but …"

"Two-fifteen is the last one." She looked up briefly. "Cut or color?"

"Cut."

Name?"

"It's Julia." What was this—"Home Alone?" "I'll just go and look around the shops till then if that's al …"

"See that you're back in time," the girl cut in, "or ye'll be waiting till next week."

Julia didn't bother explaining she'd be gone by then. She did, however, make a mental note to pick some extra strength Tylenol.

Leaving the shop, she checked her watch. It was just after one, which gave her over an hour to do a little sleuthing on her own. The girls were great to have around but they had a way of attracting attention wherever they went and she was trying to be as discreet as possible. Besides, she didn't want to get them involved in anything even remotely dangerous.

There were two places she had decided to check out. One was the Tea Store Café. She had seen one person there whom she didn't trust. Perhaps there were others. The second place was a little pub on Shore Street across from the bus stop where she'd spotted Sela earlier in the week. She'd had a funny feeling Sela had been watching for someone but hadn't wanted to confide in her at the time.

As Julia made her way down Argyle, she mentally ticked off the other suspicious characters on her list. First and foremost were the two army guys. They had admitted to being in town occasionally and with any luck their arrogance would keep them there, even with the police nosing around. The other was the oily type guy Sela had mentioned on their way to Inverpoly. Whether or not he was involved in the lichen damage remained to be seen.

A minute later she opened the door of the Tea Store Café and joined the lineup for coffee-to-go.

•◦❋◦•━━━━━◆━━━━━•◦❋◦•

Sela closed her eyes and paused for a brief break. The 1945 art section had been sketchy at best but then what did she expect—a full disclosure of all espionage activity in the art world? She sighed. She might have to go through a ton of files before anything came together and it was already approaching one-thirty. If only Dougal were here to help. She imagined his warm breath on the back of her neck. She'd turn her head and look into his eyes, he'd dip his head and then … She'd better get back to the files.

The January 15th edition had carried a short piece about a new art shop in town but the facts had been scant, no doubt overridden by the enormous wave of war news. The article had stated, however, that the shop had been opened by a woman originally from Paris, France, but hadn't included her name. Could it have been Tanika? She thought back to the elderly woman in the art shop. There might have had a slight accent but she wasn't sure.

Rising, she stretched her legs and rubbed her lower back. What if she just assumed it was Tanika and went from there? The date was right and the fact that it was a woman fit with the letter.

She once again picked up the folder. Moving her finger down the long list of entries, she stopped at the "E" section— "E" for Espionage. A few newspaper clippings had been included under a heading by that name but as she scanned through them she realized they didn't have anything to do with Ullapool. Had she really thought it would be that easy?

What had Dougal said that had made her so angry? Something about Granddad leading the Germans to a treasure. She reached up and fingered the locket. "Don't worry, Granddad," she whispered. "He'd never believe that if he'd known you."

Supposing, though, there really was a treasure here in the Highlands that the Germans had been searching for. Suddenly she drew in a sharp breath. What if Dougal had gotten it all wrong and it had never actually been found? Could that be what the neo-Nazis were looking for? The men at the Ceildh Place had talked about finding the goods. Were they referring to a treasure dating back to the Second World War? The little proprietor was old enough to have been around during that time. Shivering, she continued down the list until she reached the "T" section. Theatre, Tourists, Turks. In other words, zip. She sighed in frustration and continued on down the list.

A shadowed figure stood stone-like behind the bi-centennial quilt. After tailing the girl to the old church, he had watched from an outside window and quickly made his move when the museum woman turned her back. She hadn't spotted him though it had taken precious seconds to open the door without jingling the bell and slip over to his present vantage point. It wasn't perfect but it was at least passable. He couldn't see the girl's face but could tell by the piles of papers littering the floor that she was deep in research. What was she looking for?

After a moment she sat back on her heels, and her face became visible. Letting out an exasperated sigh, she stared straight at the quilt. The man stopped breathing. Had she seen him? Slowly, he moved his gaze away lest she felt his eyes on her and suspected she was being watched. After a moment, though, she turned back and resumed her exploration. The man let out an inaudible breath and pushed his unruly black hair away from his face. He'd wait it out and after she was gone, saunter over and see if she'd left behind any trace of her search.

•◦●▬ ▬ ● ▬ ▬◦●•

The lumpy woman at the counter removed her glasses and mopped her forehead with a Tea Store Café napkin as she squinted down at Julia. "What'll it be, miss?"

"A large triple-triple to go please." Julia counted out the change.

A minute later she meandered through the café with her steaming cardboard cup and found an empty seat close to the door. She'd spend a few minutes here and if nothing turned up she'd make her way to Shore Street. As casually as possible she scanned the room. Tourists, with their obligatory shopping bags and loud voices dominated the place but here and there clusters of locals sat huddled together. Julia looked them over from the rim of her cup and tried to catch a few phrases but nothing seemed out of place.

Near the window three workmen in grey overalls and caps were carrying on a discussion about the price of scallops. Could one of them be the oily type guy Sela had mentioned? They fit his general description but none appeared to be the womanizing sort. Trying to appear casual, she picked up the "Highland News of the Day" paper and began leafing through it. A headline on page three caught her attention and she set her cardboard cup down with a thud.

"Who's Chasing Who and What Are They After?" Letting out

a breath, she read on. "It appears we have a regular cat and mouse game going on right under our noses here in Ullapool. Clandestine meetings, the destruction of property, and people poking about at all hours of the night lead us to believe that somebody's after something—possibly something of value. What could it be? We'll keep you posted with our daily report."

Julia glanced around the room but everyone appeared to be chatting away as usual. Was there really a "cops and robbers" type drama going on around them? Was Sela mixed up in it? And who in the world would do that sort of reporting? After a few minutes she took her coffee and left.

Walking toward Shore Street, she checked her watch for the third time and noted it was already one-forty. She'd better be back to the hairdresser's on time or she'd never hear the end of it from the girls.

The park across from the pub was quiet except for a few children playing by the picnic tables on the far end. She sat down on the bench closest to the sidewalk and nonchalantly took a sip from her now tepid coffee as she looked across at the arched doorway.

The place had a secluded appearance though it was flush with the other buildings. Maybe it had to do with the door being recessed into the wall. As Julia watched, two somber looking fellows opened it and disappeared inside. Should she do the same? What would it hurt? She'd just order coffee and see what was happening.

She got up, poured her coffee on the ground, dropped her cup into the trash bin, and crossed the street. Just be cool, she told herself but her heart had already begun to thump. Lord, she prayed, please help me not to do anything idiotic.

A cloud of smoke assailed her as she swung the hulking door open. Between the smoke and the diffused lighting, it was impossible to see much of anything but after a minute her vision cleared and she was able to observe a mahogany bar that stretched the length of the left wall. Behind it, at least a dozen coats of arms were hung neatly in a row. Her eyes went to the center of the room where a luxurious pool table stood regally on top of an oriental rug. On the right side were several small oak tables around which clusters of men had ceased their conversation and were staring directly at her. Julia clasped her hands together and gave a slight cough.

"Are you looking for someone, miss?"

She jerked her head toward the voice and found herself looking into the cool dark eyes of a young black man.

"I'm, uh, just here for coffee." She could feel the weight of the men's gazes like a tangible thing. What was going on?

"You're aware this is a gentlemen's club?"

"Gentlemen's club?"

"Yes, I'm afraid the ladies meet elsewhere."

She cleared her throat. "Is it a convention or something?"

The man seemed to stifle a smirk. "An ongoing one, you might say—dating back to 1850."

Something inside her rose up at his condescending tone and for one horrific second she thought about sticking out her tongue. Instead, she forced herself to take a controlled breath and look out over the room. For someone who didn't want to be noticed she certainly had everyone's undivided attention. "So you don't serve coffee to women?" Once again she met his gaze.

"I don't usually serve coffee at all."

That was just too much. "Pardon me, Your Highness," she hissed. "I happen to be a botany professor but I'll just go card wool with the rest of the underlings. You go right ahead and serve the 'gentlemen'." She turned and flounced out the door.

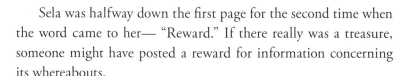

Sela was halfway down the first page for the second time when the word came to her— "Reward." If there really was a treasure, someone might have posted a reward for information concerning its whereabouts.

She grabbed the directory and flipped forward until she came to the "R's." And there it was. "Reward—April 17, 1945." Cross-referencing, she got down on her knees and rummaged through the file until she found the clipping. It read simply, "Any information concerning the whereabouts of a German WW1 metal container is to be reported immediately to the War Office. A small reward will be offered." Not exactly what she had hoped for.

Sitting down on the desk chair, she tried to sort it out. A German WW1 metal container? Could the treasure possibly date back to WW1? Of course the container might just be holding some poor soldier's love letters or boots or something. Still … She glanced up at the filing cabinet. Another full drawer had been devoted to WW1. Where would she start?

She pulled it open and decided to begin with the obvious—treasure. Flipping to the "T" section, her heart pounded wildly when she discovered a file by that name. She pulled the entire thing out and set it on the desk.

It was quite small and after a few minutes of frantic reading she realized it dealt mostly with personal treasures soldiers had brought home from their tours of duty. She shoved the clippings back into the folder.

"Havin' any luck?" The woman had come up behind her and was standing with her arms behind her back.

Sela patted the folder. "Not yet."

"I see you're in WW1. Ye must be doing some heavy research."

Sela glanced at the clock on the wall. Two-fifteen. She was running out of time. "Sort of," she answered, hedging. "I'm, uh, doing a project on war treasures." She mentally crossed her fingers. Situation ethics—again.

"I see." The woman's expression was thoughtful. "Are ye referring to precious gems or gold bullion?"

Sela sat up a little straighter. She hadn't even considered that aspect.

"Because," she continued, "there was a lot of gold bullion sunk off the coast here at the end of WW1. Too deep to recover, though."

Just then the door opened and a group of boisterous tourists entered and began mulling around the displays. "Oh my, I must go," she said. "Got to keep the museum in business you know." She strode over to the front desk and Sela could hear her begin the membership routine once again."

Placing the treasure file back in place, she began looking for something under "gold" when she came across a file entitled "Gold Bullion." Taking it out, she set it on her knee, carefully going through it piece by piece. The woman had said the incident happened near the end of the war. She leafed through till she was near the back. Nothing, nothing—Bingo! A short article had been published on March 31, 1918. It began ... "The German battleship, Scharnhorst, believed to be carrying millions of pounds in gold bullion, was scuttled off the northwestern coast of Scotland in the area of Loch Broom. Hunted by British ship HRM Kingston, it was attempting to hide after a looting expedition near Norway." The article continued on about Rear Admiral Ludwig von Reuter's bold maneuver that kept the Allies from retrieving the gold.

Sela's hands began to shake. Could this actually be the treasure? The woman had said it had never been recovered but that wasn't necessarily true. It might have been secretly retrieved years later using modern-day equipment. Then again, what if part of it had been stowed away on a life boat or something and secretly taken to shore? Suddenly her hand shot to her mouth. Could that be what the metal container thing was all about? Had they been downplaying it to keep treasure hunters away?

Placing the clipping back inside the folder she returned it to the drawer. It had given her all the help it could. She picked up her purse and waved to the woman who was once again expounding on the beauty of the bicentennial quilt. She could have hugged her. The five pound membership fee had been her best investment since arriving in Ullapool. Quietly she slipped out the door.

Twelve miles east, beside a hollowed out hazel tree, two soldiers, as they liked to call themselves, had stopped for a short break when they heard the distinct screech of metal against metal and looked up to see their compatriots grinning from ear to ear.

Chapter Thirteen

Julia edged back down Shore Street as discreetly as possible after her dramatic exit from the gentlemen's club, but it seemed that everyone along the way was giving her a look. Fifteen minutes remained before her hair appointment. She could either continue her search for suspicious characters or hide out at the hairdresser's. She chose the latter.

Entering the salon to the jingle of the bell, she caught a whiff of peroxide wafting through a wicker room divider but saw no one at the reception desk. At least the radio was no longer at a screaming pitch.

A head suddenly popped around the corner and a plump little woman in her mid-fifties, complete with burnt orange hair and smock to match, appeared and greeted her with an apologetic smile. "You're a wee bit early, luv. Just take a seat and help yourself to a magazine. We'll be with ye in a jiff."

Julia took a seat on one of the pink faux leather chairs. Hopefully the other girl was gone for the day. She lifted a magazine from the table beside her and leafed through the pages, trying to visualize herself with one of the weird and wonderful hairdos of the models. A moment later, though, she sighed and dropped it back onto the table. Try as she might, she couldn't ignore the fact that she'd made a fool of herself. What on earth had possessed her? Sure, she'd been caught off guard by the men-only policy and the waiter had been elusive and arrogant. Still …

Without warning, a renewed blast of heavy metal splintered her thoughts and the waif-like girl reappeared in a cloud of second hand smoke. "This way," she clipped, indicating by a jerk of the head that Julia was to follow her through the opening.

The back part of the salon was all business, housing two basic hairdressing stations and a couple of stainless steel sinks flanked by tables of folded towels and small stacks of magazines. The girl pointed to the nearest one. "Take a seat over there. I'll be with you as soon as I get a chance."

Julia sat down but felt herself standing on the inside.

She looked over at the orange-clad hairdresser who was adding the final touches to the fuzz-ball do of an elderly client. "That's you, luv." She stood back in admiration. "You'll be the bell of the ball."

The woman attempted to turn her head for a better view but finally gave up, chuckling, "I'll take your word for it, Sophie." Sophie helped her out of the chair and the two shuffled to the front.

Julia rolled her eyes. Frump or weirdo. What would she end up looking like? There seemed to be no middle ground. With a swish of plastic she felt a slippery cape encircle her neck and her head lowered to the dip of the sink.

"Let me know if it's too hot," the girl instructed, as a blast of scorching water shot out, dousing Julia's hair and splashing up onto her face and down her shirt.

"It's fine," she spluttered, thankful when the ordeal came to an end and she was directed by a pointer finger to one of the chairs.

Finally the girl began combing out the wet locks. "Ye've got quite a wad of hair. Do ye get it done professionally or just whack it off yourself?"

Julia's ire was beginning to rise but she wasn't about to make the same mistake twice in one day. She smiled sweetly. "Oh no, I'm not allowed to. Ever since the 'accident' they don't trust me with scissors."

The girl's mouth clamped shut and she began furiously pinning the hair into sections, standing as far back as possible.

"I'm away then, Lisa," Sophie called from the front. "Got some business to attend to. See that ye lock up at the end of the day."

The girl heaved a sigh of exasperation. "Lees—not Lisa." She glanced at the clock on the wall.

Hopefully the expression on her face wouldn't translate into a disastrous haircut. Julia's image at the moment resembled some warring tribal chief and she felt grateful that no witnesses were present. Just then the bell jingled.

"Be right back," the girl said, nearly tripping over the chair to get to the front. Julia overheard a male voice and then a giggle as the volume of the radio was turned to an even higher pitch.

She began counting the number of colored rollers in the plastic tub followed by the number of hair clips and bobby pins. Finally she gave in and stole a glance at the clock. It was two-thirty and her hair was drying to a mass of wild curly-cues intent on escaping the pins. At last she heard the bell again and the radio volume was turned down a notch. A moment later "Lees" emerged.

"Sorry about that," she said, as though trying for an air of professional annoyance. "Just a scheduling mix-up." Julia decided not to mention the fact that her lipstick was smeared halfway across her cheek.

Before her cut could begin, however, the bell sounded again. "Wait right here," the girl said—as if she'd wander off in her present state.

A minute later Julia heard her reply to a second male voice. "I can take ye right now if it's just a trim, Dr. Westcott. Otherwise it won't be till after five. We've been run off our feet today I'm afraid."

Julia felt her blood boil. Of all the shoddy business practices. She picked up a magazine, determined to keep her nose buried in it until the man was gone.

"Hope you're not in too much of a rush," the girl chuckled, turning to Julia a moment later as she settled the man into his chair. "I'm afraid some of us are a little higher on the pecking order than others."

Julia had never been a violent person but something within her was about to explode. She began counting to ten.

"Oh, I don't know," the man replied as though discussing a new warming trend. "I believe professors are fairly high up in the pecking line."

Julia's head shot straight up and she found herself staring into the amused brown eyes of the waiter from the gentlemen's club.

———○———

"Imagine that it was practically on our doorstep all the time," the soldier observed with a silly grin as they once again sealed the lid.

"Aye, and we'll be needin' a wee celebration once we've secured it," countered a second man.

"There'll be no celebrating until we've made our move," said their leader who had maintained a cool demeanor throughout the excitement. "You've read that article in that paper. Somebody's got their ears perked. One word of this and the whole of the New Thistle will be rotting in Bishop Briggs."

"Aye, he's right," another man replied, rubbing his bandaged arm. "We canny be too careful."

The leader spoke again, this time with a new fervency. "July first was my goal from the start—the date when the Scots were once again able to wear the tartan and carry weapons—the repealing of the Proscription Act." He paused, narrowing his eyes. "Now that we've got the funds behind us, that date will be in the history books once more."

"But that's tomorrow," one of the soldiers gasped, his shaved head beading with sweat. "How can we manage to get everything in place by then?"

"Everything's already in place," barked their leader. "Did you imagine you were in on all the details? At my say-so we'll join the others and storm the Royal Mile in Edinburgh. At long last we'll be a free country again—no matter what the other half thinks." He paused, looking off into the distance. "Just one other thing needs to come together and I'll see to that today." He turned and nodded toward the container. "Heave that onto the back of the truck and take it as far up as you can. You drive, Alan. You're not much good for anything else."

••◆••———◆———••◆••

Sela could hardly contain her excitement as she headed back down Argyle Street. Finally another piece of the puzzle. Things were starting to come together, but the fact remained that time was short. She began to cross the street in the direction of the Tea Store Café where she'd get a bite to eat and decide on her next move.

Suddenly, from the corner of her eye she noticed a car shoot toward her and screech to a halt. She turned to glare at the driver and realized with a start that it was Julia. Loose bobby pins were dancing from frizzy ringlets encircling her head and her eyes held the look of a caged lion.

"Get in," Julia barked.

Sela opened the door and jumped in. "What happened?" She tried to keep the amazement from her voice.

Julia stepped on the gas. "I need to get fixed up before anyone else sees me. Can you think of some place to go?"

Sela thought fast. How about the car park for the ferry? There won't be anyone there right now."

A few minutes later they darted into the parking lot. Julia turned off the ignition and let out a sigh of relief. "You won't believe it."

"Do I dare ask what happened?" She tried unsuccessfully to stifle a giggle.

Julia looked into the rear view mirror and after a moment of horror, burst out laughing. "It's worse than I thought." She tugged at some of the bobby pins hanging down on her face.

Sela reached into her purse and pulled out a small flat brush.

143

"I keep this for emergencies. If you've got an elastic band you'll be good as new in no time."

A few minutes later Julia looked almost normal with her hair pulled back into a frizzy pony tail.

Sela faced her. "Now tell me what in the world is going on. I know you didn't leave the hostel looking like that."

"It's a bit of a long story," Julia sighed, and began from the beginning. "I wasn't trying to be nosy," she concluded after recounting the events. "I just didn't want someone taking advantage of you."

"But who is this Dr. Westcott? You say he was serving tables at the old boys' club and then he turns out to be a doctor?"

"I thought he was serving tables. Obviously he just happened to be standing there at the time." She covered her face with her hands. "I think I'd die if I saw him again. It's a good thing we're leaving tomorrow, especially after flouncing out on him for the second time."

Sela smirked. "Don't worry. He probably wouldn't recognize you anyway."

Julia shot her a look. "Well, that's enough about me. I'm still worried about you. Can't you tell me what's been going on?"

Sela let out a breathy sigh. "I'd like to get it off my chest. I just don't want to give you the wrong impression about anything."

"Whatever it is I won't be shocked," Julia promised, holding up her hand like a boy scout. "Come on now—out with it."

Beginning with her grandfather's strange admission at the airport and his subsequent death, Sela recounted her reasons for traveling to Scotland including her loneliness, the anonymous telephone call, and the break-in as well as the facts she'd discovered since arriving.

Julia's eyes were full of compassion. "That's quite a story. I can't believe how well you've held up in spite of it all—and how you've kept it all inside."

"I just need to clear Granddad's name," Sela said. "I know he'd never be involved in anything like that."

"And you say it all has to do with a treasure? How could that possibly be linked to the lichens?"

Sela shrugged. "All I can figure is that somebody heard the treasure had been buried near the lichens and went digging for it."

"That would certainly account for the so-called army men shooing us out and then destroying the lichens. They probably had no interest in the lichens at all. They were just digging for the treasure." She paused. "But where would they have gotten that information?"

"Don't forget, this might all have begun at the end of World War I. Maybe the German soldiers sent a message over to their headquarters and it finally leaked out." Sela rubbed at her eyes. "It's all too confusing for me. Granddad would have figured it out in no time."

"It makes sense, though. Maybe the neo-Nazis picked up on it somehow."

Sela shifted in her seat. "Anyway, I need to check that painting again one way or the other."

"I'll help," Julia said.

"That would be great but I'm running out of time." She thought for a minute. "You wouldn't happen to be going back to Corrieshalloch Gorge, would you?"

"I could if you want me to. What would you like me to do?"

"That document at the Ceildh Place named Corrieshalloch Gorge as well as Inverpoly as one of the lichen sites. Why don't you take the girls with you. Act like it's just another excursion but try to find out if there's anything fishy going on. We'll meet back at the Tea Store Café at five to compare our findings and get a bite to eat."

***

The young man looked at the little proprietor with a measure of satisfaction. "I think we've found our weak link."

The proprietor viewed him through narrowed eyes. "What makes ye think so?"

145

"Liam was at the Ferry Boat Inn last night. Said some bloke with a bandaged arm was spouting off about having to stand guard all day instead of partying with the girls."

"Did he engage him?"

"He just suggested he should come by the butcher shop for a chat."

"Keep an eye out for him. This thing's comin' to a head sooner than we thought. You're aware of what'll happen if they find it before we do."

The other man nodded. "I know, I know."

"What about the girl? Any information as to her allegiance?"

"She's been doing quite a bit of sleuthing. Can't seem to mind her own business. Don't worry, I'm taking care of her. I'll contact you later today." With that he ducked out the back door and sauntered down the alley.

Chapter Fourteen

"What happened?" Amanda stared in amazement at Julia's pony-tailed mane. "I thought you were going to the hairdresser."

Keira looked up from the slice of bread she was buttering. "Please tell me you didn't have it done that way."

"Sorry, girls." Julia kept her eyes on the floor. "It just didn't work out. I'll have to get an appointment in Aberdeen. Anyway, we need to go back to Corrieshalloch Gorge for a few more samples. Can you get ready right away?"

The girls looked at each other. "Didn't we just go there?" Amanda asked.

"Yes, but while we're up here I'd like to get as many as possible. I'm sure we won't be coming back any time soon."

"You're the boss, as they say," Keira quipped. "We can go right now if you'd like."

A few minutes later they piled into the Rover and headed out on the A835.

Julia sat in silence and listened to the girls jabber on about the latest fashions. She was glad for the reprieve. She needed time to think and plan. Perhaps if she left them at a safe location to do a little collecting on their own she could do some snooping around.

"Good to see you again, Sebastian." The two shook hands warmly outside the Ceildh Place door.

"Good to be back. I've had enough stuffy corridors to last me a while."

"I hear you were told off right smartly at the club today."

The black man grinned, revealing a set of perfectly square white teeth. "That woman must be some kind of nut. I ran into her again when I nipped in to get my hair cut and she gave me the same treatment."

"You're sure you're not the one following her?"

"I don't have a death wish if that's what you mean."

The other man's face took on a sober expression. "We'd better be on our way. The vehicle's just down the street."

A few minutes later they were zooming east on the A835.

Sebastian turned to the driver. "So maybe you can fill me in on a few details."

The other man paused, seeming to weigh his words. "We've got a real mess on our hands. That's why I called you in. If we don't act fast I'm afraid it could lead to a battle royal."

"What makes you say that? I thought these jokers were just after a treasure."

"Right, but to what end? There's been rumors they want to start an uprising. If they find the treasure before we do, they'll be able to finance a full-scale rebellion."

"There's that many of them?" Sebastian queried.

"Enough to do a great deal of damage."

"So why don't you and your boys round them up and stop the whole thing before it begins?"

"We've got our eye on a few of them but the big fish is a still a mystery. It's pointless to reel in the others without him or the location of their headquarters."

Sebastian sat back in the seat for a minute and looked out at the clouds gathering in the distance. "So what is it you'd like me to do?"

"You're the expert on social sciences," the other man replied." If we could come up with the motivation, we might be a step ahead of them instead of a step behind.

"What have you got so far?"

"Not much but enough to make things interesting." He let his foot off the gas slightly while sorting through his thoughts. "To begin with, the possibility of a treasure has been around for a long time. According to an intercepted radio message back in WW1, some kind of German container loaded with gold bullion was hidden close to Loch Broom."

Sebastian allowed that thought to settle in for a moment. "Did no one go looking for it?" he finally asked.

"They did for a while but it wasn't that simple. The location was encrypted of course and after a while they apparently gave up."

"What about the Germans? You'd think they would've tried to retrieve it."

"No one knows what became of the ones who hid it. Possibly got themselves killed on their way back over."

"So this group—"The New Thistle"—seems to have a lead on it?" Sebastian asked.

"I'm afraid so. You must've heard about the damaged lichens up at Inverpoly."

"Who hasn't? The media has been making quite a stink over it."

"According to our sources there were army personnel in the area but oddly enough they're denyin' it."

"So you think it might have been the neo-Nazis?"

"Could be. Why would anybody go out of their way to ruin rare lichens unless they were looking for something?"

"Sebastian was quiet for a minute. "I can understand them hunting for the treasure but it takes almost a pathological zeal to start an uprising—especially during peace time. There has to be a specific reason for it."

"I should mention there was also quite an interest in the treasure during the Second World War but I'm afraid that's somewhat classified—at least for the present."

"Even after all this time?"

The driver tapped his index finger on the steering wheel. "I can tell you this; it caused the biggest internal uproar the M15 has ever seen."

"Do you think the two things are linked?"

"That's for you to figure out, pal.

Before long a sign for Corrieshalloch Gorge came into view. The driver slowed and turned into the parking lot, pulling up on the far side of a touring bus.

"So we're going on a little sight-seeing expedition since time is so short?"

"Not quite. We've discovered that the type of lichens destroyed at Inverpoly grow here as well. Maybe we'll be able to hunt up somethin' of value."

They left the car and followed the signs to the gorge.

Amanda pulled the box from the back of the Rover and grasping it with one arm, slammed the trunk shut with the other. "Don't worry about helping or anything," she muttered.

"Good job," Julia laughed. "You'll make a great botanist one day."

"I'll help as soon as I get my hiking boots tied up," Keira offered from the front seat.

"Don't worry. I know how delicate you are."

"Okay, okay, let's get going." Julia began walking ahead. "This really is our last time here and we need to make the most of it."

"So what's the plan?" Keira caught up to her as they crossed the parking lot and followed a group of tourists to the gate. "Are we going to the same spot we were at the other day?"

"I thought we might begin there and possibly branch out." Julia paused. "I might get you girls started and then try another location on my own—you know, just to make sure we're not missing anything."

"Sure," Keira sighed. "Just thrust us out by ourselves. We don't mind."

"I'm sure you'll do just fine. Anyway, I won't be far."

They continued down the path on the other side of the Kissing Gate. "It seems spooky in here today." Amanda sniffed the air around them. "It's heavy—like old-lady perfume or something."

"Perhaps it's the au de 'Vaccinium myrtillus'," Keira offered, raising her eyebrow a notch.

"Very impressive," Julia said with a laugh. But it's probably just the fungi. I hope we get some work done before it starts raining. Oh, that reminds me …" She rummaged through her pocket and held up a key. "I don't want to be blamed for anyone catching their death if it starts to rain." She tossed it over to Keira who dropped it into her pocket.

They rounded a leafy corner and saw the swinging bridge just ahead, wobbling under the weight of a couple of sightseers. Amanda made a face. "I don't blame Sela for wanting to stay away from here. That bridge gives me the creeps. One push from behind and you'd be a goner."

Keira rolled her eyes. "Thanks for mentioning it."

They waited on the viewing platform until a couple of tourists had crossed to the other side, then began making their way over. "Are you okay with that box?" Julia called to Amanda as she passed the mid-way point.

"Aye, I don't mind being the pack horse—but I might have to be rewarded with an ice cap on the way home."

"No problem."

They reached the other side without incident and continued on until the path divided. "And now," Keira said with a flourish of her hand, "to the left, as you know."

Turning toward the trees, they stepped onto the mossy undergrowth, slowing their step to avoid fallen limbs and low hanging branches of birch, oak, elm, and pine.

"That's it—just a little farther up," said Julia.

In a few minutes a crop of hazel trees appeared, their trunks and slender limbs bearing the lichen script. Amanda set the cardboard box down with a thud. "Finally," she sighed. "My arms are falling off."

"It always amazes me how they actually resemble writing," Keira observed as she gazed around. "It's as if someone took a piece of charcoal and scribbled all over the bark."

"Hence the name, of course," said Julia. "I agree though. It's a remarkable sight, no matter how many times you've seen it."

They unpacked their paraphernalia and Julia distributed the brown bags and tissue paper as well as the tools—knives, scrapers, chisels, hammers, and hand lenses—into individual pouches. "Make sure you take only samples from the untouched trees," she cautioned. "We certainly don't want to be accused of damaging anything."

"We'll be careful," Keira said. "Feel free to follow your heart."

"You're sure you'll be okay? Don't forget to label each bag."

"We're big girls," Amanda said, wafting her hand away. "Just don't be too late or we might be forced to rove somewhere in the Rover."

"I'll be back," Julia droned in her best Arnold Schwarzenegger voice.

<hr />

"So, you think the treasure will just pop up as we pass by?" Sebastian asked.

"I doubt it'll be quite that simple, but if we're in the right location anything could happen. Not only that, but we might find tell-tale marks of someone's digging."

"Hopefully not anyone dangerous," Sebastian said with a grin. "I'd hate to be chased back across that bridge at gunpoint."

"Speaking of danger," the driver said, "try not to trip over the rotten log at your feet." He stooped down and examined the bark. "Wouldn't you say those are lichens?"

"Maybe, but I'm no expert. Anyway, you said they were white, not orange."

"True, and the kind we're looking for grows only on hazel trees. This is an oak."

Sebastian gave a smirk. "So what do we do now—go over every square foot of forest until we come across a hazel tree?"

"What would you think of splitting up? We'd cover more ground that way. If you found somethin' unusual you could text me." He stood and looked at his watch. "Otherwise, we'll meet back at the car in half an hour to compare notes and go from there."

"And for this you called me from my cloistered quarters?"

"We'll be able to use your expertise when we find something."

Sebastian sighed dramatically. "Where would you like me to start?"

The other man pointed straight ahead. "You keep going west and I'll go north. Remember, text me if you come across anything unusual." With that he turned and began trudging his way left.

Sebastian stood for a moment looking out over the busy woodland. He had to admit it was a beautiful sight. Tiny red flowers speckled the carpet of mossy undergrowth and colonies of toadstools, like gnomes in funny hats, stood patrol over dead tree stumps. Suddenly a movement caught his eye and he looked up to see a cheeky squirrel peeking from behind an oak tree. "So, you'd like to play hide-and-seek," he said, and stepped toward it but it disappeared in an instant.

Taking a stride forward, he caught sight of it again on a branch just ahead. He decided to follow it. He had heard once that squirrels were fond of hazel nuts.

Julia stopped for a moment and switched her bag to the other arm. What was she actually doing out here? Sure, she wanted to help Sela but was that the real reason she'd raced back without a second thought, intent on bringing the bad guys to justice? Or was she still trying to exact revenge on Cyril? Lord, she prayed silently, help me to let it go and forgive him from the heart. Let this only be about helping Sela. Feeling a warm sense of peace, she blew out her breath and began walking toward the middle of the forest.

The girls hadn't appeared to suspect anything when she'd left them and their assignment would no doubt keep them busy for a while at least. Now to find something out of the ordinary in as short a time as possible. No big deal. Right!

She gazed at the abundance of ferns, mosses, and liverworts carpeting the forest floor and creeping up the trunks of the oak and elm trees. She would need to move west, deeper into the heart of the forest, to find more hazels. She picked her way toward an overhang of dark, leafy-lobed "Lobaria pulmonaria," which were known to thrive in the oldest sections of the woods. She was on the right track.

In a few minutes a hazel tree appeared and she stopped beside it to get her bearings. Looking down, she noticed with a start the moss around it had been disturbed. Her heart began to thump. Someone had been here recently. The army guys? Not likely—but still …

Following the crushed vegetation, she found herself in the middle of a second hazel grove. Like the first, male and female flowers bloomed in profusion among toothy-edged foliage that had taken on the yellow-green tint of summer. More importantly, a mosaic of small crustose lichens could be seen on each slender limb— "Graphideon scriptae."

Squatting down to examine the moss for tell-tale clues, her eyes went to a pile of loose black earth at the foot of a nearby tree. She crawled over to it and found a recently dug hole about four feet in length, noting with mounting excitement that it was also fairly deep. Had the neo-Nazis been digging for the treasure? What if they had left something behind? With both hands she began scooping out piles of the loose earth and heaping it to the side.

Suddenly a small round object like a marble appeared in the dirt but as Julia reached in to get it, it rolled deeper. She grabbed for it again and it slipped through a narrow trough just out of sight.

She sat back in exasperation and blew an escaped curly-cue from one eye. "Two can play that little game," she said through clenched teeth. With her face near ground level and her back end assuming a kick-me stance, she reached in once again and grabbed for it.

"Gathering supplies for winter?" inquired a male voice directly behind her.

Julia scrambled to her feet and whirled around. Seeing Sebastian, she let out a shriek and stepped backward, catching the heel of her shoe on the edge of the hole. Losing her footing, she teetered helplessly as though in slow motion and watched in horror as he rushed toward her, arms outstretched.

He grabbed hold of her hand but the center of gravity was on the side of the hole and pulled them down together in a less than dignified embrace. Before either could speak, the sky opened and delivered the cloudburst it had been promising all afternoon.

"Look at it this way," Sebastian offered, once he had regained his breath, "at least we can forgo the formalities."

"Get off me," Julia spluttered. "Are you trying to add murder to your list of felonies?" She lifted her arm and attempted to push him away.

Sebastian clambered to his feet and held out his hand to her. "At least let me help you up."

"Thanks, but you've been quite enough help already." She swiped at a soaking glob of runaway hair and tried to get her feet underneath her. The rich black earth, however, had been transformed by the rain into glue-like gumbo which stuck to her shoes in clumps. Looking up, she noticed the corners of Sebastian's mouth twitching.

"You consider this funny?"

"No—not at all. It's just that …" His voice wavered and without warning he dissolved into a roar of laughter.

Julia grabbed a fistful of mud and heaved it toward him but the majority of it stuck to her fingers like black dough. Suddenly the absurdity of the moment caught up with her and she giggled until her sides ached.

After a few minutes she held out her hand and he helped her

up onto solid ground. The rain was beginning to subside and they did their best to clean up. "Who are you, anyway?" she asked as she rubbed the remaining mud from her fingers.

"Just an angel sent to keep you humble."

"In that case you should be getting your wings any day now. Really though, who are you?"

"Would you believe I teach Social Sciences at the University of Edinburgh?"

"You're not in with that group?"

"What group?"

"The ones looking for the … uh … never mind."

"What?"

"Nothing … really. It's just that you keep popping up in all the wrong places." His smile seemed genuine enough but she wasn't about to trust him on that basis alone. What was he doing out here, anyway? He could be a walking "Digitalis purpurea"—attractive to the eye but poisonous to the heart.

"Look," he said with a twinkle in his eye, "We've gotten off on the wrong foot, to say the least. Why don't we try again. Perhaps we'd get to know each other a little better—say, over supper?"

Julia looked down. She couldn't believe he'd ask her out after she'd made such a fool of herself. "I don't know …"

"No strings attached—really. I think we have a lot in common—you being a professor and all."

She laughed sheepishly, recalling the men's club episode. Suddenly, she remembered the girls and looked down at her watch. It was four forty-five. "Sorry, I'm late. I've got to go."

Six-thirty? The Ferryboat Inn?

"Okay, then." She dashed off, wondering why her feet felt light as air.

Chapter Fifteen

Sela slowed her step, gathering her thoughts as Custom House Street came into view. She had turned over several options of how to approach the woman at the art shop but nothing seemed quite right. Finally she decided honesty was the best policy. She would simply ask outright if she knew of Tanika, explain who her grandfather was, and beg to see the painting again.

That is, if it was still there. Recalling the conversation by the little proprietor and his comrade, she had her doubts. Perhaps they'd followed up on their plan to move it to a safer location. Or, the old woman herself might have removed it. She hadn't been taking it out of the box just to admire it. Still, it was worth a try.

The wind had picked up and fat raindrops dotted the sidewalk in front of her. Thankfully her umbrella was tucked into her purse and she pulled it out now, determined to make a more favorable impression this time around.

She glanced at her watch which said three forty-five. The shop would be open. She'd have a chance to explain her situation, hopefully examine the painting and be back in time to meet Julia at the Tea Store Café by five o'clock.

As she neared the building she thought again of the photograph she'd found in Granddad's things. The woman, so pretty in an old-fashioned sort of way, had been standing at this very spot. What had she been thinking? Had she known Granddad would be shipped off, never to return? What had the two of them shared that had changed the course of their lives?

A low moan of thunder rumbled in the distance and she hurried to open the door and go in. Once again the strangely inviting aroma of musty paper and turpentine wafted toward her as she stepped into the cluttered room. Looking around, she realized the shop was empty. The woman must be in the office. Her eyes went to the row of boxes along the back wall and for an instant she considered sneaking a peek to see if the painting was still there. That, however, would earn her a curt dismissal from Miss Pinched Lips should she be caught.

She cocked her head, listening for the sound of rustling paper or some other office-type noise, but there was nothing but the tapping of rain against the window. This was strange. Where was the middle-aged woman? She hadn't seemed the type to run out and leave the door open. "Hello," she called out in a voice that sounded too high and reedy. "Get a grip," she told herself in disgust.

Sliding the umbrella back into her purse, she walked over to the office doorway. "Anybody home?" The heavy curtain separating the two rooms seemed to waft inward slightly and Sela stepped back, wondering if she had imagined it. She knew there were no windows in the other room and she hadn't noticed a door—but then her mind had been on other things. What had caused the curtain to move? Surely the woman wasn't going to jump out and surprise her. She didn't seem the type for practical jokes.

She waited, watching for another movement but the curtain hung limp as a rag. Her breath was coming in short staccato-like bursts. Why was she acting like such a coward? It was the middle of the day for crying out loud. Coward or not, though, she'd have to make a move if she was going to find out anything at all. Grabbing the curtain by the edge, she took a deep breath and flung it open, ready to dive for cover.

The office lay silent and dim before her—empty. She groped for the light switch but a new idea presented itself and she let her hand drop to her side. Why not get the feel of the place before her senses were dulled by the glare of the light?

Forcing herself to stand perfectly still she breathed deeply, taking in the stuffy atmosphere, the strong scent of turpentine—and something else. What was it? Haltingly, she stepped inside and let the curtain fall behind her. Standing motionless, she tried to isolate the scent but it ducked away from her. Her eyes followed the dim contours of the room—boxes piled up against one wall, a makeshift desk, and on the far side, faint in the half-light, the outline of a small doorway. So there was an exit. Her heart begin to thump in her chest.

She reached across and turned on the light. The door was unobtrusive—sepia in color, like the wall and shorter than a standard door with a recessed handle rather than a door knob. Was it a recent installation or had it been there for sixty years or more? She wondered if the outer side was just as inconspicuous. Shuddering, she thought of the clandestine meeting between her grandfather and Tanika. "Granddad," she whispered, "What were you up to?"

She looked at the table where she had previously examined the painting, and was surprised to find it lying in the same spot. The woman must have left it there, possibly in an effort to keep it out of the public eye. Should she risk examining it before she returned? No time like the present she decided and crept over to where it lay.

Immediately she noticed two things. One, something was different about the painting itself and two, a jar of turpentine sat at its side, complete with telltale cloth stained with blue paint.

Someone was just as curious about its validity as she was and that someone had no doubt slipped out the back door when she arrived. She shivered again, considering her close proximity to a thief—or worse. Who could it have been?

"If you ever need more art advice ..."

She closed her eyes, concentrating on the elusive phrase that danced just out of reach. What was it again?

"If you ever need more art advice, don't hesitate to ask."

Jimmy. Yesterday at the Tea Store Café. She had wondered what he was talking about. Had he been relaying a secret message? Did he want her to come in on some covert deal to steal a million dollar painting? Then again, maybe he was just rattled at the sight of Dougal.

Searching her mind, she realized there was something strange about the time he'd brought her here in the first place. She hadn't thought much about it then but the middle-aged woman had seemed taken aback—as though he'd been in the shop earlier. If so, she'd been quick to cover it up. Sela grimaced. Surely the woman wasn't in on the theft as well—if that's what it was.

She needed to check out the painting thoroughly. She darted back to the doorway and peeked through the curtain. The room was still empty. Possibly the woman had run out for a cup of tea or a crumpet break or something. Reassured, she dashed back to the painting.

Looking down on it, she took in the hastily scrubbed out right hand corner which had changed from ultramarine blue to a mixture of viridian green and burnt umber. Someone back then had known what he or she was doing.

She picked up the cloth, and adding a tiny bit of turpentine, gently began blotting an untouched section from the same corner. In a short time the number nineteen appeared. She continued on, trying her best not to disturb the original oil. The entire date soon became visible and the sight of it caused her to drop the cloth and grip the table's edge. 1945. Granddad.

A part of her didn't want to continue. What if it pointed to something she couldn't bear to accept? Not only that, if someone came in now and saw what she was doing she'd be arrested on the spot. Swallowing, she picked up the cloth. She had to know.

The area just above the date contained a small, scribbly signature—as though the artist was not nearly as important as the subject itself. Franz Triebsch or something. She didn't recognize the name at all which was strange considering how important the painting seemed to be. She moved the cloth over to the middle section. She might as well dive right in. There was no turning back now. She'd start at the bottom.

Before long a man's shoe appeared and judging from the artist's liberal use of white against the black, it seemed to illustrate a fine spit polish. No doubt someone of wealth or distinction. Left of its mate stood a pair of oxfords, dingy by comparison. What was this? She could think of no famous painting, missing or otherwise, with this type of composition. Forget the feet. She needed to move upward. She began blotting again near chest level.

The man on the right seemed to carry himself with an almost military-like bearing, at least according to the lack of slouchy-type shadows. Moving upward, the appearance of medals and insignias proved it out. Who was this? She moved to the left.

Soon a much more informal figure materialized with a hand tucked into the pocket of a casual jacket. The prince and the pauper? No, that didn't seem to be the message conveyed, though it did suggest an unlikely fellowship.

Sela stopped what she was doing and listened. Had she heard something or was it just the rain? She'd better get down to business— the faces.

Pouring a little more turpentine on a clean section of the cloth, she delicately blotted an area above the shoulders of the man on the right. A high forehead soon came into view, sliced diagonally by a slash of dark hair. She continued downward, noting the deep furrows between the brows. Not exactly the friendly type. As the eyes began to emerge she suddenly stepped back in shock and let out a gasp. She had seen those eyes in old war pictures—cold and cruel and callous. Before she could change her mind she reached out with a swipe and uncovered the thick, short mustache together with the unrelenting lines of a ruthless mouth. Staring back at her was the cold blooded face of Hitler.

She couldn't breathe. This was no famous million dollar painting. It was an obscenity. Who would want to own it? And more to the point, why was it hidden away at the art shop?

She knew what she had to do but her hand didn't want to co-operate—as if it revolted against the idea. Discovering the identity of the second man could take her into deeper waters than she'd bargained for.

Diffidently, she picked up the cloth which had again dropped to the floor. If she didn't take the next step she'd be uncertain for the rest of her life. Her hand shook as she poured a dime-sized drop of turpentine onto the cloth. She held her breath and blotted.

A grayish tweed cap appeared which seemed in keeping with the rest of the relaxed figure. She blew out her breath and continued. Soon a set of reddish eyebrows came into focus and she felt her heart begin to thump double time. Stop, she told herself. Half the population has a little red in their eyebrows. It's no big deal. The dread, though, was too overwhelming and she had to stop for a minute and take a deep breath.

She began again with the chin. Soon the clean jaw line of a young man emerged and as she moved upward she saw that the lips were spread into a cocky grin. A bead of sweat trickled from her forehead down past her cheekbone and dropped onto the canvas where it mingled with the paint. …"*as it were, great drops of blood*." The unwelcome phrase disturbed her. She knew it was from the Bible.

It would take only one last blot to reveal the man's identity and as the cloth hovered between knowledge and ignorance she felt as though her soul itself was trembling. Nothing had prepared her for this. If it turned out to be her greatest fear she wasn't sure she'd be able to live through it. Her own life would be meaningless. In one jerky motion she grasped the cloth tightly and swiped at the image, exposing the remainder of the face.

She stared in horror, her shoulders beginning to heave uncontrollably. A ragged sob worked its way up and escaped her throat. Smiling up at her with his high-up dimple in full view was the youthful face of Granddad.

In that moment she knew what it was to die. Every hope, dream and promise perished in the face of the new-found facts. His life had been a lie. Her life was a sham. There was no true goodness—only deceit, treachery, and betrayal. In a sudden rage she reached up and ripped the locket from her neck. The picture inside was nothing but an affront.

"Aunt Therese? Are you in the office?"

Hearing the voice, Sela froze on the spot, then flew to the little door, flung it open and charged through like a bull on a rampage. Out on the street she ran like mad, her breath coming in gasps and her feet kicking up water and debris. The rain pelted her skin like arrows but she couldn't have cared less. In fact, she welcomed it. Anything to match the pain in her heart.

She ran full tilt for several minutes, not bothering to slow down at the amazed stares of other pedestrians. Now her feet refused to oblige and she slowed to a walk, panting furiously. Her nose dripped and she realized with relief she'd had the presence of mind to retrieve her purse. Opening it, she pulled out a Kleenex.

Where was she anyway? Somewhere downtown. Shaking from head to toe and soaked to the skin, she had to find a place to rest before she passed out and complicated matters further.

Just ahead stood an open door and she rushed through it without thinking. She needed to sit for just a few minutes. Maybe then she could slip back to the hostel, collect her things and catch a bus to Glasgow. She wouldn't stay—not even for Dougal. She'd get a plane back to Minneapolis and figure out what to do from there. One thing for sure—she'd sell the house and everything in it. She wanted no reminders of her past.

The building she entered was fairly roomy with rows of chairs facing a bit of a platform at the front and covered tables set out across the back. On the platform two girls seemed to be preparing for some kind of concert. They looked up when she entered. "It doesn't start for another half hour," one of the girls called out. "You're welcome to stay for the practice though. There's coffee at the back."

Sela nodded without making eye contact. She spotted a lone chair and pulling it over to the farthest corner, sank down onto it, attempting to appear calm. After a few minutes her breathing slowed but she was chilled to the bone. Seeing the coffee pot on one of the nearby tables, she hobbled over to it on shaky legs, poured herself a steaming cupful, and returned to her secluded spot. The warmth of the first gulp rushed to her stomach and spread outward. That at least was somewhat comforting. As to the rest of her, it would take a lot more than coffee.

The girls at the front were busy setting up the mike and tuning a violin and hopefully had forgotten about her. A minute later, though, the mike screeched loudly and one of them turned to her with a sweet smile. "Sorry, luv, we'll try to keep it down."

Sela attempted to return the smile but at the small show of kindness her chest convulsed in a quiet sob and tears rolled down her cheeks. She picked up the Kleenex and pressed it to her face, thankful the girls had turned back around, seemingly unaware of her state. Why, Granddad? What possessed you to side with that monster? Didn't you care that it would ruin your family? She wanted to hate him but it wasn't hatred she was feeling. It was a terrible loneliness.

Almost imperceptibly the melancholic strains of the violin began to play, echoing the depth of her grief. Fresh tears ran down her cheeks and as she wiped them away she heard a voice so sweet and clear a chill ran down her spine. She listened as the girl sang.

> How deep the Father's love for us,
> How vast beyond all measure
> That He should give His only Son
> To make a wretch His treasure.
>
> How great the pain of searing loss,
> The Father turns His face away
> His wounds which mar the chosen One
> Bring many sons to glory.

Something about the words wrenched her heart in almost physical pain. She had never thought about God in that way—as a Father losing His only Son. After a brief interlude the girl continued.

Behold the Man upon the cross,
My guilt upon His shoulders
Ashamed, I hear my mocking voice
Call out among the scoffers.

It was my sin that held Him there
Until it was accomplished
His dying breath has brought me life
I know that it is finished.

Suddenly the enormity of Jesus' sacrifice on the cross struck her
as she comprehended for the first time that He had actually died in
her place. The phrase, *"great drops of blood,"* came to her once again.
He had sweated blood just knowing what was ahead of Him but He
had gone through with it anyway—for her.

It wasn't just Granddad who was guilty. She was guilty, too. She
was self-centered and rebellious—quick to assign blame and lacking
in compassion. She covered her face with her hands and cried quietly.
Oh God, forgive me, she prayed. All these years Granddad tried to
teach me about You but I refused to listen. I blamed You for letting
my parents die. I turned my back on You but You loved me anyway.

I will not boast in anything,
No gifts, no powers, no wisdom,
But I will boast in Jesus Christ,
His death and resurrection.

Why should I gain from His reward,
I cannot give an answer
But this I know with all my heart,
His wounds have paid my ransom.

The violin continued to play for a few more minutes but the strains seemed to be reaching directly from heaven into her heart. She couldn't explain the change she felt because outwardly, nothing had changed at all. But the awful dread had lifted and for the first time in many years she had an unexplained security—like the encircling of a warm blanket, wrapping her in love. She knew with all her heart she was not alone.

Hearing voices, she looked up and caught sight of a group of people chatting together as they ambled through the doorway. Suddenly aware of her disheveled appearance, she glanced about for an exit and noticed one of the musicians walking toward her. When the girl reached her, she took Sela's hand and squeezed it warmly. "I'll be praying for ye," she whispered.

Sela could only smile and nod. The girl pointed to a door at the side of the stage. "If you're needin' to leave right quick, that's the best way."

"Thank you," Sela said. "Thank you for everything." She hurried across the room and out the door. The rain had passed and a warm breeze was blowing. She felt like dancing. She looked across the street and saw the "Tea Store Café."

Chapter Sixteen

Exhilarated yet ravenous, she took a seat at one of the few remaining café tables and set down her tea and sandwich. She was beginning to feel like a regular. Using both hands, she picked up half of the whole-wheat bun stuffed with tuna, lettuce, tomato, bean sprouts, and pickles, and stretched her mouth wide to accommodate the sheer volume. Sorry, Julia, she thought, chewing ravenously, but if I don't get something in my stomach, somebody will be picking me up off the floor again.

She took a slurp of her king-sized tea to wash it down and looked at the door. It was just after five but she couldn't wait to recount to Julia the events of the afternoon, not to mention what had taken place in her own heart. Julia would be thrilled. Even though they'd known each other for such a short while, they had developed a kinship that couldn't be measured in time.

Sitting alone for a few minutes, she had the chance to process what had happened and think about the implications. Something inside her had changed in a split second and she wasn't the same. She felt lighter, but that may have had something to do with missing lunch. Anyway, she was different. For one thing, she was able to analyze the situation more objectively. Perhaps things weren't exactly as they appeared. Maybe Granddad actually was the man of faith he had always seemed to be. "Please Lord," she prayed silently, "help me find the truth." She smiled, recalling how Great-Grandma had asked her to do that very thing.

Taking another bite, she glanced again at the door and saw Julia bustling through at top speed. She waved her hand, making squeaking noises as she tried to swallow the bread whole. Julia saw her and maneuvered toward her, side-stepping an elderly patron who was holding court in the middle of the floor.

"Wait till you hear what happened," they both began at once and burst out laughing.

"You first," said Julia.

"Why don't you get your food and we'll talk when you come back," Sela said.

Julia shook her head, wearing a mysterious grin. "I'm afraid I won't be eating at the moment ... due to having a supper date and all."

"What?" Sela gasped. "I thought you were out looking for suspicious characters. How in the world did you end up with a date?"

"Believe me when I say that truth is stranger than fiction. First, though, I want to hear your news. You look like you found something exciting."

"Since you insist," Sela began, and filled her in on the horrid discovery she'd made at the art shop, her initial reaction, and then what had taken place in the building across the street.

Tears misted Julia's eyes. "Oh, Sela. The Lord must have brought you there at exactly the right moment."

"I know," she agreed. "I'll never forget the words of that song as long as I live. I think they're eternally etched in my brain."

They sat for a minute trying to take it all in. "So now you're a fellow believer." Julia gave her hand a squeeze.

"I wish Granddad knew. It's my only regret."

"Don't be so sure he doesn't," Julia said. "So how do you feel about the painting now that you've got your head on straight?"

"I've been mulling that over in my mind. There's got to be another explanation. The whole Hitler thing—it's just too incongruous with Granddad's Christian character. Maybe he was over in Germany as a spy for Britain or something."

"Anything's possible. But do you think there's a connection between that and the person sneaking around the art shop?

Sela made a face. "I'm almost afraid to find out."

"He—or she—didn't leave anything behind, like a hat or sweater or anything?"

"Not that I saw." She thought for a minute. "There was one thing, though. I got a whiff of something when I first went into the office. It seemed familiar but I couldn't put my finger on it."

"Not anything to do with art supplies?"

"That's just it—it seemed out of place." She shook her head as if to rearrange her thoughts. "Oh well, it'll probably come to me. I want to hear about your adventure now. Who are you going out with and what did you find at Corrieshalloch Gorge?"

⁂

"Are ye daft, man?" the driver exclaimed, as he negotiated the puddly road, spraying muddy brown water up onto a white Volvo in passing. "I couldn't believe my eyes when I got your text— "No clues, just a beautiful woman." I thought you said that woman was a nut case."

"She may be, but a good-looking one none the less."

"And you're not afraid she'll slip something into your drink or plunge a sharp object in your back?

"Now who's being daft?" Sebastian tapped his index finger on the seat. "The thing is, she seems the genuine type. Whatever she's up to, I think her intentions are noble."

"Noble, huh? Just make sure there's more than noble intentions between you and a 9mm Glock."

"I promise. I won't turn my back on her for a second. But enough of my love life." He paused for a minute. "I should also mention … someone's been doing a little digging around out there by the trees."

The driver raised his eyebrows a notch. "And you never thought to bring this up to begin with?"

"I had a few other things on my mind."

"Apparently." He rolled his eyes. "Was there evidence of somethin' heavy being dragged?"

"No, nothing like that. I'm sure it was just an exploratory search if anything. What about you? Did you find out anything about an uprising?"

"Not exactly, but I may have stumbled onto something by accident, though I'm not sure it's got much to do with the "New Thistle.""

"Well, out with it, man. Don't keep the doctor waiting."

"My, my," the driver chuckled. "That little lady's got you in quite a stir." He rounded a corner on the inside lane and continued. "It's just a bit strange. I was walkin' back toward the bridge and noticed an old steel building half hidden by some bush. Not that it was suspicious in itself. As you know, there's umpteen buildings scattered here and there throughout the Highlands."

"What was it then?"

"It just struck me as odd that someone would tie up a Rottweiler outside a building in the middle of nowhere."

"Surely it's not that unusual to have a dog."

"A sheep dog, no. A Rottweiler, yes. And believe me, this one wasn't the petting variety."

Sebastian snickered. "Did it try to sample you for dinner?"

"It would have if I'd gotten any closer. Anyway, I didn't want to give away my hand to anyone in the building so I just kept moving."

"So now what do you do?"

"Nothing till I drop you off. I've got a couple of things to take care of. As soon as I find something I'll get back to you. Like I said before, I have a hunch we don't have much time.

Liam stretched a wide length of butcher's tape over the brown paper package and looked up with a smirk. "I'm sure I dinna have to tell ye this cut is best for roasting or stewing. Most flavorful if it's done correctly."

"I was stewing fore shanks before ye were out o' yer nappies," the elderly woman rejoined. "What's the damage?"

"At 2.49 a pound, that'll be L4.98, if ye please."

"Highway robbery." She reached into her purse and pulled out a L5 note. "Keep the change. Ye must be needing it more than I do."

Liam chuckled. "Tell Robert we'll have to get together for a wee pint before long."

"Aye, that I will." She turned to leave and nearly collided with a dour-faced young man just entering the shop. "Ye better hold onto yer wallet if ye don't want to be skinned," she smirked, elbowing him in the arm and causing him to grimace.

"Good day to ye, Mrs. McMurphy. Come back soon." The door closed and Liam looked across the counter to a face he'd been hoping would show up before long.

"Are all your customers that friendly?" the man asked. His closely cropped hair was black and his eyes a lifeless brown.

"Not all," Liam said. "Some are downright nasty." He removed a cigarette from the pocket of his stained apron and eyeing the man warily, placed it loosely between his thick lips. "Mind if I smoke?"

"It's your shop."

Liam reached behind the counter and held out a pack of Imperials. "Care to join me?"

"Sure." He took one and stuck it into his mouth.

Liam produced a lighter as if by magic, flicked it and held it out, his eyes never leaving the man's face. "Nothin' like good old-fashioned freedom, eh?" The man sucked in a lungful.

Liam narrowed his eyes as he lit up his own and blew a billow out into the room.

"Aren't ye afraid of getting fined?"

Liam chuckled quietly. "It's not a problem. Ye just have to have the right connections, so to speak."

The man looked up with a sly grin. "I get you—a few chops here, a roast there …"

"Sounds like ye know the ropes."

The man took a puff before continuing. "Only too well."

"We do what we have to do." After a moment he continued. "What brings ye to the butcher shop today? I hope yer not the police."

"Hardly. I just feel the need to get away from work every now and then."

Liam butted out his cigarette, wiped his hands on his discolored apron, and began rearranging a pile of ribs. "What is it ye work at, then?

Taking one last drag, the man dropped his cigarette onto the floor and crushed it with his foot. "Just a bit of security."

"So ye are with the police."

"Not that kind of security."

"The bank, then?"

"No—it's more of a private nature."

"Ye find it gets to be a bit hum-drum, do ye?" Liam turned to the cooler and drew out a container of loin chops.

"Ye might say that. Every now and then I wonder if I'm in the right line of employment."

"Ye don't like keepin' things safe and sound?"

The man smirked. "All depends on your point of view."

Liam turned back around and with his eyes trained on the other, leaned both elbows onto the counter. "Sounds like you're in need of a change."

<hr />

Sela lifted her purse and made her way out of the Tea Store Café. Julia had already gone, anxious to get back to the hostel to prepare for her date. Hopefully, this Sebasian guy would finally get a chance to see her in the right light—not as some wild woman on the loose.

She smiled as a picture of Dougal popped into her mind. Wouldn't it be amazing if both she and Julia found the man of their dreams? Unconsciously, she reached up to finger the locket around her neck but her hand came away empty. The locket was gone. With a groan she stopped in her tracks, recalling the moment she'd torn it from her neck and flung it onto the art shop floor. Her face grew hot. "So sorry, Granddad," she whispered. "I should've trusted you."

"I see ye've now taken to conversing with yourself," said a nearby voice. "Ye must be finding it difficult without your sidekick."

Sela's head shot over to the cocky face just inches from her own. Jimmy. His scruffy appearance stood out in sharp contrast to the previous image in her mind and she took a step back. "Unlike some people, my brain doesn't continually run on empty."

"Aye, there's a lot who say the same thing, but they're usually on the inside looking out."

"Is there a point to this little chat or are you just trying to antagonize me?" She turned to leave but he fell into step beside her.

"I was just wonderin' when we could enjoy our lunch date together."

Sela snorted. "I'm afraid that won't be possible now. I'll be leaving soon."

He opened his eyes wide. "Ye don't say. Back across the pond?"

"Not yet. First we're going to ..." She stopped, irritated that she was explaining herself to him again. "Let's just say I won't be around."

Jimmy ignored her lack of civility. "I'd hoped we could have a wee conversation at one of the cafes before you left." His eyes twinkled but Sela was convinced she saw something beneath the surface.

If only she could feel repulsed by his cavalier attitude and grubby attire. His quick wit and brawny physique, however, had a way of capturing her attention and making her heart beat faster. She looked away. "Sorry," she said. "It just came up."

"Did ye ever find what ye were looking for at the art shop?"

He stared at her intently and she wondered if there was a hidden meaning. Glancing down at his hands, she checked for any sign of blue paint but as usual, they were spotless.

"Don't worry," he smirked, lifting them high for her inspection. "I'm not wearing a wedding band if that's what you're concerned about."

Sela jumped back. "I'm not the slightest bit concerned about your marital status, thank you. I couldn't care less if you're married, single, or anywhere in between."

"That's good, then," he grinned. "Just the kind of girl I like."

"I didn't mean it that way," she stammered, her face heating to crimson. Seeing him chuckle, she spun around and forged her way into a group of tourists, hoping to lose him in the crowd. The tourists, however, dissipated on the spot, leaving her standing alone, exposed to his apologetic grin.

"I'm sorry," he said. "I tend to get a wee bit carried away."

"Just leave me alone," she snapped. "I really don't have time for your nonsense. I've got things to do."

"As you wish then," he replied slowly, his eyes boring into her own. "But remember, things aren't always as they appear." He turned and made his way back in the direction of the café.

Sela stood for a moment, looking after him. What was he talking about? Was he delusional—or could he actually be the leader of a subversive gang?

She shuddered but a twinge of guilt caught her off guard. If that was the first test of her new-found faith, she'd failed it miserably. Granddad would never have reacted that way. *Sorry, Lord*, she prayed silently. *Help me to be courteous—even to people who bring out the worst in me.*

What should she do now? Time was running out. Sure, she knew about the treasure but what good would that do if she couldn't connect it to anything? Maybe she should pay another visit to the art shop. If the woman said anything about the painting she'd just play dumb and see if she could pick up any more information. At the same time she could keep an eye out for the locket. At least it was worth a try.

The shadows were growing lengthy as she made her way toward Custom House Street. Julia would be meeting up with Sebastian any minute now. A pang of envy swept over her at the thought of it. She should be with Dougal. Oh well, it was no one's fault but her own. He would have taken her back to Glasgow long ago if he'd had his way.

She rounded the corner to the art shop and stopped dead. Yellow police tape, the kind she'd seen on detective shows, was stretched across the front of the store. On the far side, a police car had pulled into a makeshift driveway and a bobby stood to the side of it, arms folded across his chest.

Sela's heart began to thump. What were they doing here? Looking for her? Maybe the woman had seen her racing away earlier and called the police. Cautiously, she reversed her course and began slinking back down Ladysmith. Was there an ABC, or whatever it was called, out for her? She picked up the pace as she approached Argyle Street. Thankfully, the swell of tourists rendered her virtually invisible and she was able to slow down and think. What she'd done wasn't such a monstrous crime was it? After all, she'd just continued what someone else had begun.

Reaching Shore Street she glanced around. No police. She turned the corner and hurried toward the hostel. At least she'd have a place of refuge while she figured out what to do. Maybe the girls would help her. Then again, she didn't want to involve innocent parties in her clandestine activities.

With a bang, the door of the hostel swung wide and a man barreled through, his head down and his face partially covered by the hood of his jacket. He glanced at her, then turned and sprinted off in the opposite direction. Sela's hand flew to her chest and she stopped to regain her breath. He looked familiar somehow. Had she seen him before or was she just becoming paranoid?

Entering the hostel, she noticed the woman at the desk viewing her with pursed lips.

"You certainly have quite an entourage," she smirked.

Sela had no time for niceties. "Meaning?"

"Meaning, I've never seen anyone with so many boyfriends all at one time."

Sela ignored the jab and shot down the hallway to her room. The door was unlocked and she turned the knob with a shaky hand and went in. An eerie stillness seemed to pervade the room. Quickly she turned on the light and went over to her bed. Her mouth flew open as she caught sight of a crumpled note lying on top of her pillow. 'Leave Now!' Above it lay a long, tangled thistle.

Chapter Seventeen

Julia sat across from Sebastian in a snug little alcove at the Seaforth Inn, watching his dark eyes sparkle with amusement. "Really, I thought you were one of those snooty-type waiters."

He raised an eyebrow in feigned shock. "And do you treat all waiters with such disdain?"

"Only those who refuse to serve me." She flicked her hair, sending the newly brushed curls springing back as though in agreement.

He raised his water glass in a mock toast. "To snooty waiters everywhere."

Julia laughed, clinking his glass with her own. She glanced around the room and took in the soft white stucco walls, dark wainscoting, and arched doorways which seemed to overflow with customers. "How in the world did you manage to get a reservation on such short notice?"

"Oh, just a little academic pull."

She narrowed her eyes.

"And also the fact that I know the owner."

"I should've guessed," Julia said. "You probably know everyone in town."

"Except for the tourists of course—but even those, I attempt to become acquainted with." He threw her an impish grin and his square white teeth gleamed in the light.

She took another sip. "Have you always lived here?"

"We actually moved to Aberdeen when I was sixteen but the family keeps a small cottage just outside of town. I try to get up here every summer." He paused, a smirk forming on his face. "So what brings you to the Highlands—just getting to know the lay of the land?"

"Very funny, she said, recalling her embarrassing pose by the hazel trees. "I'm actually here with a couple of students trying to finish up a project."

"So you actually are a professor."

"Part time, anyway." She crossed then re-crossed her leg.

"And the rest?"

"To be honest, I spend most of my free time looking for other teaching assignments."

"Ah," he said. "The plight of the young instructor."

She shifted in her seat. "So … you're officially on vacation now?"

"Sort of. I'm working on a bit of a project myself."

"Here we are," crooned the waitress, her face beaming as she swooped in on them balancing two steaming plates of food. "Salmon bisque for the lady, and for you, Dr. Westcott, haddock in crab sauce." She placed the plates meticulously before them and stood back in admiration. "Anything else I can get ye?"

"It looks like you've got it all covered," Sebastian said, returning her smile. "Tell Patrick I said to give you the night off."

"I don't think it would do me much good. As ye can see, we're pretty swamped. Enjoy your meal." She left in a swish of rayon.

"No snootiness there," said Julia when she'd gone.

Sebastian laughed. "That's where we men come in."

Julia automatically bowed her head to give thanks but when she'd finished, she found that Sebastian had lowered his head as well. Waiting, she felt a warm glow. Was he, too, a believer?

He looked up and a slow smile spread across his face. "Looks like we've got more than one thing in common."

The buxom waitress rolled her eyes as she listened to the voice at the other end of the line. "Hang on and I'll get him." Without bothering to turn her head, she roared out, "Theo, it's that grimy-lookin' butcher. Says he wants to talk to ye pronto."

Theo bustled out from behind the bar, his face a thunder cloud. Grabbing the cordless receiver from her hand, he strode to the back door and disappeared through it.

"Liam?" he roared, as he reached the office and closed the door with a thud. "Is that you?"

"Well I doubt the Queen of England would be referred to as that grimy-lookin' butcher."

"Sorry about that. Any word?"

"Seems we have a person of interest."

"Interest in what?"

"A wad of cash."

"In exchange for?"

"A golden opportunity, ye might say."

The little proprietor took a breath, glancing down the hallway. "Any chance he'd know what happened to Therese?"

"I'd give him an eight out of ten. He knows about the ammo box. Chances are they've found it."

Theo paused again and when he spoke, his voice, for once, was close to a whisper. "What's he offerin'?"

"Specific information. He made it sound like it might be out of date shortly."

Theo grunted. "Why didn't he come to ye before, then?"

"Says it just came up."

"And how did he figure you'd be the one to come to?"

"Guess he just put two and two together."

The little proprietor scratched his chin, thinking in passing that he was getting too old for this nonsense. He'd never have agreed to it if he'd thought it would put Therese in danger. "Send him over," he said. "Tell him to sit at the booth nearest the bar. I'll be waiting fer him."

"Righto … And Theo, don't worry. The boys are good at their job."

⋯•◦◦◦⋯——◦——⋯◦◦◦•⋯

Jimmy slumped into a chair at the Tea Store Café. Would he never learn to keep his mouth shut? He downed a gulp of the strong black coffee, savoring its bitter aftertaste. Making the girl feel like a fool wasn't exactly the way to win her trust. At best she thought he was an imbecile—at worst …

Her eyes, as usual, seemed to observe everything. Why had she looked straight at his hands? He'd better watch his tongue or he'd never learn a thing.

He sat back with a sigh. Much as he hated to admit it, his interest in her was becoming less and less about the business at hand. "Focus," he told himself. He couldn't afford to mess this up. Too much was riding on it.

Not only that, but his old boss was givin' him the beats every chance he got. The man didn't trust him—that was as obvious as the bulbous nose on his face. And who could blame him. Jimmy looked down at his cup, a renewed surge of shame running though him as the events of that day played out in crystal clear detail. They'd been backed into a corner, literally—the underground parking lot jammed with every imaginable vehicle, the stench of gasoline and diesel putrefying the air around them. Only one car had separated them from their pursuers—that and the one gun between them. He had insisted on carrying it but had promptly forgotten everything he'd learned at the first sign of clear and present danger. Thunder now reverberated around the lot and a metallic taste rose up in his mouth. He couldn't breathe. He had to get out. As if by magic, a truck began backing up and idled momentarily between him and the car. Not needing further invitation, he threw the gun at his boss and raced ahead. Just as he reached the opening, several loud bangs erupted but he didn't look back. He ran like his life depended on it.

It was a thousand wonders he hadn't been taken out on the spot when the crew showed up at his apartment later on that day. The boss had suffered a shoulder graze—much less than the opposition—but had stated in no uncertain terms, if Jimmy was to stay on, he was done. He wasn't about to get himself killed for the sake of some cowardly young chump. For some unknown reason, Jimmy was given a reprieve by the higher-ups—though his pride kept him from a full admission. With that, his boss had turned on the spot and thrown in the hat. Now, years later, when the tables were turned, it was like prying teeth to get the man to cooperate. Jimmy would have to bite the bullet and straighten things out with him whether he liked it or not. Confession, he'd been told, was good for the soul.

<hr />

Julia bit into an asparagus spear, closing her eyes as the butter melted slowly in her mouth. "Delicious," she sighed.

Sebastian pointed with his fork. "Wait till you try the salmon. I've had it here many a time and haven't regretted it yet."

"So I take it you do a lot of eating out?"

"Only when I get tired of stale cheese sandwiches and luke-warm tea."

She laughed and took a bite of the bisque. "Mmmm. Well at least you have good taste in restaurant cooking."

"Aye, and it tastes even better in the company of a lovely lady."

"Thank you."

"Did I happen to mention that you definitely clean up well?"

She blushed at the compliment but smirked to cover her pleasure. "You too. Mud just isn't your color."

After taking another bite of the fish, she went on. "So what project did you say you're working on?" His upper lip gave a slight twitch and she looked down at her plate. Was he nervous? Was it some kind of university venture he wasn't allowed to discuss? For a second her mind flashed to Dr. Hendricks and Cyril. Get over it, she told herself in disgust.

"Just helping out a friend," he said. I actually teach social sciences which seems to fit in with an investigation he's working on."

Julia's ears perked up. "Sounds fascinating. Do I dare ask what it's about?"

He looked directly at her and she had the uneasy sensation he was sizing her up.

After a moment he dropped his gaze. "I'm not really at liberty to say."

"No problem." Her tone held a bit too much vigor. She pushed the salmon around the plate with her fork.

"But that's not to say I can't talk about hypothetics."

"Hypothetics?"

"You know, that's where you—"

"I'm familiar with the term."

"Right." He coughed and wiped his mouth with the cloth napkin. "Well let's just say someone was looking for the motivation behind some unscrupulous goings on."

"You mean like a burglary?"

"More like something that would affect a lot of people."

"And you—or rather someone—needed to find out why it was happening?"

"You've got it."

"So how would you go about doing that?"

Sebastian took a bite of his asparagus. "You were right," he sighed. "This is heavenly." Swallowing, he caught the look in her eye and continued. "Anyway, one way would be to look for a pattern."

"As in the type of articles being stolen?"

"Something like that."

"So, if there were a rash of diamond thefts, for instance, you would presume it was the same person doing them."

"Are you sure you don't operate a detective agency?"

"Quite sure."

"Another way, of course, would be to get into the perpetrator's mind and discover what makes him tick."

"Which would be hard to do if you don't know who he is in the first place."

"Ah, but that's where you're mistaken, my good woman."

Julia giggled. "Then please enlighten me."

"Fingerprints."

"Don't you think the police would have covered that?"

"Not the same kind of fingerprints—the unseen variety where the perpetrator unknowingly leaves a trail of hidden clues—like a signature."

"As in the methods he uses?" She pushed back her plate, feeling suddenly full.

"Possibly."

"What about beliefs?"

"Such as ..."

"Well, what if he believed he should rid the world of certain people?"

"Jack the Ripper revisited."

"You catch on fast."

"Touché." He thought for a moment. "Or supposing he was convinced he'd been wronged."

Julia's mind whirled. "Like a disgruntled employee perhaps?"

He nodded.

"Or someone who felt the whole world was against him."

His eyes slowly narrowed. "Maybe not the whole world. What if it was just part of the world?"

"Like here—Scotland."

Sebastian coughed again and sat up straighter. "Of course we're still speaking hypothetically."

"Of course." She continued on. "And what if he wanted to take revenge, like blowing up buildings and what not."

"Or take control." He leaned forward, his elbows planted on the table and his hands resting under his chin.

Julia hesitated, swallowing. Did she dare plunge in? "What if he had to find something first?"

"Something like what?"

"You know—something to help his cause."

"Like?"

"Like a treasure."

In the thunderous silence that followed, he lowered his arms and folded them in front of him, piercing her with a stare. "What is it you do, exactly?"

Julia's eyes fluttered. "Like I said, I teach botany."

"Coffee?" The beaming waitress had returned with a steaming pot in her hand. "Piping hot, just as ye like it, Dr. Westcott."

Sebastian sat back, his eyes never leaving Julia's. "That would be lovely, Aggie."

Aggie took her time filling his cup three-quarters full. "I've just left a wee bit of room for cream. I know how ye love your cream with coffee, Dr. Westcott. Not too light and not too dark as ye always say. And you, miss? Coffee?"

"Please. Black—straight up."

The waitress left with all but a curtsey and Sebastian poured a dollop of cream into the coffee and stuck his spoon into the swirling contents. "So … it seems we're not speaking hypothetically after all."

Julia lifted her cup and faced him over the rim. "I also have a friend."

"And …"

"And she's doing a little investigating of her own. But I'm afraid she's in a lot deeper than she thinks."

"She's not the one putting those ridiculous articles in the paper, is she?"

"No, of course not. Anyway, wasn't there just one article?"

"There's a new one out today. It hints that the goings on around town have to do with a treasure hunt. Someone appears to know too much and I'm afraid they'll find themselves in a lot of hot water if they're not careful." He took a sip of coffee.

"That's not Sela's style. She just wants to clear up the past."

"How so?"

Choosing her words carefully, she filled him in on a few of the details, including the soldiers at Inverpoly, and Sela's discovery of a missing treasure.

When she'd finished, Sebastian shook his head, incredulous. "It's a wonder the two of you haven't been shanghaied what with all this amateur sleuthing."

"We can take care of ourselves."

His mouth twitched again. "Yes, I've noticed that on a few occasions."

Sela looked down at the note, her hands trembling like twigs in a windstorm. Whoever was responsible for this was becoming bolder by the hour.

As her eyes shifted to the tangled thistle, she thought about her introduction to that prickly weed just days before. If it hadn't been for Dougal, something terrible might have happened. If only he were with her now. As usual, though, she was trying to figure it all out on her own. She swiped at her eyes as tears broke the surface and rolled down her face.

Suddenly the song she'd heard earlier that day floated into her mind like a fresh breeze and she began to sense God's presence once again. "How deep the Father's love for us, How vast beyond all measure." Hadn't she felt His love envelope her like a thick blanket? Hadn't she entrusted Him with her life from that moment on? Couldn't she continue to trust Him? "Thank you, Lord," she prayed aloud. "I see I'll have to work on my memory."

The thing was, that man could return at any moment. She needed to go somewhere else for now, at least until the girls got back. Grabbing her purse, she headed to the door with a quick "Show me what to do, Lord." Before reaching it, however, another thought occurred to her and she rushed back into the room. Tossing her sketch book and a couple of pencils into the canvas bag, she let out her breath. She knew exactly where she would go.

Twenty minutes later she turned off the main road onto the steep incline that would take her to Postie's Path. She had wanted to take advantage of the panoramic view since the first time Dougal had brought her here and now was the perfect opportunity. The sun was sloping westward, casting lengthy shadows and there was only a slight chill in the air but still, it was a beautiful day.

Reaching the path, she took in the heathery hill above and filled her lungs with the salty aroma. She exhaled slowly. Whether it was her newfound sense of peace or simply the beautiful view, she didn't know, but suddenly something inside her bubbled to the surface and she burst into an off-key rendition of "Joyful, Joyful We Adore Thee." So, she thought while furtively scanning for observers, all those years in church haven't been wasted after all.

Reaching the place where Dougal had given her the locket, she plopped down on the grassy slope and began taking out her art supplies. The view of the loch was breathtaking with sunbeams skipping over the water and glinting off the purple mountains of the Summer Isles. The only thing to complete the picture would have been Dougal himself with his beautiful green eyes and blond hair, his lips closing in on hers. She sighed, reaching up to touch her throat. Somehow she'd have to find the locket.

Before long she was lost in the drawing. Her hand moved swiftly across the page to keep up with the ever-changing cloud formations. Sea gulls screeched and dove for their supper and she captured their flight with quick impressionistic strokes. Remember, she reminded herself with a lesson from art school, less is more.

Thunder rumbled somewhere in the east. How could it possibly storm on such a glorious day? She didn't have time to worry about it, though. The sun was dipping fast and she'd like to have at least three sketches to bring home and paint—a good start to her project.

Abruptly her hand dropped to her side. Where was home? Was

it back in Minneapolis at Granddad's house, or here with Dougal? Hadn't he implied they should be together? She sighed and turned back to her sketch. She'd cross that bridge when she got to it.

She finished the first one and turned the page, viewing the loch from a slightly different angle. Violet clouds were now overtaking the coral. She'd be lucky to complete even two drawings before darkness set in.

Once again, she moved her pencil from one side of the page to the other as deeper shadows crept over the distant hills. She'd have to hurry. Focusing on a patch of wild roses in the foreground, she heard a sudden "Swoosh" and turned to see several small stones roll onto the pathway beside her. What in the world? She looked back up at the hill but the dwindling light seemed to confuse the landscape.

She turned back, hurriedly sketching the delicate petals. Suddenly a thunderous roar reverberated from the hill above. Spinning around, she stared in horror as a boulder the size of an arm chair hurled down the rise directly in her path. She screamed and flung herself out of the way. A second later it smashed into the very place she'd been sitting and plummeted to the loch below.

She gasped, staring down at her ruined work. Her hands began to shake as she took in the implications. It could have been her.

Hardly daring to turn, she glanced back up at the hill. At the very top, stark against the sky, a man-like figure seemed to be standing with hands on hips. But then it might just have been a tree. It didn't matter. Finding her feet at last, she dug the toes of her shoes into the earth and spinning around, flew back in the direction she'd come.

Chapter Eighteen

The little proprietor took a slow sip of his tea and eyed the unshaven galoot across from him. The weak link. Still, he'd have to play his cards right if he hoped to get information concerning Therese. She'd disappeared nearly three hours earlier and there was still no sign of her. Added to that, he wouldn't trust the one in charge with his pet goldfish.

"So," he said, "you're fed up with your working arrangements."

The man nodded. "I can see it's time for a change."

"It comes to us all."

The man lifted his cup and held it in both hands. "Some more than others, I'm sure ye'll agree."

"Aye, depending of course on the level of dissatisfaction." He shot him a look. "And what would yours be, if I might ask?"

"Let's just say I'd have to look up to see bottom."

"What did ye have in mind then?"

The man took a sip, swilled it around in his mouth for a bit, and finally set down the cup. "Depends on what's being offered."

A long silence followed during which Theo examined the condition of his fingernails and glanced around the room. He'd never been accused of jumping the gun.

The man crossed and uncrossed his arms and finally picked up his cup again. "So what do ye say?"

Theo looked back at him. "I'm afraid I'm not authorized to deal without seeing at least a partial hand."

"What do ye need to know?"

"For starters, what do ye know about an old ammunition box?"

The man smiled. "Only that it was buried beside a grove of trees at Corrieshalloch Gorge.

Theo paused. "So it was found, then. How did they know where to look?"

"The leader somehow got hold of an ancient telegram with a vague description of the trees. Don't ask me how he got it. Anyway, they did a lot of digging before they were able to come up with the correct location."

"They weren't the only ones who did a lot of digging."

"Aye, but evidently the other bunch was missing the proper info."

"What info is that?"

"The telegram spoke of the 'writing trees.' There's a special kind of fungus on some trees that looks a lot like writing. That's how they found it." He sat back as though he'd been solely instrumental in figuring it out.

Theo decided not to mention the damage to the lichens. "And what did they find inside?"

The man smirked. "Now that would be tellin', wouldn't it?"

Theo drummed his fingers on the table in front of him. "This leader," he said at length. "Would ye be willing to give his name?"

The man shifted in his seat. "I'm afraid I'd need more than a few monkeys fer that one. It could mean my own death sentence if I didn't get off the island right quick."

"I can assure ye, we wouldn't let that happen."

The man looked away. When he spoke, his voice was barely audible. "I don't think ye understand what you're up against."

"I've got a good idea," Theo said. "It wouldn't be the first time I've dealt with his kind." He felt his stomach churn though his gaze remained steady.

"Then ye know what a risk I'm taking just sitting here with you."

Theo eyed him warily. "Ye must have had your reasons for taking such a risk in the first place."

"Aye, but they're not all mercenary."

"Is that a fact?"

"It's true. But surely ye don't expect me to come out of this in the hole."

"No," Theo said. "I'm not that daft. You'll be paid for your trouble."

"Then tell me what ye need to know and I'm away."

Sela's lungs were bursting but she wasn't about to stop. What had she been thinking, coming out here this close to dark? Ghostly trees now ushered her back into the woods and an eerie wind whispered in her ears. The hair on the back of her neck stood up. Twenty minutes more and she'd be in town. Could she hold out?

Her breath was coming in gasps and she slowed to a trot. At least it was better than stopping altogether.

"Seeelaaa."

She stopped dead and froze to the nearest tree, a band of sweat popping out on her upper lip. Had she imagined it or was someone calling her name?

"Sela, are you there?"

Her heart pounded and she slid down the trunk into a crouch. Was it the man on the hill? Had he come to finish her off? She covered her face with her hands and tried to hold back a sob.

"Sela, it's me. Are you there?"

"Dougal?" She peeked out from behind the tree and saw his shadowy form jogging toward her.

"What are you doing?" he called when he spotted her. "Are you alright?" Running to her side, he knelt down and cradled her in his arms. "What happened? Are you hurt?"

"Oh Dougal," she cried. "Somebody tried to kill me again." Her voice quivered and she broke into a sob.

"Let's get you out of here," he said, helping her up. "You got a scare, that's all."

"No, it's more than that. There was a man up on the hill … He sent a boulder flying down toward me. It ruined my drawings."

"Oh sweetheart." He placed his arm firmly around her shoulders. "That place is known for rock slides. I'm sure that's all it was. You shouldn't be out here at this time of day."

Sela allowed herself to be half-carried along to the road, enjoying the warmth of Dougal's arms.

"I've got the company truck," he said. "You won't have to walk back to town."

"How did you know where I was?" "I didn't tell anyone where I was going."

"Just call me your guardian angel. When I got back, I went to your room and saw that awful note. I thought you might have come out here to get away. Sorry. I know I shouldn't barge in when you're not there."

"As if I care." She tightened her arms around his waist. "You've rescued me so many times."

He gave her a squeeze. "Here's the truck. You're okay now."

"I'm always okay when I'm with you."

He opened the door and guided her onto the seat before going around to the driver's side. "Are you sure you're alright?"

"Yeah, I'm fine now," she said with a little laugh. "I was convinced there was a man up on the hill but you're probably right. Maybe it was just a landslide."

"I'm worried about the note, though. I really think we need to take it to the police."

She sighed, snapping on her seat belt. "Let's wait until tomorrow night. If nothing turns up by then we'll hand it over to the first bobby we see."

He patted her knee. "That's my girl … Now, do you feel well

enough to go for a little trip with me? I just have to run to the warehouse for a bit."

"Sure." She smiled over to him. "I'm up for that. Just don't drive too fast."

He laughed. "Surely you trust me by now."

"Of course."

He pulled onto the road in the opposite direction of town. "It's just down this way a bit."

Sela sat back. At least she didn't have to do any more walking. It had been a full day to say the least. She watched in silence as shadows overtook the landscape, gradually darkening it from indigo to black.

Dougal looked over. "Comfortable?"

"Definitely.

"You seem a bit quiet."

"It's been a long day—but a good one."

He threw her a rueful grin. "I'm sorry about your drawings."

"It's okay. I might even be able to redo them from memory."

"You really are quite an artist." He slowed the truck to round a sharp corner.

"Thanks." She opened her mouth to relate the whole landslide episode but her mind abruptly jumped back to the art shop. "I had quite an experience today," she said.

"Sounds like you've had more than one."

"You haven't heard the half of it. At one point I wanted to run away and never come back."

"How so?"

She paused for a moment, gathering her thoughts. "Well, to begin with, I found out there really is an oil painting underneath the acrylic at the art shop."

"You're not serious."

"I am. And when I saw what it was, I felt like my whole life was in ruins."

"Surely it couldn't have been that bad. Do I dare ask what it was about?"

She took a deep breath and let it out. "It was a painting of Granddad as a young man … standing next to Hitler."

"Oh Sela, I'm so sorry." He cast her droopy-eyed glance as they rounded another curve in the road. "But to be perfectly honest, I was afraid it might be something like that—at least judging from the old rumor I had heard."

"Thankfully, that's not the end of the story."

"Really? What do you mean?"

She smiled. "Someone came into the shop just then and I took off in a panic, running like a banshee, not caring where I went. Eventually I ended up at some sort of hall where two girls were practicing for a concert. One of them sang the most beautiful hymn I've ever heard."

"And how did that change anything?"

She turned toward him, her face beaming. "It changed my whole view of God.

"But the painting was still there."

"That's just it. I can't explain it but I suddenly realized that even if Granddad was guilty of betraying his country, that isn't the worst sin in the world."

"Really? What is then?"

"My sin of rejecting Him is worse. God sent His Son to take the punishment for my sins—all of our sins in fact. But when my parents died in the crash, I turned my back on God and refused to believe He cared about me. No matter what Granddad told me, I wouldn't listen. Sure, I went to church and played the part of the good girl, but inside I harbored a deep anger. It was only when I heard the words to that song that I realized how much I needed God's forgiveness for my own wrongdoings."

Dougal's fingers gripped the steering wheel as a heavy blanket of silence hung between them. At last he spoke. "I'm glad you feel that way, Sela. Really, I am. But I tend to believe we can't undo the deeds of others. We can only choose our own destiny.

"But don't you see," she said, touching his arm, "we have to let God do the choosing."

"But what about your granddad? Wasn't he banished from his own country for good?"

"Maybe, but he still turned out to be a wonderful man who trusted God for everything."

Dougal sighed as he glanced out the side window. After a few seconds he let out a weary-sounding breath. "We're nearly there," he said, as if to himself.

They turned left onto a narrow path. Scrawny branches seemed to reach out and paw the truck as it bounced from one pothole to another. Sela gripped the dash. "This place sure is out in the sticks. Where are we, anyway?"

"Sorry," he said. "The company likes to keep its warehouses as private as possible. Competition can be fairly keen with this type of merchandise."

She laughed, determined to bring a lighter note to the conversation. "I hope you don't have to pay for any damages to the truck."

"Oh no," he said. "The company takes care of everything."

Suddenly from between the trees, the muted glimmer of old metal shone out from the headlights and Dougal slowed and pulled up to a building. It was long and low, constructed entirely of corrugated tin with only two small windows— out of place in such a woodland setting. "Here we are," he said. "I'm afraid it isn't too pretty."

"It's a little spooky alright, out in the middle of the forest and all. I'm glad I'm not alone."

"Just stay with me," he said, and came around to open her door. "And don't worry about the dark—the headlights stay on for a couple of minutes after the truck shuts off."

She climbed out, wrapping her arms tightly about herself as the heady scent of the forest wafted her way. "It must have rained here today. The atmosphere is almost oppressive."

"Scotland at its finest."

She followed closely behind as he made his way toward the building. When he reached it he pulled a ring of keys from his pocket and held it up to the light, selecting the one he wanted. "Here we go," he said. "We'll be inside in a jiffy."

Before he could insert the key, however, the headlights clicked off leaving them in abject darkness. At the same moment, a low growl emanated from somewhere on their right. Sela screamed and flung herself up onto Dougal's back.

His voice cracked like a whip. "Get down!"

Not knowing if he was talking to her or the animal, she scrambled off him and lunged for the door, her heart thumping like a crazed drummer.

Without another word, Dougal sprinted to the truck, flicked on the lights, then ran back and unlocked the door. Sela shoved it open and dashed inside, panting like a marathon runner.

"You're alright now," he said, following her into the building. He felt along the wall for a light switch and turned it on, revealing a small Spartan office. "It's just a dog that hangs around here occasionally. Sorry. I didn't mean to startle you."

"I thought you said the headlights would stay on," she huffed.

He smiled. "You know how it is with technology. Just when you think something will work it proves you wrong."

She gave a sheepish laugh. "I'm sorry, too. I guess I'm just spooked. I didn't expect it to be so black."

"Not to worry." He walked over to the desk and lifted a swivel chair from behind, placing it close to a small counter. "Here you go. I've got a few things to do in the warehouse and then I'll be back. There's a plug-in kettle here and all the makings for a good cup of tea."

"Sure. I'll be glad to just sit and rest for a while."

"There may be a delivery truck coming which would mean I'll be a bit longer but I'd appreciate it if you'd just stay here. The warehouse isn't the coziest of places and like I said, the company likes things kept private."

She plunked down onto the chair and waved to him as he disappeared through a door on the other side of the room.

After a few minutes of sitting still, though, her legs began to cramp and she got up to stretch. No doubt her mad dash from Postie's Path was taking its toll. She walked over to the desk and ran her hand over the smooth mahogany top. Its pristine appearance was a far cry from the desk in her bedroom back in Minnesota. Oh well, to each his—or her—own.

The room itself was no more than ten by twelve—small for such a sizable company—but then this wasn't the main office. To the right of the desk stood a metal filing cabinet, and off to the left, a tiny bathroom. Reaching over to the filing cabinet, she gave the top drawer a tug but it held firm. Just as well. Dougal probably wouldn't appreciate her snooping around.

She walked back to the counter, made herself a cup of tea in a Styrofoam cup and sat back down. Opening her purse, she took out the makeup mirror and pushed her hair around till it looked half decent, then reapplied her lipstick.

After a few minutes, she began looking at the door Dougal had gone through. What was keeping him? He'd been pretty secretive about the warehouse but surely he wouldn't mind if she just peeked inside. It wasn't as if she was going to tell the world what kind of kilts he was selling.

Hesitating for a minute, she blew out her breath, then marched over, turned the knob, and pushed. The door was heavier than she'd thought. Hearing nothing, she put her weight into it and pushed again. It hesitated for a second, then swung wide, revealing a scene that caused her jaw to drop and her hands to fall to her sides.

<hr />

"We need all the information ye can give us," the little proprietor said. "For your sake as well as our own."

The man looked up with thin twitching lips. "And I'll be compensated handsomely?"

"That's what I said, wasn't it?" Theo's nerves were unraveling by the second though he dared not show it. If he could just get the blighter to reveal the location.

"Well, let's see," the man said, sticking out his fingers as though recounting a list of groceries. "I've told ye where they found the container, I've told ye about the telegram, and I've told ye about the danger. What do ye still need to know?"

"Let's put it this way." Theo added a little sugar to his now tepid tea while staring him full in the face, "That all adds up to about a bob's worth. If ye want more than that you'll have to come up with some specifics."

"Okay, okay, I wasn't meanin' to be coy. How would ye like to find out some of the other men involved?"

"Not good enough."

"What, then? I've told ye—I'd have to have a bundle to give away the name of the leader."

"What about the headquarters?"

"What about it?"

"Where is it?"

The man smirked and dropped his gaze. "Ye must realize that would be worth as much as the name."

Theo's hand involuntarily moved to the Enfield revolver by his pant leg. It had been years since he'd put it to use but the reaction seemed effortless. "Would it be worth your miserable life?"

The man's eyes opened like saucers. "Come on now—you're supposed to be one of the good guys."

"And you're one of the bad ones. Her Majesty wouldn't mind one bit if ye ended up with a hole in your knee the size of an egg."

"Okay, okay, I'll tell ye then," he whined putting up his hands like a robber caught in the act. "But ye have to promise me enough to live on once I get to some other location."

"Ye've got it. Now out with it."

The man gave a deep sigh, the picture of piety divested of its honors. "As I said, they did a lot of digging."

"Aye."

And when they finally found the container at Corrieshalloch Gorge they were ecstatic."

"Because?"

"Because …"

Suddenly from the kitchen came the clatter of breaking dishes rising to an ear-splitting crescendo as though an entire shelf had given way. A second later a female voice belched out a string of fiery expletives. Gasps as well as loud guffaws could be heard throughout the restaurant as customers rose to their feet to witness the spectacle.

Theo's attention had been diverted no more than five seconds. He turned back to the man and stared in horror at the scene before him. The man lay slumped across the table, his mouth caught in a half-formed word, his eyes open though vacant. An ever widening pool of blood oozed from his shirt onto the table cloth and dripped to the floor below.

A woman at a nearby table caught sight of the macabre sight and let out a blood-curdling scream, throwing the room into pandemonium. The terrified crowd jumped up from their seats, stared at the spectacle and rushed for the door, upturning chairs and knocking plates of food onto the floor as they forced their way to the exit. Theo jumped up, too, and bellowed for calm. He ripped a cloth from a nearby table and tossed it over the body but it instantly became a sogging red mass.

Bounding up onto a chair like a man half his age, he roared to the crowd. "Ye'll all be quiet this instant. File out to the nearest exit without another sound or ye'll be up on charges."

Whether from shock or simple fright, a morgue-like hush, thick as a blanket of snow, fell upon them. Theo locked gazes with Hazel, his waitress. "Get me the phone," he mouthed and collapsed onto the nearest chair.

Chapter Nineteen

"Here, take a wee sip of water," Liam said, handing a glass to Theo. "Ye haven't seen this much action in a while." He'd arrived just minutes after the commotion and had taken Theo into the office, leaving the police to sort through the carnage on their own.

"It's not me I'm concerned about," Theo answered. "If they're this desperate to keep their whereabouts hidden, what have they done with Therese?"

"The sooner we piece together their motive the sooner we'll find her," said a third man as he entered the room and slumped down on the chair next to him. "Let's go over what the poor bloke had to say before they popped him."

Theo set the glass down on the cluttered desk and rubbed his face with both hands. "Just bits and pieces of things is all. He didn't get a chance to say much."

"He wouldn't budge on their location?"

"No. He said that would cost as much as the leader's name. Little did he know I was willing to pay double."

"Did he give any hint at all?" asked Liam.

Theo narrowed his eyes in thought. "There's one thing that might be of some help. He said they were ecstatic to find the treasure at Corrieshalloch Gorge."

"So they've found it, then." The other man dropped his gaze. "Ye know what that means."

"Of course," Theo snapped. "And no doubt our anonymous newspaper reporter spurred them on."

"Can we not put a stop to that?" asked Liam.

"We've tried. They're within their rights as long as they don't put down a specific name."

"True enough. But getting back, what was so wonderful about finding the treasure at the gorge?"

"I don't know. The bloke was just about to tell me when it all went down."

"Wait a minute," the other man said, sitting up a little. Maybe they were ecstatic because it was close to their own headquarters. Just the fact that they wouldn't have to move it far might have thrilled them to no end."

"Makes sense," Liam agreed. "The thing must weigh a ton and if it was out in the middle of the forest they'd have to carry it by hand."

"Remember the old building I told you I came across this afternoon at the gorge—the one with the Rottweiler tied up beside it?

The other two nodded.

"I'm wonderin' if that could be it."

"Do ye think it's big enough?" asked Liam.

"Like I told Sebastian, I didn't stick around to have a good look. It may be bigger than I originally thought—at least big enough to house an arsenal of weapons."

"Did ye say it was metal?" asked Theo.

"Aye. Like an old war barracks or something."

Theo closed his eyes and leaned back in the chair, thinking.

"What is it?" Liam asked.

"I was pulled out of retirement because I'd worked on that spy ring during the war, correct?"

The other man nodded. "You and your cronies knew the Nazis had been after the treasure to help finance their war effort. Plus you knew about the painting and the people involved. So when you alerted us to somebody sniffin' about for details, we knew we needed you on board."

"Right. But how did this group— "The New Thistle"—come across all the information? And how did they tie it together?"

"Who knows," Liam answered. "These things eventually always come out."

"But why would they care about anything but the treasure? After all, the painting's nothin' but a liability."

The other man chewed his lip. "Of course we've all wondered that ourselves. It doesn't seem relevant but there must be a connection."

"Maybe they thought the painting had a map on the back of it," Liam offered.

"Possibly, but what if there's an actual connection between "The New Thistle" and the Nazis of World War II?"

"I thought the whole espionage thing went away when they caught the spy." Liam rubbed his stubbly chin.

"Not necessarily," Theo said. "There's those of us who hold to his being framed regardless of the charges against him."

"Is that what all the commotion was about in the M15?"

"Aye, I'm afraid so. In the end, he was forced to leave the country and all association with it in exchange for his freedom. Thankfully, I was able to get him a lifetime pension for his trouble. They couldn't argue with it, having suspicions only and no real proof." He paused as though coming to a decision, throwing the third man a furtive glance. "I suppose I should tell you something else. When I first heard what was goin' on here I contacted him."

The two looked over in amazement. "Did ye think that was wise?" Liam asked.

"Under the circumstances, yes."

"And did ye come up with anything useful?"

Theo took a deep breath and tapped his gnarly fingers on the desk top. "Possibly, though he was reluctant to divulge it."

"What was it then?"

Theo sighed. "Ye have to understand that Joseph was a protector— no matter what it cost him personally. We always wondered why he didn't jump to his own defense and bitterly deny the allegations against him."

The other men waited for him to go on.

"But since the thing had raised its ugly head once more, he felt constrained to talk."

"About?"

He paused. "About the possibility of the real spy being his brother."

"His brother!" Liam's eyes went wide. "Why didn't ye tell us this before now?"

"Because there's no real proof for that either, just coincidences that caused him to suspect his brother. Besides," he added, "Joseph made me promise not to say a word unless absolutely necessary. He wanted his granddaughter protected at all costs."

"Do ye think the brother would still be involved?" asked the third man.

"He'd be a bit long in the tooth, to be sure. But who's to say someone close to him didn't pick up on the information and begin where he left off?"

"Someone with enough emotional attachment to take the historical theme to heart."

"It's definitely a possibility," Theo said. "And who's to say someone hasn't made a deal with the granddaughter?"

The other man thought for a minute then took out his cell phone. "Let's see what Sebastian can come up with."

<hr />

Julia looked into the face of the man across from her and tried to gauge how far she could trust him. Something about his gentle humor and kind eyes told her this wasn't another Cyril Branford but still, everything didn't quite add up, such as what he was doing out in the middle of the forest that afternoon.

"So you'll be adding treasure hunter to your list of accomplishments?" he asked, grinning.

"Hardly. What about you?"

"What about me?"

"Isn't that what your investigation's all about?"

He shifted his weight. "It's really not my investigation. Like I said, I'm just helping out a friend."

"Helping him do what—find the treasure?"

He flashed her a Denzel-like smile and she bit her bottom lip to keep from grinning in triumph.

"Okay, that's certainly part of it, but there's a lot more to it which, as I said, I'm not at liberty to discuss."

"But don't you see?" Her voice held a touch of exasperation. "The two things must be linked in some way. Besides, there might be a time element. What if something's going down today?"

"Going down?"

She fluttered her lashes. "You know—as in happening."

"Oh, that going down."

"Very funny. But it won't be quite so humorous if something happens to one of them."

He took another sip from his coffee cup and nodded to a passing waitress for a refill. "Believe me," he said after she'd gone. "my friend is more than capable of looking after himself."

"Good for him," Julia huffed. "My friend just thinks she is."

He tapped his fingers on the table. "You don't think she'd do anything foolish do you?"

"Foolish? Possibly. Outrageous? More than likely, from what I've seen of her so far."

He looked down at his cup as if trying to come to a decision. "Fine. Far be it from me to endanger a fair maiden. You ask the questions and I'll answer them if I can. But remember, this is strictly between you and me."

Julia let out her breath as she pushed her plate away. "Okay, then. You said yourself there's more to this than just a treasure. Did your friend say it had anything to do with the war?"

Sebastian visibly winced. "War?"

"Yes, war."

"I can't say he didn't."

"Then I'll take that as a 'yes'."

"As you wish."

"Have you ever heard of 'The New Thistle'?"

At this his eyes widened and he set down his cup with a thud. "Where did you hear that name?"

"Just answer the question, doctor."

He hesitated, then sighed. "Yes, I've heard of it but before you go any further, let me ask you something."

"Fire away." Her eyes reflected the glint of the table candle.

"Do you two have any idea what's going on here, because this isn't some 'Nancy Drew'-type mystery for amateurs."

"We're well aware of that." Her eyebrows arched and she lowered her voice before continuing. "That's the main reason we're not broadcasting it all over town."

"My friend isn't in the habit of welcoming the general public into his investigations, either."

"Who is your friend?"

"Sorry, I'm not at liberty to say. He works undercover."

"Anyone I've met?"

"Possibly. I can't say for sure." He took a small sip. "Why exactly is this Sela girl looking for the treasure, by the way?"

"She … a …"

"Remember, there might be a time element."

She studied his face again, wondering if she dare confide in him. He looked strong … trustworthy. If he were a plant he'd likely be a "Quercus." "Okay, I'm going to go out on a limb and trust you on this. I hope you won't disappoint me."

"Julia," he said, reaching for her hand. "The last thing I want to do is disappoint you."

She looked him in the eye to see if he was joking but he appeared serious. Just in case, though, she withdrew her hand.

In the next ten minutes she disclosed everything she knew about

Sela's secret, including Tanika, her grandfather's forced immigration to the United States, and the theft at her home in Minneapolis. When she finished, she realized she was shaking.

"What is it?" he asked.

"Nothing. I just want to help her. She's all alone in the world." She paused. "I know firsthand what that's like."

Sebastian looked directly at her. "You know, there's Someone who's there to help her even more than you can."

"I'm aware of that," Julia said, her lips curving upward. "And she actually found that out for herself today."

"Really?"

Just then a jazzy version of "Beethoven's Fifth" sounded and Sebastian reached into his shirt pocket and pulled out his cell phone. "Excuse me for a second," he said with a grin, but as he listened his brows knit together.

A minute later he clicked the button and stuck the phone back in his pocket.

"What is it?"

"Nothing good."

"Just tell me."

"Alright, but I don't want to alarm you." He straightened up in his seat. "There's been a shooting."

Julia's hand flew to her mouth. "It's not Sela is it?"

"No, no, nothing like that. Apparently it was some would-be informer over at the Ceildh Place."

"The restaurant?" she asked, incredulous.

"Aye. I guess somebody didn't want him giving away too much information."

"It wasn't the old man who works there, was it?"

He shook his head. "No, but he was the one taking the information. I guess he's pretty shook up."

"I don't understand. I thought he was involved with the neo-Nazis."

"Theo?" He raised his eyebrows. "Not him. He's one of us."

205

"But Sela thought …" she began, her expression bewildered.

"Just trust me on this one. There's more. The team is sure there's a historical twist to 'The New Thistle'."

"Right. Something to do with the World War II Nazis."

"Aye, but I'd say it would need to be fueled by something in the present as well." He paused for a minute, allowing the server to clear their plates. "We all know what the Nazis think of any other race but their own."

Julia blinked, feeling a jolt of déjà vu. Somewhere recently she'd experienced a hint of racism.

"What is it?"

"Nothing. Just a feeling. Go on."

"Anyway, I'm sure they're none too happy with Scotland's current flexible immigration policy. What if their agenda is to transform Scotland into a completely Aryan nation?"

Julia's eyes went wide. "To do that, they'd have to take over the government and break all ties with England, with no regard for the recent vote."

"Exactly."

"And if they're so intent that they'd actually kill one of their own …"

Sebastian looked over at her. "It could get ugly—just as my friend predicted."

"So when will they make their move?"

He scratched his head. "According to what I've read, this kind of group usually follows a pattern. They wouldn't pick just any day to strike. They'd probably choose some meaningful date in history."

"You mean like July 4th—Independence Day?"

"Something like that but more to do with Britain than the U.S. of course. Maybe even some obscure date."

She sighed. "I'm sure I won't be able to help you with that one, unless it has to do with Scotland trying to break away from England way back when."

His head shot up and he jabbed the air with his finger. "That's got to be it."

What?"

"Bonnie Prince Charlie. After the uprising, the Scots were forbidden to wear their tartan or carry weapons but a few years later that law was repealed. If I'm not wrong, a new law was put into place called 'The Repealing of the Proscription Act'."

"Do you think they'd strike on that day just to prove a point?"

"It makes sense, doesn't it? Even the name, 'The New Thistle' suggests something along those lines. Maybe their leader fancies himself as a modern day Bonnie Prince Charlie, freeing the Scots and setting up his own Nazi standards."

"What was the date of that law?"

"To tell you the truth I can't remember off the top of my head. Sometime during the summer, I know that." Abruptly, he reached for his phone and began punching in numbers.

"Who are you calling?"

He held out a finger. "Kelly? Yes, yes, I'm fine. Aye, the family as well. I just need some information. Can you look up the date when the Proscription Act was repealed. It was somewhere in the late 1700s." He held the phone away from his mouth. "My teaching assistant. She's a good egg."

"So where do you think they'd attack first?"

"My guess is they'd want to take over the Scottish government in Edinburgh." Suddenly his jaw fell slack. "I just remembered. There's supposed to be a special session of parliament this weekend. The Prime Minister was planning to be in attendance at the Royal Mile."

"In Edinburgh?"

He nodded, then brought the phone back up to his mouth. "Yes, Kelly. You got it? He paused, then closed his eyes with a deep sigh. "July 1st, 1782. Tomorrow."

Sela gawked at the scene before her. The room was narrow but much longer than she had first imagined. It wasn't the size or shape though, that drained the blood from her face causing her to lean against the door frame for support.

Army-type cots, neat as a pin, lined both side walls. On the left hand side, toward the back, four computers sat on immaculate desks with a huge map of Scotland hovering above them. On the right hand side, at the far end, a garage-like door stood open with at least thirty men milling about.

Suddenly, from the other side of the building came the sound of an engine and a truck appeared out of the darkness. It backed into the doorway, then stopped, revealing several large wooden crates.

Sela crouched down and watched, awestruck, as Dougal motioned for the men to carry them inside. When the crates were stacked against one of the walls, he gave a command and the truck retreated back into the night before the door was shut.

What was going on? Who were those men and why were they all acting like Dougal was some kind of general or something? Surely this wasn't all about kilts. Suddenly a horrifying thought collided with all reason and she felt as if she'd been punched in the stomach. Please, no.

Abruptly Dougal gave another command and the men lined up in three straight rows, each standing smartly at attention, facing him. Sela was glad she hadn't eaten lately. Her stomach was on spin cycle. Still, maybe she just didn't get it. What if it all just had to do with his company?

He was speaking now, his voice low except for the odd stab of punctuation. She had to hear what he was saying. She took a deep breath and crept slowly forward, careful to keep down, out of sight.

"Anybody who wants out now had better think twice if they don't want to end up like Alan."

What was he talking about? Who in the world was Alan?

"You are my chosen leaders. We've planned well, we've covered our ground, and now we stand at the apex of history."

A general cheer went up from the group and Sela's heart began to jack-hammer with fright. The apex of history? What in the world did that mean?

"And now for the crème de la crème—our last piece of the puzzle." There was a pause and this time a mighty roar erupted— "Heil! Heil! Heil!"

Sela raised her head eye level to the cots and stared in disbelief as the men stabbed their right arms into the air. Her eyes moved to Dougal who stood before them, saluting. On a chair to his right, still half draped in a billowing sheet, stood the painting—the faces of Hitler and her grandfather clearly visible where she had swiped away the acrylic. Sela took one look at it and dropped to the floor, her head spinning like a top.

She had to get out of there but she'd never make it back to the door. If she fainted she wouldn't live to see another day. "Lord," she prayed. "I need Your help right now—and a huge dose of courage." She lifted her head and looked across the room. Between two of the beds, a narrow recess in the wall revealed a descending staircase. She couldn't believe her luck—or was it an answer to prayer? It would get her out of immediate danger and maybe she'd be able to get back to town and contact the police. She'd deal with her emotions later.

She had to act now before anyone saw her. She rose unsteadily on all fours and inched her way across the empty span, resisting the urge to jump up and run. Her heart continued to thump but a curious sensation came over her that was hard to describe. It was as though someone stood just ahead, urging her slowly forward.

She reached the stairs, thankful that the commotion was still going on, and started down. Almost immediately she felt a change in the air—cool and dank—like a root cellar. It didn't matter. At least she was out of there.

With every step the air grew colder. Maybe there was an opening to the outside—an escape route. If that was the case she'd be gone in a flash. She stepped down onto the bottom and looked around. It was a cellar alright, complete with dirt walls and floor.

A bare light bulb, probably forty watts, wobbled from the ceiling casting dancing shadows onto a pile of boxes, crates, and in the far corner, an old Victorian style couch. The couch was piled high with raggedy blankets but as her eyes darted from one side of it to the other, she staggered back in disbelief. Cloaked between the shadows, cast in a strip of reflected light, another set of eyes stared back.

Chapter Twenty

Amanda barged through the archway of the Seaforth Inn with Keira close on her heels, both apparently oblivious to the stares leveled in their direction.

Julia looked up, her eyes wide. "What's wrong?"

"You won't believe it." She reached the table and slid down onto the vacant chair in front of her. Keira stood behind her gasping for breath.

"This had better be good," Julia said.

"Believe me, it is." Amanda looked over at Sebastian, giving him a quick up and down. "You must be the guy Julia met at the gorge." Without waiting for an answer, she barged ahead. "You won't believe what we just found in the room."

"We might if you tell us," Sebastian offered.

She rifled through her pocket and pulled out a crumpled sheet of paper. "Take a look at this."

"I've got the other part," Keira announced, producing a wilted thistle from her purse and holding it up like second prize.

"We found them both on Sela's bed but we can't find her anywhere."

"Let me see." Sebastian pulled the paper over to himself. He read it and slid it across to Julia, his face a blank.

Keira waved the thistle in front of them. "Don't forget about this."

"Why would someone want Sela to leave?" Amanda asked.

Julia looked down at the table. "I'm sure it's nothing to worry about."

"Sorry, Professor but I can't buy that." Amanda folded her arms in front of her. "I heard the two of you whispering together. I know you're both in on something."

Keira scurried around to the other side of the table and plopped onto the remaining empty chair. "We checked the Tea Store Café and a couple of other places. We can't find her anywhere."

Julia sighed. "Listen, I'm sure she's just out somewhere but I'm going to be honest with you. There is something going on but I don't want you two mixed up in it."

"We're not babies," Keira intoned. "Sela's our friend, too."

"I'll tell you what," Sebastian said, "I'll treat both of you to a dessert if you let Julia and I discuss what we're going to do."

Amanda unzipped her jacket and began shrugging it off her shoulders. "Fine by me."

Sebastian caught the waitress's eye on her way past the table. "Aggie, I wonder if you'd provide the girls here with a dessert menu. I believe they'll be sitting over on the other side."

"Ah, yes," Aggie said, her face beaming. "I've got the perfect spot for them now that the place is clearing out a bit. Just follow me, ladies." She turned and strode off across the room.

Amanda narrowed her eyes. "It's a good thing I'm in the mood for dessert." Reluctantly, they gathered their things and followed Aggie through the room.

Sebastian waited until they were out of earshot. "Well, that complicates things."

"Not necessarily," Julia said. "I have an idea. Keira's always taking pictures wherever she goes. Maybe she captured something interesting without knowing it."

"Right. Or someone."

"I'll send them back to the room to check it out. It'll at least keep them busy for a while."

He flashed her a grin. "I see you're more than just a pretty face."

She stood up to leave but quickly sat down again. "Who do you think put that note on Sela's bed?"

"Probably one of the gang members trying to scare her off. I'm sure she's alright. You go talk to the girls about the photos and I'll see if my friend has any news. After that, we better get over to the Ceildh Place and compare notes."

••••———————•———————••••

Sela stared into the shadows as the two eyes peered back at her. They blinked twice and she realized she was being summoned. She glanced about at her surroundings, hoping for a quick exit but nothing presented itself. There was only one thing to do. Carefully, she picked her way forward.

Who was this and why was he or she lying there like a sack of flour? Was it friend or foe? Obviously, whoever it was had fallen out of favor with "The New Thistle" which at least was a positive sign.

She reached the couch like a knight in tarnished armor, reluctant to free the captive. "Are you okay?" she whispered.

The eyes blinked furiously. Getting the message, she grabbed a handful of the rags and shoved them onto the floor. When she looked back, her hand shot to her mouth. Bound and gagged, white hair splayed out across the cushion like an aged ballerina, was the old woman from the art shop.

"What are you doing here?" Sela gasped. The woman's eyes bulged and muffled sounds broke free of the gag. "Okay, okay, just a minute." Sela dropped to her knees beside her. She loosened the gag and pulled it out of her mouth.

"What were ye waiting for—Christmas?" the woman spluttered.

"No … I … What in the world are you doing here?"

"Take these ties off me. We don't have all day." Her accent was a strange mixture of Scottish and something else. French?

Sela reached down and quickly began undoing the knots.

213

"There," she said when her arms were free, "I'll help you sit up and then I'll get your ankles." She took hold of the woman's shoulders and lifted her with a grunt. The woman let out a gasp of pain.

Sela winced. "Sorry. I didn't mean to hurt you."

"It's alright. My shoulder might be out of joint, though, thanks to that hooligan."

"What hooligan? What did he do?" She steadied her once again on the couch.

"You're a lot like your grandfather, I see. Full of curiosity."

Sela's arms dropped like stones. "What?"

"Undo my ankles. I'll explain when we find our way out of here."

"I want to hear it now." Sela said. "Who are you?" Tears began to blur her vision. "Are you Tanika?"

"No, dearie. I'm Therese McLeod. But if we don't leave soon, neither of us will live to right a terrible wrong."

Sela nodded and reached down to undo the ties but instantly jerked upright when a deep voice resonated behind her.

"Well, well, isn't this an interesting little tete a tete."

Dougal. In the fraction of a second between standing and turning, several responses played out in her mind. She could act dumb and pretend she didn't know what he was talking about, fly at him like a banshee and attempt an escape, or try to reason with him and buy some time. On the basis of sheer survival she chose the latter.

She willed her face to remain placid as she turned to look at him. "Dougal, what's going on?"

He was standing calmly by the foot of the stairs, his green striped shirt tucked neatly into his gabardine pants, a pistol in his right hand, and a wicked grin creasing his handsome face. "That, my dear, is the question of the day." He shook his head as though reprimanding a naughty child. "I told you to stay in the office where you'd be safe, but instead you found it necessary to snoop. It seems the old woman is right. Your grandfather and you do have a lot in common."

"And what would you really know about my grandfather?"

"Enough to realize he was a fool."

"He was a wonderful man, which is more than I can say for you at the moment." Her legs wobbled with fright but she wasn't about to let it show.

"Tsk, tsk," Dougal said. "And I was becoming so fond of you."

"Was it all a show, then? I thought we were … Besides," she spluttered, "what did Granddad ever do to you?"

Dougal waved the gun nonchalantly toward the old woman. "I'm sure your friend over there would love to fill you in on a few of the details."

"Dougal," she said, "What possible reason could you have for getting mixed up in this?"

The expression on his face hardened and she felt a cold tingle run through her spine. It seemed like all the warmth had drained out of him.

"Two words," he hissed. "Honor and control."

She looked at him, dumbfounded. "Where's the honor in trying to steal a box of gold? And what are you controlling—a gang of crooks?"

He laughed but she knew he wasn't amused. He sounded crazy—mad, as the British liked to say. "The honor is in continuing my step-father's failed mission."

"Your step-father? What are you talking about?"

He shook his head with a savvy smile. "Oh, the danger of a little knowledge. You thought you had it all figured out. You came to Scotland to set everything straight and ended up in a fine kettle of fish."

With sudden boldness, she strode over to where he stood and looked up into his eyes. "I don't understand, Dougal. What did your father begin that you think you have to finish?"

He chuckled again. "Have you actually taken a good look at the painting that interests you so much?"

"What do you mean?"

"I mean, if you hadn't leaped to all the wrong conclusions, you might have realized the man standing next to Hitler isn't your grandfather at all."

She gawked at him stupidly. "It isn't? Who is it then?"

"My father."

"Uncle Alec?"

"Very good. Yes—Uncle Alec minus the beard. Now do you get it?"

She stood rooted to the spot, trying to wrap her mind around the idea. "Your step father looked like Granddad? But why would he …" Her voice trailed off as the thought began to sink in. "He was a spy for the Nazis?"

"That, of course, is the crude way of putting it. He was merely trying to get out from under the confines of British Imperialism."

"On his way to a wad of cash, no doubt."

"Sela, Sela, let's not get cynical," he said. "After all, you've been such a help, informing me of the painting and all. I'd been on the lookout for it ever since Dad let it slip one day when he was plastered."

"But why do you think you have to finish what he started—he isn't even your real father." Dougal shot her a murderous glare and she knew she'd gone too far. "At least by blood … that is."

His voice grew deathly quiet. "Have you ever tried pleasing the unpleasable? Did you grow up accountable for someone else's sin? Well I did, and finally I've found a way to prove myself to him. I'm going to finish what he started."

"But Dougal …"

His head snapped up as though he'd just emerged from a stupor and he let out a harsh laugh. "Oh, by the way, after you left the shop I went back to retrieve the painting—no thanks to the old woman, of course. Fortunately I'd taken her along for a bit of insurance."

A familiar fragrance wafted over her and she realized with a start what had eluded her at the art shop. It was the scent of his aftershave.

She swallowed, hoping he wouldn't see through the thin veil

of bravado. "So what you're saying is that your step father sold out his country and betrayed his brother, and you want to follow in his steps.

"He was a realist who gave up when things went sideways. I'm simply carrying the torch."

"The torch of bigotry and hatred?

"The torch of Bonnie Prince Charlie."

"Bonnie Prince Charlie? Her voice screeched like a violin on steroids. "He was trying to free the country from British rule when things were terribly wrong."

He smirked. "And I'm not?"

Sela's mouth dropped open. "The country?"

"Of course, darling. While I'm fond of Ullapool I actually have bigger fish to fry."

She blinked hard as the reality began to dawn on her. "You think you're going to bring about Scottish independence with a group of neo-Nazis? Do you actually believe that's what the people want? They already voted it down."

His face hardened. "That's what they're going to get whether they want it or not."

"And that's where the container of gold comes in."

"Very good," he said, as though encouraging a small child in spelling. "And now that it's ours … well, let's just say the takeover is falling neatly into place."

"Dougal, you can't be serious. You think you can actually take over the country? The military would squash you like a bug."

"Unfortunately the military doesn't have quite the fire power I've acquired."

She stared at him. "What fire power?"

Again he chuckled. "The fire power that can be bought with millions of pounds of gold bullion."

"You're using the gold to buy weapons?"

"Well, just for now until we get it all squared away. What did you think I'd buy—a crown?"

"And you'd blow up your own country?"

"Tsk, tsk, sweetheart. That won't be necessary. Parliament's in session this weekend with the Prime Minister in attendance. It's perfect. On the anniversary of the Repealing Act—the day the Scots once again bore arms—a ghastly little surprise will be waiting for them."

Sela felt tears dampen her face. "But what about Great-Grandma and the rest of the family? And what about me? I thought you actually cared for me."

His mouth twitched and for a second she thought she detected an element of remorse. "I did care for you. I tried to scare you off several times but you were too obstinate to leave."

Sela's mouth went dry. "It was you who broke into my house in Minneapolis, wasn't it."

He paused, chuckling. "Well, not in person, of course. I had to send others to get what I needed. Oh, by the way, it was good of you to leave the address book in full view. It gave us quite a complete list of who to keep track of."

Sela gritted her teeth together. She'd never felt such anger.

"And the other things?" she whispered. "The note, the boulder?"

"I can't take all the credit. I had a little help from my friends." He smiled and his teeth gleamed like the big bad wolf. "You must realize I simply can't allow you to hold me back."

A chill ran through her but as she contemplated his meaning, another voice crackled from behind.

"Let her go."

They both turned to see Therese tottering toward them.

"There's not a thing she can do. Why don't ye just let her go."

Dougal's mouth turned down. "Get back to the couch, hag. I should've finished you off at your shop instead of bringing you here to cause trouble."

"Leave her alone," Sela snapped. "Is that all you can do—pick on old women? You've already hurt her shoulder."

With a speed akin to lightening he grabbed her around the

waist, pinning her arms to her sides. "No, I'm also able to pick on young stupid women."

"Ow! You're hurting me," she screamed and landed a solid kick on his shin.

He laughed. "You would've been so much fun if you'd only known your place."

She twisted to the side and managed to sink her teeth into his arm. He let out a yelp and released her, backhanding her across the face. She crumpled in a heap to the floor, a sob erupting from her throat. "Dougal, I can't believe this is really you. It's like your evil twin has taken over."

"Sorry, my dear, but I am the evil twin. Glad I could put on such a show for you, though." Still looking down at her, he barked out a command. "Wagner, now!"

A second man trooped down the stairs and snapped to attention behind him. "Yes sir," he shouted.

With dismay, Sela took in the thistle tattoo reaching from his wrist to the top of his arm. The man from the bus and the Barrows.

Seeing her startled look, Dougal smirked. "Yes, you've once again guessed correctly. He's one of us." Without turning his head he addressed the man. "Constrain them for now. We'll take care of them before we go."

Sela felt her composure melt away like yesterday's ice cream. "Dougal, you don't have to do this. You can still change your mind."

"Don't waste your breath," Therese whispered. "He's already made up his mind."

Dougal turned without a backward glance. "And not too loudly, if you don't mind, Wagner. I've got a splitting headache."

The man smiled maliciously. "Don't worry, sir. I'll keep them quiet." He lunged forward as Sela scrambled to her feet and ran back toward the couch. "Get away from me," she shrieked. Spotting a broken board, she picked it up and jabbed it toward him. "I'm warning you. I already hurt one of your friends—very badly," she added for good measure.

The man laughed and grabbed it away from her.

She raked at him with her nails, managing to scratch him across the face, but he swiped her away like a bear with an open paw. He was toying with her.

"Give it up," Therese said. "Don't let him have any more pleasure than necessary."

"Alright," Sela said, facing him. "If I stop fighting will you just tie us up and leave us alone?"

"That depends on what's in it for me." He lunged for her again, grabbing her by the shoulders and planting a soggy kiss on her lips. Disgusted, she bit down hard. He jumped back with a string of curses.

"Wagner!" Another man stood at the foot of the stairs. "Just get them tied and get back upstairs. Dougal wants us pronto."

With a scowl, Wagner grabbed hold of her and threw her onto the couch. Producing a nylon line from his pocket he quickly tied them back to back. "And if yer thinkin' of escaping, think again," he spat, wiping his bloodied lip with the back of his hand. "You'd be dead before ye could say 'Jack Robinson'." He turned and ran up the stairs.

Tied up against Therese, Sela shook from head to toe. Was the whole world evil? First Dougal, now Uncle Alec. Was there no one to be trusted? As she quietly sobbed, Therese tried to pat her hand.

"There, there," she said. "I've been in worse places than this and the Lord delivered me."

Sela twisted around as best she could. "You're a believer?"

"Long before ye were born, dearie."

Sela sniffed. "Did you actually know my granddad?"

"Yes I did. He was a fine young man."

In spite of the situation Sela broke into a grin. "Young?"

Therese smiled. "He was when I knew him. Young and dashing."

"Really?"

"And honorable. He could never have betrayed his country."

"So, you knew about that?" Sela asked incredulously.

"Yes, and I also know it's not true."

"But why didn't they believe him? I don't understand how it could've happened."

Therese let out a sigh. "You have to understand that the war made people jumpy. They wanted answers. When an incriminating note was slipped to the M15, everything seemed to point to him. Of course, they wouldn't listen to what I had to say since I'd worked for the Nazis. It was only due to another agent's word that he got off without life imprisonment or …

Suddenly a loud thump sounded overhead and they both jumped.

"What was that?" Sela gasped.

"They must've dropped some piece of artillery. Don't worry. They've got a lot to do before they come back for us."

Sela shuddered. "I wish Tanika was here so I could ask her about the whole thing."

"Sela," Therese said with a sigh. "I don't think you understand. Tanika wasn't a person—it was a mission."

"A mission?"

"Yes, an M15 mission. The Nazis had gotten hold of an old German WW1 message saying that an ammunition box of gold bullion had been hidden close to Ullapool. Since Hitler desperately needed funds during the Second World War, he came up with a plan to find the container."

"I read about it," Sela said, a sudden surge of excitement running through her. "But how did you get involved?"

The woman sighed once more. "My family owned a small art gallery in Paris. They took my parents captive and forced me to become an agent for them. I was sent to Ullapool to open an art shop and find someone willing to hunt for the treasure—in exchange for my parents' lives."

"And you found someone?" Her heart began to thump.

"Yes, but I never actually saw his face. He always contacted me at night wearing his hat pulled down and his collar up."

Sela swallowed. "You're sure it wasn't Granddad?"

"Positive. Somehow the M15 had gotten wind of what was going on and your granddad and Theo were sent to Ullapool to investigate."

"Theo?"

"Another British agent. After the war he bought the Ceildh Place—and while he was at it, he married me."

"The little proprietor is your husband?"

Therese nodded her head.

"So Tanika was the name of the mission to round up whoever was working for Germany and find the gold?"

"That's it in a nutshell."

"But I have a picture of a woman with the name 'Tanika' on the back."

Therese sighed. "So he kept it, did he?

"Sela paused. "Were you that woman?"

"Aye," Therese answered. It was taken when we first began working together. I gave it to him to remember me by. Imagine that he kept it all these years."

"But I still don't get it," Sela said. "How did Granddad end up getting framed?"

Therese tutted. "The boys convinced me to work as a double agent on the side of Britain, so whenever I got new information I'd leave a note for Joseph under the old side door."

"The door to the art shop office."

"Aye. The last time we communicated, I told him the Fuhrer would be sending new orders for my contact—and also a payment."

Sela felt her throat tighten. "I know. I have the note."

"Ach, Lassie, it must've sounded awfully incriminating to anyone reading it. If only I'd thought of it that way when I wrote it. Unfortunately, it was intercepted and sent to police headquarters—no doubt to throw suspicion away from the real culprit."

Sela thought for a moment. "And the painting?"

"I can only imagine that's what the new orders were all about—to smuggle the spy to Germany and get his picture painted next to

Hitler. While he'd think it a great honor, the Nazis would actually have him in their pocket. He'd be forced to feed them more and more information or they'd produce the painting." She chuckled quietly. "The Germans later sent it over to me to keep him in line but I thought it was a portrait of your granddad and covered the entire thing with a coat of acrylic."

"You never knew until now that it was Uncle Alec?"

"No, dearie, I had no idea it was his brother. But I wasn't willing to give it to the M15 at the time, either. I knew there had to be some twist—just didn't know what it was. As you know, the war ended soon after and the treasure wasn't found—until now, that is." She sat up a little straighter. "And now I think we'd better make our move and leave this dungeon while we still can."

Sela sniffed. "If only we could."

"It's not a problem," said Therese. "These young galoots nowadays haven't the faintest idea how to tie a real knot. Since he was daft enough to leave our hands relatively free, I've been workin' away at it with my one good one." She yanked on one of the ties with her fingers and the knot fell open.

Sela gasped. "After all these years you've still never lost the touch. Now all we have to do is manage to find our way out of here without being caught."

Chapter Twenty-One

The back door to the Ceildh Place swung open and a blubbery-lipped man appeared and motioned for Julia and Sebastian to enter. They followed him down a dingy hallway and through a door to their left where two others sat in quiet seclusion—one old, one young.

Julia was sure the old man must be the spunky little proprietor Sela had mentioned. A gray pallor now marked his lined face and he acknowledged their arrival with a curt dip of his head. The other one also seemed familiar, as though she'd seen him in passing. He was good-looking in an unkempt sort of way and didn't look like he missed much. Was this the undercover agent?

"Glad you could come," he said, pulling a couple of chairs over for them. He looked at Julia with a mischievous grin. "Ye must be Sebastian's new friend."

"Sorry, I'm completely forgetting my manners," Sebastian apologized. "This is Julia Kalahadi, Botany professor, presently with the University of Aberdeen." He waved his hand across the little group. "I'm afraid, Julia, you've fallen into the hands of the British Intelligence … although I'm sure Theo here would love to get back to civilian life as soon as possible."

"Just as soon as Therese is safe and sound," Theo answered. "Nice to meet ye, Julia."

"The bloke next to him is Liam," Sebastian continued, indicating the thick lipped man who'd let them in the door. "You might've seen him around town. He operates a butcher business but gets pulled into service occasionally."

"I believe your reputation precedes you," she said, laughing.

"Liam reached across to shake her hand. "Guilty, I'm sure."

"And finally, our fearless leader, agent MacLauchlan."

Julia took in the chaotic shock of dark hair, greasy shirt, and scuffed shoes.

"Like I said, he works undercover."

"Sorry, I didn't catch your first name."

"It's just a common old Scottish name," the man grinned, but his look told her there was nothing common about him. "The name's Jimmy."

"Jimmy?" She attempted to look unfazed though her mouth insisted on falling open. Was this the one supposedly in cahoots with the neo-Nazis? So far Sela had been batting zero.

"I'm sure your friend had me figured for one of the baddies," he said, reminding her never to play poker.

"Well, Sela thought maybe …"

He laughed. "I'm afraid that's my fault. I didn't exactly instill too much confidence in her. I sometimes have that way about me." He glanced over at Theo before looking back at Sebastian. "So what's the scoop? Have ye come up with a possible date?"

Before Sebastian could reply, the door burst open and a middle-aged woman in a black dress and white apron stumbled forward, followed by a tall, elderly man who appeared to be nudging her on. The group looked up, wide-eyed. "What's goin' on, Jock?" Theo asked, looking from one to the other.

"Seems we've found our reporter," the man answered.

"Maggie?" Theo rose from his seat and stared. "Surely not."

"It's true," the woman answered, avoiding his gaze. At this, she covered her face with her hands and sobbed, mascara streaming down both cheeks like black rivers. Julia pulled a tissue from a box on the desk and handed it to her.

"I didn't mean nobody no harm," the woman spluttered through a series of sniffs and hiccups. "I just needed some money to see me through after my husband took off with that hussy and all."

Jimmy brought over another couple of chairs. "Have a seat. We just need to know what's goin' on."

"It was her idea to confess," Jock offered. I was on my way in and found her hovering in the hallway."

"Could ye not have asked me for the money?" Theo said. "Surely ye know I would've helped out a long-time employee."

"I thought it was a harmless way to make a few extra quid without bothering nobody."

"Let's put that aside for now," said Jimmy. "Tell us where you've been getting your information and who else is involved."

The woman sniffed a couple of times and heaved a loud sigh before continuing. "My friend over at the Hair Today Beauty Salon has been seein' some suspicious goings-on. One of the girls who works there has an unsavory boyfriend who's been whispering something about a treasure."

"Go on," said Jimmy.

"Well …" She cast her eyes in Theo's direction. "I just happened to hear a couple of you talkin' about the same thing here and noticed some of you keeping odd hours …" She looked toward Jimmy through narrowed eyes. "Anyway, it seemed like a harmless way to earn a bit on the side—until all this happened." Once again her face crumpled and she burst into tears.

"So that's the extent of it?" Jimmy asked.

"Aye," she sniffed, dabbing her eyes with the tissue. "That's it—except for their meeting place, of course."

The men's eyebrows shot upward in unison. "Meeting place?" asked Jimmy.

"Aye. My friend overheard the bloke say they meet in some old abandoned tin building out at Corrieshalloch Gorge."

"Ahem, ah, well then," harrumphed Theo, clearing his throat

and mopping his face with his hand. "I, ah, hope ye've learned not to go snoopin' for information and posting your findings in the paper."

"Does that mean I'm not fired?" she asked. "I'll clean up the mess myself if I have to."

"You're not fired, Maggie. Jock, maybe you can take her home. She's had quite a day."

"Thank you, Theo," she cried. "Oh that poor man. I hope I didn't get him killed."

"It wasn't your doin'. Now go home and get some rest."

When the door closed behind them, Jimmy let out a long breath. "Can ye believe it?"

"I can't imagine how she ever heard us talkin'," said Theo, shaking his head in wonder. The others peered silently at the floor.

Jimmy looked across to Sebastian. "So did ye manage to come up with a possible date?"

"I'm afraid it's worse than we thought," Sebasian answered.

"Let's have it then."

"A definite possibility is The Repealing of the Proscription Act, the day the Scots were allowed to carry weapons again after the Bonnie Prince Charlie uprising. July 1st—tomorrow." He crossed his arms in front of him with a sigh. "I'm sure they'd consider it the height of irony, especially with Parliament open and the Prime Minister in attendance."

The others sat in silence. They could have been discussing the weather.

Finally Jimmy spoke. "It makes sense, though. We've been told of a large shipment of ammo on the move. With the amount of gold they've got, they'd be able to attract all kinds of dealings in a short period of time."

Theo grunted in agreement, giving Jimmy an appraising look.

"Still no word on the leader?" Sebastian asked.

"Not exactly, but we're thinking he might be connected to Joseph."

"Sela's granddad?" Julia cut in.

"Aye, though we're sure Joseph had no knowledge of it before he died."

Julia's brows arched. "It would've been nice if Sela had been informed." She looked pointedly at Jimmy.

Theo chuckled. "My sentiments exactly, lassie, though I have to say in our defense that no- one knew for sure where she stood what with all her snoopin' and carryin' on. She could've found out about the treasure from Joseph and been working with the neo-Nazis to recover it."

"I guess that's possible," she conceded, realizing for the first time how closely monitored they'd been. "Although one look at her would tell you she's not the type."

"Quite right," Liam agreed, "but we had to treat everyone with equal suspicion."

Suddenly, a loud banging came from the direction of the back door and a familiar voice called out Julia's name.

Julia closed her eyes, her color deepening. "Sorry, we told my students to come over if they found anything. They've been checking out some photographs."

"I'll get them," Sebastian said, heading for the door. A minute later Amanda and Keira rushed into the room like twin balloons ready to burst.

Without waiting to be introduced, Amanda blurted out, "We solved the whole thing and you won't believe who it is."

"Let's see what you've got," Jimmy said, reaching for the camera in her hand, but she made a bee-line for Julia.

Julia took it from her and peered into the small screen. "It looks like one of the side streets in town."

"Aye. Keira was snapping shots right and left when we first got here. Good thing she hadn't gotten round to deleting some of them."

"You see this group of guys sitting together on the patio," Keira butted in, pointing to a group of men at the left of the picture.

"They're not really clear," Julia said.

"Here, I'll zoom in and you can take a closer look. Ye might recognize the one in front."

Julia looked closely. "It's still not focused but it could be one of the army guys from Inverpoly."

"Right." She paused dramatically. "Now look at the one just off to the side. He's blurry but I'm sure you'll recognize him."

Julia squinted, then let out a gasp.

"What is it?" Jimmy asked.

"I don't understand," she said. "It's Sela's cousin, Dougal."

⁘⸺⸺●⸺⸺⁘

Sela and Therese stood at the bottom of the stairs, listening to the muffled thumps and thuds from above, accentuated by the occasional curse.

"It sounds as if they're loading up a ton of stuff," Sela whispered.

Therese nodded. "Aye, that'll be the ammunition."

Sela shuddered. "Do you think he'll actually go through with his insane plan?"

"I don't see him backing down now. He wouldn't want to lose the respect of his men."

Suddenly a voice rang out from the top of the stairs and the two stumbled backward, nearly falling over each other as they scrambled for the shadows.

"Get those boxes from the corner, Willy. We don't have all day."

Sela's heart catapulted with fright and she grabbed hold of Therese's hand.

"It's alright, dearie," Therese whispered. "They're too busy to be bothered with the likes of us right now." She paused before continuing on in a more ominous tone. "We'll have to be makin' our move soon, though. When they're done loading they'll need to figure out what to do with us."

They stood still until the footsteps finally faded away. Sela looked at the older woman doubtfully. "How's your shoulder? I wonder if I should try to bind it before we go."

"Aye, that's a good idea," she said. "That way it won't be bobbin' all over."

Sela bolted back to the couch, returning a minute later with a long piece of discolored muslin. "This'll have to do," she said, quickly winding it around Therese's arm and shoulder, forming an ungainly sling.

Therese glanced down at it. "I trust you're not in the medical profession."

"Beggars can't be choosers," Sela sniffed. "Are you able to make the stairs?"

"I've still got a bit of spunk in me, though I have to admit to feeling a bit weak. Maybe if I rest a minute I'll be able to make the climb."

Sela cast her eyes around the shadowed area. "There's something over by the wall that looks strong enough to sit on." She led her to a low, rectangular box, covered by a tarp. "Sit here for a minute and we'll see how you're doing."

"Aye," the woman answered, lowering herself down onto it. After a moment, though, she quietly chuckled. "I think it's time to get up. This seat's a bit hard on the old backside."

Sela took her by the elbow and helped her stand. "Sorry, I didn't realize it was …" She glanced back and abruptly stopped. The tarp had moved and a dull metal patina now shone from the uncovered portion. A padlock hung open from a latch in front. What in the world? She knelt beside it and whipped off the cover.

Her heart began to pound. Before her sat a rusty ammunition box, its stamped lid dented and its handles hanging at ungainly angles. World War 1? She pushed on it with both hands but it didn't budge. Slowly, with trembling fingers, she slid the padlock from the fastener, opened the latch and raised the squeaky lid. Therese let out a gasp and muttered something in French.

Sela stared, dumbfounded at the shining yellow bars filling the container. The treasure. Letting out a low whistle, she stuck out her hand and caressed their smooth, cold surface. They had to be worth more than a few million. Imagine what a person could do with …

"Just think," said Therese, "the damage that was caused by that very pile of bricks."

Sela looked up at her, noting the intense look in her eyes. "You're right." She shut the lid with a snap. Rising, she dusted off her knees. "Let's get out of here."

A moment later they stood by the stairs once again. "If we can make it outside we'll head for Dougal's truck. I'm almost positive he left the keys in it. Wait here and I'll see if the coast is clear."

She tiptoed up the stairs but froze on the spot when a board suddenly whined beneath her feet. Once at the top she listened again. Hearing nothing, she poked her head out into the open.

The garage-like door still stood ajar but this time an old holiday trailer filled the opening. Wooden crates lay strewn across the floor as the men pried them apart, removed their contents and placed them carefully into the underbelly of the trailer.

"See that you clean up after yourselves," she heard Dougal bellow from the other side. "We're starting an uprising, not a rubbish heap." Three of the men immediately pounced on the crates, lining them neatly against the side wall. There weren't many left to open.

Sela crept back down the stairs feeling like a terrified cartoon figure. Reaching Therese, she whispered, "Here, take my arm and we'll go together. We'll have to leave now while they're all still busy."

Therese locked her good arm in Sela's.

"Quietly now. When we reach the top we'll stop for just a minute to see if anyone's there."

The two women inched their way up the stairs, hardly daring to breathe. Halfway there, Therese pulled back, her face gray in the half-light. After a few seconds, she nodded and they proceeded on.

When they reached the top, Sela peeked out. Seeing the men were still occupied, she pulled Therese ahead. They had to get to the office before they were spotted. Right now they were sitting ducks.

Suddenly a man's voice called out from across the room. "Willy, ye must have left another of those boxes over by the corner. Go back and get it, ye lazy lout."

"Don't get your shirt in a wad," the other snarled. "I'm on my way."

Therese yanked on Sela's arm and pulled her down toward the nearest cot. Crouching beside it, they heard his languid footsteps approach and stop.

"I don't see it anywhere," he called back.

"I hope I don't have to come and find it for you," warned a familiar voice. Dougal.

Sela looked at Therese and pointed under the bed. Somehow they'd both have to wiggle into the small space without making a sound. If Dougal came, he wouldn't miss a thing.

Thankfully, the cots were fairly high but Sela made a mental note to apologize for the pushing and prodding. She pulled her foot in and held her breath just as a second set of footsteps drew near.

"Where were the others?" Dougal demanded.

"Right over there, sir. You'd see it easily if it was there."

After a slight pause, two sets of feet approached and stopped directly in front of them. Sela's heart thumped like a base drum. "Dear Lord", she prayed silently while squeezing Therese's good hand and listening to Dougal chew out the underling for his laziness. "we're in Your hands. You're the only One who can protect us."

She stretched her neck and recognized Dougal's shiny black loafers. A smudge of dirt now graced the toe of one and for an absurd moment she was tempted to reach out and wipe it off. At the thought, a hysterical giggle welled up inside her and she bit her lip till she tasted blood.

At last Dougal seemed satisfied that the box was no longer where it had been and the two moved off, back towards the trailer. When she was sure they'd gone she crawled out and helped the struggling old woman to her feet. With a quick glance over her shoulder, she planted her arm firmly around the woman's waist and half carried her the remaining distance to the door.

••❊❊❊══════════❊══════════❊❊❊••

"Are ye sure?" Jimmy probed.

Julia blinked and peered again at the photograph. "I'm just about positive."

"I knew it," Amanda scowled. "I knew he was a dirty no-good—"

"Let's not judge him before we know the facts," Julia cautioned. "He might be completely innocent."

"More than likely, though, he's not," said Jimmy.

They all turned and looked at him. "Why is that?" Julia asked.

"Nothing we can put our finger on. He just shows up in all the wrong places." He paused and scratched his chin. "Put that with the fact that he's related to Joseph and now pictured next to one of the known gang members …"

"Like I said," Amanda smirked, "we solved the whole case."

"But he didn't even know Sela's granddad," Keira said. They lived on different continents."

"True." Jimmy gave his head a scratch. "Could there be another relative?"

"Wait just a minute … I've got something here." Liam sat at the computer, clicking furiously. "Seems Dougal's not actually his father's son."

"What?" The others looked over in disbelief.

"Apparently, Alex Lamont adopted him when he married his young single mother, Agnes Duffield. Dougal was only three at the time."

Sebastian blew out his cheeks. "That could be a good chunk of the motivation right there—that he could never measure up and had to prove his worth as a son."

"Anything else?" Jimmy asked.

Liam continued reading. "He graduated from Oxford."

"In what discipline?"

"British History."

"That would make sense." He paused for a moment in thought. "I take it the father must be retired. Can ye find out where he worked?"

A few clicks later Liam continued, "He retired from the railroad fifteen years ago."

"And where do they live?"

"In a rather high-end neighborhood in Steppes."

"A little too high for a retired railroad worker?"

"It would seem so."

Jimmy turned and paced the length of the office. "Get him on the line. He may be our only hope of preventing a blood bath."

"But what about Sela?" Keira asked. "How do we know Dougal doesn't have her? We looked everywhere we could think of."

"If she's missing," Theo said slowly, rubbing his large nose, "it's more than likely she's been taken along with Therese."

"Ye might be right," Jimmy answered, turning his full attention to the old man. "But I promise you I'll do everything in my power to find them both. I'm not the huddy I once was back when you were my boss. I'll move heaven and earth if I have to. Dinna fear, Theo, we'll get them."

Theo took a long moment to look Jimmy in the eye, then slowly nodded his head. "I believe ye, lad, I believe ye. I've seen the changes in ye and I know ye'll do what ye say."

━━━━━◆━━━━━

Alec took a long pull on his cigarette as he stretched out on the chaise lounge. The sun room was the only place Agnes would allow smoking and he wasn't about to put up a fight. He was done with all that.

The air was sticky—not good for the lungs—especially after yesterday's report. He'd have to let Agnes know eventually. Dougal, too, of course, so things could be arranged. He sucked in another lungful and his chest erupted in a deep cough. Sighing, he butted out the cigarette, thinking of the old sixties' song, "I Can't Get No Satisfaction."

He was an old man. When had that happened? He'd lived a full life, and except for a few indiscretions during the war, a fairly decent one. After all, he'd made an honest woman of Agnes and given her son a good life.

His mind suddenly went to the inquisitive dark eyes of his grand-niece and he shifted uncomfortably in his seat. Surely he couldn't be held responsible for Joseph's troubles. After all, it was each man for himself back then.

"Did ye not hear the phone?" Agnes stood over him holding the cordless phone, a look of distaste clouding her florid face.

"Who is it?" he whispered.

"Someone by the name of Agent McLaughlan. Are ye sure the taxes are paid up?"

He took the phone from her hand, wafting her away with a look of exasperation. "It'll be nothing." He waited with palpitating heart until she shuffled back into the kitchen. What was the matter with him? It was probably just some government agency begging for money. Still, why would they be calling on a Saturday night? He forced his voice to remain calm. "Alec Lamont. How can I help ye?"

<hr />

Sela closed the door silently behind her and leaned forward, her hands gripping her knees.

"Don't give up now," Therese whispered. "We're half-way there."

"I know, I know. I'm just so relieved to get out of that room." She stood up, a silly grin pasted on her face. "Do you think Granddad would be proud of us?"

"I think your granddad would be very proud—but unless you want to ask him face to face, we'd better leave now."

"Are you sure you're up for it?"

Therese threw her a wry grin. "There's not much choice in the matter, is there?"

They tiptoed across the room to the outside door. Sela turned the knob and with both hands, pushed it slowly open. Cool humid air mingled with droplets of rain fell across her face and lifted the ends of her hair. The fragrance of honeysuckle filled the air. She'd never been so delighted to experience the Scottish outdoors.

"It looks awful dark out there," Therese said. "Are ye sure the truck's not far?"

"It's just over there a bit." She took the woman's good arm and guided her through the door, closing it silently behind them. Together they picked their way across the stony path, spotting the sharp outline of the truck just ahead. The wind was picking up and the sound of raindrops pelting the tin building grew steadily louder. Thin ribbons of fog hung in the air like rags. She could feel her hair begin to frizz.

Suddenly from behind, the sound of a menacing growl cut through the din. "It's that dog," Sela cried. "Hurry!" She clutched Therese's arm and pushed her ahead.

Seconds later the snarling canine hurled itself up onto them, saliva dripping from its jaws as it snapped viciously at whatever it could seize. Sela screamed and covered her face.

"Va t'en, chien!" Therese commanded. Abruptly the snarling ceased and Sela looked in amazement as the creature's head came down and its tail shot between its legs.

"Va!" she ordered, pointing, and it slunk off in the opposite direction.

Sela looked over at her in awe.

"Just a wee something I picked up in France. Shouldn't we be going? We're gettin' awful wet."

A few seconds later they were at the truck. Sela opened the door and helped Therese climb into the passenger seat before scampering around to the driver's side. She was soaked to the skin and shaking like a leaf but at the sight of the key stuck in the ignition, she nearly wept with relief. There was little time for theatrics, however. Vapor from their breath had already begun clouding up the windshield and she gave it a quick swipe with the palm of her hand. Any second now, thirty terrorists could be pounding toward them.

She looked over at Therese who was cradling her arm. "Are you okay?"

"I'll be fine. I hope you're able to drive a standard."

Sela looked down at the gearshift in dismay. "I tried it once, years ago. It's got a clutch, right?"

Therese let out a sigh. "I won't be able to do it with my shoulder in this shape. I hope you're a fast learner."

Sela swallowed, her hands shaking.

"Press down on the clutch," Therese ordered, "and I'll try to shove it into gear. Then, when I tell you, push on the gas pedal and at the same time, let your foot off the clutch."

Sela threw her a blank stare and turned the key. "Okay. Here goes."

"Push in the clutch," Therese said. She waited, then grasped the gear shift with her good hand, pushing over and up. "Now let it off gently."

The motor let out a deafening roar and the truck jerked forward like a bucking Broncho and stalled.

"Gently," Therese hissed. "I said gently."

Sela glanced over her shoulder through the rain-drizzled pane. "I sure hope they didn't hear that."

Therese muttered something about hearing it on the moon. "Try it again," she said. "This time more slowly."

Once again Sela pressed in the clutch. She blew the hair out of her eyes and grasped the steering wheel with both hands. "Okay, I think I've got the hang of it." She shoved the gas pedal half way down, wincing as it emitted a bellow like a wounded bull.

"The clutch—the clutch!" Therese gasped.

Sela let it part way up and the truck shot forward, narrowly missing a tree.

"Keep going!" Therese shouted.

Releasing the clutch completely, she rammed the gas pedal to the floor. The truck shuddered violently and bounded ahead in a series of leaps and roars and finally ground to an undignified halt.

"I think we'd better try Plan B." Therese attempted to crane her neck backwards.

Suddenly from behind came a shout and Sela turned to see the beam of a flashlight bouncing toward them followed by several others. "We'll have to make a run for it," she gasped.

"No, dearie. I'd just hold ye back. Go now and ye'll make it to the road."

"But I don't even know where we are," she cried. "Dougal wouldn't tell me. I don't know where the road is."

"We're at Corrieshalloch Gorge. Not far ahead there's a bridge. Cross it and ye'll …"

Sela felt her mouth go dry. "Corrieshalloch Gorge?"

"Yes. Now go before they're on ye."

"But I can't leave you here."

"Quick! It's our only chance." She pushed on Sela's shoulder. "Go! Do it for yer granddad."

Sela's eyes filled with tears but she opened the door.

"God be with ye, luv."

Sela clambered out, slamming the door behind her. With a final look over her shoulder, she took off running.

Chapter Twenty-Two

Sweat dripped like rain down Alec's forehead and he knew there was no point in denying the facts. They had him. "So why are ye bothering me after all this time? I'm a sick old man."

Agent McLaughlin met his eye. "I'm afraid you aren't the central theme of the investigation."

"Then why all the shenanigans, bringing me here in a helicopter and all? Who is the 'central theme', as you say?"

There was a pause. "Your step-son."

At this, Alec sat straight up. "Dougal? Why on earth would you think that?"

"Look, I don't have time for explanations right now. But we need your help. There's a slight chance ye might be able to redeem yourself for some of your past and save yer son in the process."

Alec sighed. "What is it ye want me to do?"

<hr />

Sela sloshed wildly through the slimy grass, her hair a frantic mass that caught on every protruding branch, her clothing soaked and tattered. The path was long gone but the direction was right. The roar of the waterfall had grown steadily louder. She wished for a hole to crawl into and hide. How could she face the bridge alone, in the pitch dark, in the middle of a storm with a gang of terrorists at her heels?

"*Lo I am with you always.*"

The words seemed to drop into her head from nowhere.

"Sela, it's no use, you know," called the taunting voice not far behind. "Remember the last time you were on that bridge?"

Shaking like a leaf, she ploughed forward through a cluster of scratchy weeds and slipped precariously, righting herself at the last second.

"You know there's no use trying to stop us. Who are you against 'The New Thistle'?"

He was right. Who was she anyway—or who did she think she was? Did she actually believe she could escape their clutches and stop an insurrection?

"*One shall chase a thousand.*"

Again, the phrase slipped into her mind from somewhere in her Sunday School past. But was it true? Could God rescue her from a dilemma of this magnitude? "Please God," she cried aloud, "get me out of here!"

Slowly, a warm energizing glow beginning in the pit of her stomach worked its way through to her fingertips and her shaking quieted. Was it a figment of her imagination—or God Himself?

A moment later she sensed the ground beneath her slope downward and realized she was nearly at the bridge. Keeping her arms stretched out in front, zombie style, she felt for the safety fence that spanned the length of the canyon. Not that it would stop Dougal. She had to get to the bridge and cross it or she'd never make it to the other side alive.

A flashlight found its mark just as she took a quick glance over her shoulder. The beam alighted on her face and she shrieked and scrambled ahead.

"Oh, Sela," Dougal mocked over the roar of the falls, "you look so cute bumbling about in the dark like that. Aren't you getting tired?"

Her fingers abruptly touched on the wire of the fence and she let out a sob of relief.

Following it with her hands, she clawed her way through the brambles that had grown up alongside it. She could hear the scraping of the bushes close behind. They were nearly on her. Her lungs were exploding.

In what seemed like an hour, though it was only a matter of seconds, the fence made a sharp turn and she found herself standing on the edge of the bridge. It seemed a lifetime ago that she'd stood on this very structure, paralyzed with fear and uncertainty, though mesmerized with Dougal's charm. If only she'd known then what she knew now. The wind, roaring through the canyon like a ravenous thing, had transformed the rain into driving pellets that pounded her skin and twisted her hair like a crazed rag doll. "Lord," she screamed. "help me! I can't do this alone." She grasped the sides of the creaking bridge and took a step forward.

The rushing of the waterfall far below threatened to vaporize her courage but she moved ahead with small, jerky steps, her breath following in staccato-like bursts. Before long a weightless sensation came over her as the bridge swayed sideways. She clutched the slippery railings and held on for dear life.

"So far so good," called the voice behind her. She felt the metal beneath her feet dip with his weight. So it had come to this. Could she make it to the other side before he reached her?

Suddenly the bridge rocked crazily and her feet nearly flew out from under her. With a shriek she grabbed tighter onto the railings and tried to balance herself.

"What's wrong? You don't like excitement?" He laughed as he rattled it once more, causing her to pitch forward in terror. "Just listen to those falls," he continued like a mad man as he moved toward her, "And imagine yourself hurling toward them. It'll be such a rush."

"*I am with you.*"

"Lord," she cried, "If You're really here, do something."

The wind and rain continued their barrage all around her, but in that instant a surge of power coursed through her veins and her fear gave way to faith. She turned and faced him.

A flash of lightening lit the sky just then, revealing the man before her. He was drenched to the skin like she was, but his face held such profound misery it took her breath away.

She inhaled in shock, overcome by a rush of compassion. "Dougal ..."

He looked into her eyes, but then his mouth twisted down in contempt. "Don't Dougal me," he spat. "You're going to pay for causing me all this trouble." He lifted his hands from the rails and lunged at her, grabbing her roughly by the arms.

Suddenly, from the opposite side of the bridge came a strangled shout accompanied by a strong beam of light and they twirled as one toward it.

"Don't do it, Dougal!"

"Who's there?" he roared, loosening his grip. "This is none of your concern."

"Yes, it is," the man called. "A father's always concerned about his son."

"Dad, what are you doing here? This has nothing to do with you."

"Yes it does," Alec cried, his voice cracking with grief. "You found out about the gold and wanted to finish what I started long ago."

"That's right, so get out of my way so I can finally prove I'm worth something."

"Son," Alec cried. "you don't have to prove anything to me. I was wrong to treat you the way I did. I love you. Besides, I was nothing but a greedy turn-coat."

"No!" Dougal screamed. He snatched Sela again before she could react and hoisted her up toward the railing. She kicked and clawed but he held tight. "No one stops 'The New Thistle'."

"Don't do it," another voice called out as a flood of lights erupted around them.

Dougal squinted, trying to identify the source of the voice.

Suddenly he began to chuckle. "Oh now I get it—the scruff—AKA the bobby."

"Agent McLaughlin to you."

"Well, I wouldn't be too proud of that title if I were you. You're a mite late on all accounts."

"Put her down," Jimmy said.

"Or what? If you shoot me she'll go right over the top. Is that what you want?"

"'The New Thistle's finished, Dougal. My men are on the other side rounding up the rest of your gang. It's over."

"You don't know the half of it."

"And the army will be swoopin' in on Edinburgh any minute now. Like I said, it's over."

In the dead silence that followed, Sela grasped the railing with both hands and tried to brace herself.

Suddenly an animal-like scream emanated from Dougal's throat and he lurched forward with renewed vigor and heaved her up and over the top. Her hands flew from the rails but in a mad scramble she managed to grip the bottom side wire with one hand. She let out a startled yelp and hung on for dear life. Floating between heaven and earth, an inexplicable calm settled over her and the strains of the violin and the voice of the young vocalist echoed through her brain. "How deep the Father's love for us, how vast beyond all measure, that He should give His only Son to make a wretch His treasure."

Her fingers cramped and trembled as the wire cut into her flesh. She couldn't hang on much longer. "It's okay, Lord," she whispered. "I'm ready to be with You and Granddad. Please, just make it quick."

"Hold on Sela!" came a shout. In the next second Jimmy clambered over the rail, all swagger and bravado gone. He gripped the railing with one hand and crouching low, clamped his other hand tightly around her wrist. She craned her neck upward through the fog-drenched darkness and as their eyes met for a split second, she saw his unveiled desperation. The next instant he turned and shouted through the torrent, "Sebastian, a little help!"

"Right here, boss," Sebastian bellowed, grabbing Jimmy around the waist and bracing himself against the rail. "I've got you. Just don't let her go."

"Not a chance." Grunting from exertion, he rose and pulled her straight up and over.

She tumbled over the side, her hair slicked down and her clothes ragged beyond repair. That, however, was the least of her concern. "Thank you," she cried and sank like a stone into his muscular arms.

"Shhhh," he whispered, putting a finger to his pursed lips as he held her tightly with his other arm. "You can thank me to your heart's content tomorrow over a wee fish tea."

"But what are you doing here? Who are you?" Before he could answer, the bridge dipped and shook as Julia, Keira, and Amanda, rushed forward and wrapped her in a big group hug.

Jimmy laughed. "Let's get off this thing before we all land in the drink."

As they helped Sela onto solid ground, she looked over at the bevy of policemen and M15 agents escorting Dougal, handcuffed and shackled, down the path to a waiting police car. He turned and for a second their eyes met before he dropped his gaze. What would become of him? His choices had left his life in ruins but as she well knew, that wasn't the worst sin in the world.

Three Months Later

Sela felt her knees quake as the Lord Chamberlain, standing to the right of Queen Elizabeth II, announced her grandfather's name. A regally attired usher stepped to her side as she rose and walked to the front of the ornate chamber in the Palace of Holyroodhouse. Lavishly carved woodwork—door casings, picture frames, and swags—lined the walls on either side but she kept her eyes straight ahead.

Since receiving the formal invitation nearly a month earlier, she had thought of little else. At long last Granddad would be recompensed.

"Presented posthumously to Joseph Calder Lamont," he proclaimed. "For services rendered above and beyond the call of duty during and after World War II—the Defense Medal."

She lowered her head and curtsied as she'd been instructed. Looking up, she saw in the Queen's right hand the silver disk attached to a green and red ribbon. The Queen held out the medal with a motherly smile and Sela enfolded it in her hand.

As she turned to walk back to her seat, her eyes locked on the twinkling orbs of her great-grandmother. How long she had waited for this moment. Sela knelt by the side of the wheel-chair and pressed the medal into the old woman's palm. "For you, Great-Grandma," she said. "For believing in him when no one else did." Her great-grandmother leaned over and hugged her fiercely. Then Sela once again took her seat.

Along the same row sat Theo and beside him, Therese, Julia, Sebastian—and Jimmy. He had pulled a few strings to allow double the number of permitted guests. She sat down beside him with a contented sigh and cut her eyes to his. From that moment on the bridge, even before he explained who he actually was, she had felt an almost palpable bond with him—as though they understood each other from the inside out.

He looked at her now with a cheeky grin and cocked his head to the side while reaching for her hand. "What are you doing?" she whispered.

"Just giving ye a wee something to make up for the medal."

"What?" She opened her hand and caught sight of a golden chain slipping silently through her fingers. Attached, was a delicate, heart-shaped locket. She stared in disbelief, ignoring the loud "Ahem" from behind. "How? When?"

He hesitated for a mere second, then cupping his mouth with his hand, whispered in a loud stage voice, "How about we beat it out of here as soon as this thing's done. There's a great fish and chip shop just down the road where I'll let ye in on a few tricks o' the trade."

About the Author

Born in Glasgow, Scotland, Iris grew up in Windsor, Ontario, Canada. After high school, she attended Canadian Bible College in Regina, Saskatchewan, where she met her husband, Karel.

After graduation, she and her husband ministered for ten years in eastern Kentucky where three of their four sons were born.

After returning to Canada, they pastored several churches in the west. They now own and operate a B&B where Iris spends her time writing, painting, leading a women's Bible study, acting in a local drama group and trying her best to visit their sixteen grandchildren who are spread from one side of the country to the other.

Printed in the United States
By Bookmasters